Praise for Where Monsters Lurk &
Magic Hides

"You can find me lurking, looking for people to throw this book at because this magic should never be hidden!"
 – **Sonora Reyes**, bestselling author of *The Lesbiana's Guide to Catholic School*

"I didn't know how much I needed an anthology like this to exist. Just bursting with originality, beauty, and Latinidad; WHERE MONSTERS LURK & MAGIC HIDES is an undeniable showcase of extreme talent providing some fresh perspective to genres that desperately need it."
 – **Angel Luis Colon**, author of *Infested, An MTV Fear Novel*, and editor of *¡Pa'Que Tu Lo Sepas!*

"One story that magnifies the many shades of grief, madness, and a desperate wife's blood-soaked attempt to cover it all. Another that contemplates the meaning of first kisses and familial love with humor and relatability. A haunting story of a deserted girl who takes back her own life...even if it means letting her lover perish. WHERE MONSTERS LURK & MAGIC HIDES is a collection of captivating stories, melodic prose, and beautiful illustration all immersed in unapologetic cultural glory. These captivating worlds detail first love, loss, heart-wrenching grief, and a deeper meaning that begs to be pondered within every word. Read and discover the magic that lies within each of us to unashamedly write our own stories & let our culture shine forth like gold."
 – **Charity Alyse**, author of *Other Side of the Tracks*

"WHERE MONSTERS LURK & MAGIC HIDES edited by Lauren Davila is a gripping collection of triumphant speculative fiction. At turns haunting and devastating, it flawlessly encapsulates a variety of Latinx experiences that will surely speak to many."
 – **Sandra Proudman**, editor of *Relit: 16 Latinx Remixes of Classic Stories*

Where Monsters Lurk
& Magic Hides

Where Monsters Lurk & Magic Hides

A LATINE ANTHOLOGY

Edited by
Lauren T. Davila

Published by Bee Infinite Publishing
Los Angeles, CA

Collection © 2022 by Lauren T. Davila
Illustrations © 2022 by Mazziel Coello

"La Piedra Suerte" © 2022 by Carolina Flórez-Cerchiaro. "Fragile Bodies, Stained Glass" © 2022 by Shayna Conde. "In Mis Own Palabras" © 2022 by K. Victoria Hernandez. "Carlos and the Immortals" © 2022 by Sabrina Prestes. "The Ivory Brush" © 2022 by K.C. Amira. "L.A. Llorona" © 2022 by Jaelin St. Clair. "Calle Verde 4 O'clock" © 2022 by Mariel Jungkunz. "For Every Flower, A Bird" © 2022 by Kiara Medina. "Besitos" © 2022 by Ashley Jean Granillo. "Under A Sea of Stars" © 2022 by Jarrard Raju. "The Larimar Experiment" © 2022 by Judy Fernandez Diaz. "They Outdid the Gray Sky" © 2022 by Nathalie D. Medina. "Beyond the Mist" © 2022 by Taylor Ramage. "When They Come" © 2022 by Linda Raquel Nieves Pérez. "Dark Space" © 2022 by Stephanie Slagle. "Breaking News" © 2022 by Lauren T. Davila. "Written In Sand" © 2022 by Alexandra Campos. "Currucus" © 2022 by Flor Salcedo.

ISBN 978-1-7360038-5-5
www.beeinfinite.org

Printed in the United States of America
First Printing, 2022

Contents

Contents

Introduction

Mermaids and fairies and sorcerers and goddesses.

Portal fantasies and holidays and alternate worlds.

Retellings and cultural mythos and nightmares.

First kisses and falling in love and misunderstandings and puppy love.

I've always been drawn to genre stories.

While friends were concentrating on homework or sports, I was rereading *The Chronicles of Narnia* and *Percy Jackson & the Olympians*. I looked for fairy circles in woods or secret mermaid caves that would grant me a tail. I never had a quinceañera or went to prom, but I could read all about them. I devoured Nancy Drew stories and imagined I'd solve mysteries in houses that maybe weren't as haunted as they seemed.

But most of the time, these portal fantasies were British. The prom queen and king were the white cheerleader and quarterback. And my girl Nancy was driving a cute little convertible courtesy of her attorney father on her way to solve mysteries. It seemed almost impossible to find myself, my friends, my family in the stories I read. In genre writing, there seemed to be a gap missing, especially for Latine/x writers and characters. If people who looked like us, like our parents were included, they took on stereotypical roles: gardeners, or maids, or a smooth-talking charmer with an indistinguishable Latine/x accent. Our characters were not fleshed out, were not living, were not actually human. Instead, we were only added for some spice.

This anthology is my hope to change that a bit. In the last few years, there have been some wonderful novels and short stories across genres. But I have not seen an anthology that pays tribute to multiple genres within the same manuscript.

Introduction

In this collection, I have gathered 18 culturally-specific stories across three genres: gothic horror, romance, and sci-fi/fantasy. Some authors are well-established in their genres, while others are just starting out. Either way, I hope you find some amazing new authors who you'll be able to support for years to come.

I also want to note that I have another Latine genre anthology publishing in tandem with this one. It is an adult anthology entitled PLACES WE BUILD IN THE UNIVERSE from Flower Song Press. While you are reading this one, maybe your parent or mentor would enjoy that anthology instead! It's just as representative, but has some older themes and content.

With my previous anthology, I asked my contributors what it meant to be part of a diverse project. I'm planning to continue this tradition for all of my anthologies from here on out. So I asked this question—how is your specific Latinidad expressed in your story and this anthology as a whole? Here are just a few of their answers:

- "Latinidad feels like a kaleidoscope of colors, fragmented pieces of myself gilded with gold. It is an aspect of myself as a product of diaspora. I wanted to write a fragmented perspective as someone who dances between these worlds." – Jaelin St. Clair

- "The indigenous people of Puerto Rico were wiped out a few years after colonizers came to the Island. Sharing their stories is my way of feeling connected to those that came before me, and to make sure they are remembered." – Kiara Medina

- "Latinidad, the word holds so much complexity for so many of us. For me, it speaks truths weaved together from those before me to now, an expression of who I am and the stories I choose to tell to highlight such complexities. I am steeped in diaspora and these complexities, like me, are melded into my stories and words." – Jarrard Raju

- "For me, Latinidad has often felt like running to stay in the same place. My Mexican-Guatemalan heritage will always be mine, but my relationship with it is as much informed by what has been lost as it is with what remains. I wrote this story in the wake of my paternal grandmother's passing, so my feelings of personal and cultural loss are prominent, but I hope with them comes the good haunt, the joyful memories that keep us attached to our heritage and the people who define it for us." – K. Victoria Hernandez

Introduction

- "My story is a second-world fantasy story set on an island loosely based on Puerto Rico. One side of my family goes back several generations in the mountainous area of Puerto Rico and it's one of my favorite places to visit. Feeling 'allowed' to write fantasy based on this part of my culture is still new to me, given the assimilated diaspora experience I've had most of my life."
  – Taylor Ramage

- "This story was born out of yearning to feel more authentically Mexican. But Latinidad gives me the freedom to experience what was kept hidden from me out of fear. Now, I can embrace my cultural identity, without fear of someone invalidating my lineage, my truths." – Ashley Jean Granillo

I hope you enjoy this anthology, full of genre stories in all of their wonder. As always, I am so grateful to all of the authors who agreed to be a part of this collection. Thank you to the wonderful team at Bee Infinite Publishing for taking a chance on this anthology in your first few years of building your book list. And most importantly, I am grateful to you, the reader. Whether you are Latine/x, from a diverse community, or love genre (or maybe you are none of the above), thank you for supporting a collection built around diverse authors for diverse communities. Representation matters and the voices we allow at the table, especially in genre spaces, are so important. Whether romance, sci-fi/fantasy, or gothic, I hope these stories stay with you long after you place this book back on your bookshelf. I know they will linger with me forever.

Gracias por todo.

– Lauren T. Davila

{Gothic Horror}

{ 1 }

La Piedra Suerte

CAROLINA FLÓREZ-CERCHIARO

"Come back con una bolsa de esmeraldas and maybe I'll consider your request."

The simmering rage in Manuela's stomach was beginning to boil over but she fought her natural tendency to talk back. Instead, she stumped out of Doña Petrona's oficina and down the rackety stairs of el bar de mala muerte.

Of course, Manuela didn't have a bag of esmeraldas to spare. No. She didn't even have a ring, or an emerald necklace like her cousin Azucena did after marrying a rich emerald miner. Manuela's parents made sure that she didn't see a single peso of their fortune when they locked her in a convent, accusing her of being a disgrace to her family, stripping her of all her inheritance rights and dooming her to a life of abnegation and solitude.

Alas, not having esmeraldas, or enough money to àcquire them wasn't her only problem. She also had no time. With the nuns' plan for Manuela's relocation in motion, she'd be shipped off to a cloistered convent in Gran España in a matter of weeks. But what Manuela did have was access to the biggest financial center in Santa Fé de Bogotá: El Convento de Santa Clara.

She strode down through the gravel path, framed by delicate bloomed bromelias and lush thicket, that contrasted against the backdrop of weathered encenillos leaning into the muted, late afternoon sun rays. Two-story homes, clad in yellow and green painting, with thick triple-latched wooden doors kept the uninvited outside. The scent of wild nogales prickled her nostrils, the dampness from a thunderstorm still lingering in the cold air.

Manuela marched up to the only four-story structure in the city: the one with gold ornate moldings, pointed arches, and flying buttresses. El Convento de Santa Clara, the place that Manuela begrudgingly had been calling home for the past twelve months.

With a temperament matching a brisa de invierno, Manuela slammed the door open and marched up the stairs to the second story, ignoring the ceramic statue of Jesús on the landing. She didn't cross herself; she never did. Padre Juan was wrong: she was not going to heaven. Jesús hadn't put her name in the guest list.

A spear of fear ran down her spine as she struggled through the spiral staircase. The utter silence within the whitewashed walls muted and muffled every sound, making her feel exposed. Exposed to what? She didn't know. But she missed the loudness of the city, it made her feel safe, like she always had company. Inside the convent's walls, she felt alone and forgotten.

She threw open the door that led to her chambers. At least her parents had gotten her the best accommodation. The dowry they'd given to La Madre Superiora was generous enough to buy Manuela some special treatment and privileges.

The chestnut door was ajar, revealing the unwanted presence of someone—a man—inside.

"Are you insane?" Manuela whispered angrily.

Ignacio sat at her narrow cedar table, the dim from the kerosene lamp gilded his profile. "Why would I be?"

Manuela shut the door behind her. "This is a convent. You are a *man*, and not a priest precisely..."

He reached for one of his coat's pockets and pulled out a stone. A gem wrapped tightly between his gnarly fingers. A green one.

Recognition sparkled in Manuela's eyes. Her gem. Su Piedra Suerte.

His voice was low. "I've been told you want to escape—"

"That's my gem," Manuela said in an exasperated voice, fighting the urge to throw herself at him and snatch her esmeralda from his nasty hands.

"Today is your chance to get it back."

Manuela's lips parted in surprise. "How come you have it? After the last time, I thought—"

"You'd never see me again?" he chimed in, stealing the words away from her lips. Was he able to read minds now? "Making you believe that we'd run away together on the eve of your sixteenth birthday was foolish and mean..."

Manuela's stomach twisted. She remembered exactly what happened that night. It had been a year since, certainly not enough to forget. Being in el convento reminded her how tonta she'd been for believing in the first jovencito who promised to take her to the moon and back.

"I want to apologize. If I had done things differently, you wouldn't be here."

"Apology accepted. Now, why are you *really* here? And why—no, how—is it that you have my gem?"

He flipped the stone between his fingers, the sight of it almost hypnotizing her. "Necesito ayuda con un último trabajo—"

Help with one last job? What made him believe that Manuela was willing to help him?

"Tú sabes lo que esa esmeralda puede hacer, why don't you use its powers for your own gain?"

Manuela locked her gaze on his coffee-brown eyes. Perhaps her gem could be her key out of the convent and the city. If only she could get it back...

"What does that have anything to do with you? And why haven't you given it back to me yet?"

He scoffed and when he spoke his voice was sharp. "I can't make it work," he spat out. "But you know how. And you know it can grant you anything you ask for."

If he really wanted to help her, why hadn't he come earlier? And why did he just stand there while they took her away?

Ignacio stared at her as if trying to find the right thing to say. "I heard you coming up the stairs con la furia de un huracán—"

"Of course! Doña Petrona is asking for esmeraldas I don't have," she said between gritted teeth. "She thinks that just because I'm Manuela Soler, I'm able to grow coins in my chambers." She gestured around mockingly.

"I was lucky to be born in a golden crib," she continued. "But rather unlucky to be born the last child. It's the curse of the youngest daughter."

Ignacio cocked his head to the side. "I'm not sure I follow. When it comes to rich people's protocols, my knowledge is rather limited."

"The youngest daughter belongs to the church, the middle one to the parents, and the eldest to marriage," she explained. "When my older sister Catalina died, papá y mamá reconsidered giving me away to the church. But then you happened—*we happened*—and here I am."

When her parents discovered she wasn't as virtuous as they expected her to be, they put her in the only place where she'd find forgiveness. Forgiveness they weren't going to grant her because only God could forgive a woman's ultimate sin.

Ignacio clutched the emerald-like a greedy child. "You know how to use it. You can get us both out of the city."

The gem belonged to an ancient curandera in her mother's family. She'd found out about it through her abuela. Abuela wanted Manuela to have it, but she warned her not to use it ever, or else its powers would cause her infinite misery. But Manuela didn't listen. And here she was, locked up in a prison of her own, with her ex-lover, now the man she hated the most, sitting in front of her.

"Doña Petrona would take that in exchange for a passage out of the city," she said stoutly.

Manuela knew what the gem could do. But that wasn't what she wanted it for. She needed it to get her escape; her freedom.

"I've heard rumors that there's a cavern filled with treasure some-where below this floor," Ignacio muttered, ignoring her statement. "Treasure that could secure both our futures outside of Bogotá."

"I'm well aware."

"You'll get your esmeralda back if you sneak us both down there..."

Manuela stared down at him. His gaze locked on the glowing stone. "I know about the treasure," she said curtly. "I'll guide you."

Ignacio frowned. "See? Not too hard—"

Manuela shrugged. "I just want mi piedra suerte back."

He smirked at her as he vanished from her chamber. But she knew who would be smirking last.

***

The next day Manuela told La Madre Superiora that she'd volunteered for the convent's renovation plan with Ignacio. She told Doña Petrona that she was expecting to collect a particularly hefty bounty that would grant her the esmeraldas she wanted. And, of course, she confirmed to Ignacio that her plan was ready to go.

"I heard this place is supposed to be haunted," Ignacio said, breaking the silence slowly settling in between them as they walked down the narrow spiral staircase descending into the convent's basement.

"Oh please." Manuela glared at him briefly. "Don't tell me that you believe in such things."

When Ignacio spoke, his voice echoed in the openness below. "You know all the nuns are buried here, don't you?"

"So what? They're dead."

Below the convent's structure, the atmosphere was underwater thick. A marshy stench curled in the wintry air, and the gravel path snaking across the makeshift graveyard was covered in dirt and grime. Cold sneaked in through her woolen skirt and wrapped around Manuela's bones like a heavy blanket she couldn't get out from.

Ignacio's bushy brows raised high. "How has this remained a secret for so long?"

"Not only women are buried here," Manuela said pointing her kerosene lamp at the rackety path, careful not to step on one of the tombs.

"What are you—"

Manuela drew her gaze to his and stared at him a bit. There'd always been a naïve little kid hidden behind that young man's face. When Manuela finally spoke, her voice was cold. "It's not by the congregation's good heart that the convent is able to withhold such fortune."

Ignacio's expression was puzzled. "What—"

"Necromancy," Manuela revealed, not certain by the blankness of his expression that he understood what that meant. "Magia Negra? The manipulation of death and the dead, through an occult ceremony. Invoking spirits if you will."

An unpleasant grimace cut Ignacio's face. "You're telling me the nuns are witches?"

The cold stinky air thickened, threatening to drown them.

"*Necromancers...*"

"Think about it," she added quickly. "We, the girls, are the perfect subjects. Most of us don't have families, and the ones who do, won't be missed by them. If we die, no one notices. We're the perfect prey to sacrifice."

And it was true. The place held more secrets than it let on, and moreover it held the key to the nuns' fortune. Spilling innocent blood in exchange for wealth and power. It was, after all, one of the oldest tricks in the book.

He rubbed his faint beard. "But the nuns are supposed to be good people?"

Manuela scoffed. "Well, that's the point. That's why no one will suspect whatever happens here in the after-hours."

Ignacio didn't utter a word, his expression vacant as though her words were taking him longer to process. As though they'd landed nowhere yet.

"And that's also why I need out. I'd rather be a predator than prey."

"So the treasure is a pile of innocent women's corpses?"

Manuela shook her head and motioned to the tall decaying structure standing several steps from them. "The treasure is in the fortress. But no one is willing to go inside."

"We are."

Manuela gulped down a breath before she marched behind Ignacio. He rushed down the dirty path and Manuela didn't try to keep up. Manuela choked on the putrid smell, growing stronger as they strode along. Verdant leaves the size of elephant ears burst from the path thick with centuries-grown moss. The path ended abruptly at a rocky crag on the flanks of a derelict fortress.

Ignacio wavered at the high wooden doors. Manuela stood beside him, waiting for him to make a move. She opened her mouth to say something, but he interrupted her.

"I'm just readying myself for when everything goes wrong." Ignacio mumbled, pulling out a leather-bound book out of the pocket of his robe.

A bible?

Manuela pulled out a short knife from under her robe. "Keep your negativity to yourself, will you?"

Manuela rolled her eyes at him and slid the metal latch on the thick weathered wooden door. She pressed hard before it shrieked open, revealing the utter darkness from inside. A marshy stench flowed from inside and into her nostrils, bile pooling in the pit of her stomach. She swallowed.

She motioned inside with her kerosene lamp. "I know. This doesn't seem like a place where someone would hide a treasure," she said, stepping inside. The dim glow of both their lamps barely allowed them to see a few steps in front of them. Soon they were walking down a narrow long corridor and Manuela's lungs were intoxicated with the putrid smell. "But it is rather the perfect place to keep people out."

"So where is it?" His voice rolled like thunder in the hollow stucco walls of the fortress.

Manuela hadn't thought of her plan so thoroughly. She knew there was no treasure underneath the convent. At least not the kind that Ignacio was hoping to find. Only a pile of corpses and an even bigger pile of rather dark secrets.

But Ignacio still had her stone and she was good at thinking on her feet.

"You wanted me to bring you down here"

"I will blow this place up, if needed," he pressed.

"Careful with what you do. This is a *sacred* place."

"How are we going to find it? Do you even know where it is?"

"No," she blurted. "We just need to look. It must be somewhere." Under the black canvas they found themselves in, there was no place to look. Manuela wouldn't even know where to start. The fortress seemed as hollow as Ignacio's head.

"Instead of that knife of yours, you should've brought agua bendita instead. A crucifix, at least. No knife is sharp enough to protect us from what can't be killed."

When Manuela spoke, her voice was gaily. "I'm assuming your grandma's copy of the bible will serve us well?"

"Yes."

"The dead don't die again. That's why they can't be killed."

"But spirits can be sent back to hell." Ignacio chimed in. "You should know about these things."

A disembodied voice came from behind Manuela, stealing her away from Ignacio's conversation, but she didn't turn around. She wouldn't let the darkness of the place get to her too.

But something—no, someone—yanked her back.

¡LARGO!

The voice was so loud, she jumped back. "What the—"

Manuela looked up at the sound of a sizzle. Ignacio had lit one of his bombs. Sulfur and smoke filled her nostrils moments before a bright light filled the room.

"You weren't supposed to do that..." She yelled.

"You wouldn't tell me where the treasure is, and I told you, if I ought to blow this place up to find it, I will."

From where she stood, Manuela saw a viscous green slime oozing from the staircase and quickly making its way toward them. What had La Madre Superiora said? *The spirits ought not to be disturbed. They must remain within these walls.* But now? What would the consequences be?

Her heart hammered in her chest, threatening to escape her ribcage. She struggled to get away from the viscous slime quickly spreading in the open space. Vines slithered through the cracks in the stone bricks, wrapping around her ankles and the debris from the crate his bomb had exploded.

"What the hell is happening?" Ignacio bellowed.

She looked up again. Fear seized her throat, and she couldn't utter a single word.

"Manuela, what is this?"

"I warned you there was a lot more that goes on in this place than you're able to imagine," she said in an exasperated voice.

She tried to scream this time, but her voice came out faint. "*¡Dame la piedra!*"

"I will not."

"We'll die. Give it to me."

It took Ignacio a few seconds, but he diligently threw it at her. She caught it still in the air and Manuela held on to it and manifested the slime and vines dissipating. She knew the legends were real and this place and they—no, *she*—needed to get out.

Ignacio waded through the slime to her as she bent down to cut at the vines. But then the slime and vines stopped, retreating to where they came from.

La esmeralda worked.

Ignacio grabbed a huge wooden plank and threw it to the side, face flushed. He crawled to her. "Are you okay?"

"No!"

She smacked him across the chest harshly as she struggled to keep her balance. With her nostrils caked in dust and her lungs burning, she surveyed the damage. The entrance was blocked. If she remembered correctly, she could exit from the balcony on the second floor, she just needed a way to get up. With la esmeralda in her possession, she was going to run until her legs could hold her no more.

Before she gathered enough strength and oxygen to run, she heard a scream. Ignacio. The green slime was draining him. The vines erupted from the ground, and she didn't hesitate. The necromancy had taken a hold on the fortress. It was to not be disturbed, and she should've warned him, but she didn't. Vines whipping her back and forth as she struggled through the long corridor. Her hand protected the pouch as she dropped onto him. The air was knocked out of her as black dots blurred her vision. Something smacked her across the temple, maybe his elbow and their bodies crashed into the hard floor. Fire bit at her ankle and even breathing came with white-hot pain.

Once she opened her eyes, she noted his face inches from hers. She forgot how full his chapped lips were.

"The place was going to get us killed. *You* bringing us down here was going to get us killed."

"I don't want to kill you."

The way he looked at her, as if he didn't quite believe her, made her heart tense.

Manuela shook her head. "This isn't about killing you," she admitted, her eyes falling away from his questioning gaze. "It's about getting myself out of here."

He backed away against the stone wall behind him.

When Manuela looked up again, La Madre Superiora's silhouette came into view. Terror washed over Manuela, raising fine hairs at the back of her neck. Her heart throbbed in her ears as the old nun approached them.

Nasty white hairs on the nun's chin escaped the brown coif out of the habit and swung along with the damp wind sneaking in from the outside. Manuela squirmed, her toes curled up inside her black leather shoes, and she forced herself to not look away. The air got thicker with every lazy step the nun took around the room. Her feet sagged and the dusty stench of the robe wafted inside her nose. Realization hit her. She'd done it.

Ignacio had taken the bait.

The nun's voice rolled over the weathered structure. "Manuela, darling, you've done an outstanding job."

"Manuela, what does this mean—"

"I think you know what this means." She moved toward him, chewing on her lower lip to distract from the pain.

He held her gaze. Manuela didn't think herself able to turn him in like this. She didn't think she'd be able to put her feelings away. To turn her ex-lover into prey. But it was always better someone else than her; she'd learned that the hard way. And Ignacio owed it to her for having taken away her freedom.

"Manuela—" his eyes bulged out in terror. Manuela looked away. She didn't think she was able to lead her ex-lover into a necromancy sacrifice. But she'd learn she always ought to put herself first. "You can't do this to me."

"My family pushed me away, exiling me to a place where I don't belong. It was all because of you. You fooled me, you made me believe you loved me and that you were worth everything. Even my freedom, even my well-being... You let them take me away, you stood there and watched..." Her voice trailed off. Warm tears seared her cheeks, but she didn't look away.

"It's not my fault you fell for me, Manuela. Your love for me, your infatuation...it's not me you should blame. I wanted money, you and your family had it. You were okay with that."

Manuela didn't let herself falter at the sound of his words. She wouldn't allow him to make her feel guilty.

"Your plan won't work," he continued, anger flaring in his brown eyes. "Your luck charm will bite you right in the ass. And meddling with the darker side will haunt you forever."

Manuela grabbed the pouch and shot up to her feet. "I'll proceed at my own risk."

"Manuela, there must be a way in which we can both get out of this. Alive. You can't be serious..."

Manuela drifted briefly to her own thoughts. She'd turned in the villain of the night stories she used to fill her cousins' heads with. The woman-like one-legged creature who wandered at night with a sack of male bones in a tow, punishing all kids who disobeyed their parents, but also luring men into the woods with her to drain them from blood and life.

Manuela, just like La Patasola, had become a punisher. She'd lured Ignacio to this place. She'd turn him into her prey, into her key to freedom. Manuela had become a heroine. Her heroine.

Remnants of slime and vines surrounded Ignacio. Manuela watched as Ignacio struggled to rip the vines off his wrists, but he failed. He shrieked and crowed. The more he struggled, the tighter they enveloped his limbs.

Not a drop of regret in her expression, Manuela turned to La Madre Superiora's sunken eyes.

"We're done here. He's all yours."

And with that, ghost-like figures swarmed around him—their faces hidden behind thin dark veils. Soon chanting began, muffling Ignacio's screams and Manuela was glad.

She stared outside the fortress door and back up to a new life without looking back.

{ 2 }

Fragile Bodies, Stained Glass

SHAYNA CONDE

The blue-black water of Lake Erie shimmered with long white snakes of light and the puckering kisses of distant stars. It was the September of 1899 and the summer air still lingered among the trees around the lake. There were no boats that bounced upon the waves, nor campfires or laughter in the woodland across the expanse. There was just a single bird floating on the calm waters, distracting a troubled girl who looked out of her window—too terrified to sleep, too tired to cry. Lacey's pitch-black eyes she inherited from her mother glittered like fresh ink. She peered into the gentle midnight sky in search of a distraction from the horrors that echoed every night in the corridors of her mind. Her eyes glanced behind her, making sure she had not disturbed the other peaceful children within the room.

There were five beds although only three were used. Eden and Adam, who have been in the house for a year and four months, shared a bed. With red hair, green eyes, and a light dusting of freckles, the five-year-old twins were a recessive sight to behold. However, beneath their heavy-cheeked faces and laughter festered a sadness that was only visible when one half was separated from the other. They slept on the bed closest to the door. Next to Eden's empty bed was nine-year-old

Kimberly with her smooth braided hair and her chestnut brown eyes. In another life, she and Lacey may have been friends. Along with being the only Black girl in residence, Kimberly was the only other child to never speak about life before the manor. There was an understanding between them. Some nights, Lacey would wake up and see her staring out the window, too.

An empty bed mirrored Kimberly's on the opposite side of the room. An empty bed in the Goodin Manor had two implications: someone was in the bathroom or parents had come to claim them. An unmade bed usually meant a bathroom visit. A bed as pristine as the one that laid next to Lacey meant that Gretchen was gone. She'd been adopted out of the Manor the day before. Nobody knew much about her other than that she was quiet and nervous with greenish-brown eyes.

Lacey scanned the room for a moment and exhaled out envy of her peacefully resting "brothers and sisters." Sleep would come and go, but rest would never entertain her. She planted her elbows on the window-sill and looked outside at the glittering midnight world. A grand and beckoning world that hummed her name on the wind and invited her to dance with each changing season. It was the world that she feared and loved and wanted to despise but admired with a grin and starry eyes.

She stayed up until the morning sun peeked over the Erie horizon, lighting up the face of the Manor. Madam Goodin always woke up the children about an hour after sunrise so Lacey raced to her bed and closed her eyes. She forced herself to sleep for half an hour before Madam's wake-up call rang through the room, gesturing for the children to start their Friday activities.

Fridays were Lacey's gardening days. The front and back yard of the Manor was littered with splotches of open dirt amidst the flowers and healthy grass. Every few weeks, on a Wednesday, the children of the house would have to dig a hole in the yard, as a togetherness exercise, which the Madam would fill in again the next morning. They tried to keep the holes relatively close together since Lacey's job was to decorate the patches with flower arrangements. Everyone in the Manor had chores and everyone had their favorites—hers was gardening. Kimberly had preferred foraging and the twins preferred washing the car. Adam would splash Eden; Eden would make bubbles. The vehicle was never actually clean. Gretchen had never vocalized which chore was her favorite. Lacey assumed that she liked washing the windows, especially the stained glass windows of the viewing room, which was full of untouchables. On tables and shelves were ornate vases, crystal roses and daffodils, and antique plates painted with pictures of women riding on horseback in their circus tent shirts and ballooning sleeves. Madam maintained the untouchables, but the windows were for Gretchen. She would spend hours quietly wiping the colorful windows. Every now and then, Lacey would walk past her as she pressed herself heavily against the glass—as if, by sheer will, she could dive into the blues and greens and yellows to the world beyond. Gretchen always had sad eyes, but they came alive when she cleaned the windows.

After chores, the children ate a lunch of rotisserie chicken, greens and rice. Then there was learning time. This occurred every day in the living room. Each child found their selected seat among the grandiose furnishings to read their books, finish their calculations from the day before, or continue their essays or stories. That is until Madam made her way over to them to teach them something new.

"The mind is a terrible thing to waste," she would repeat under the auburn lighting. Lacey attempted to finish *Frankenstein* but the words blurred on the page. She rose from the plush Victorian loveseat and gently tugged at Madam's sleeve, who was teaching the twins subtraction.

"I'm sorry, Madam, but I really need to talk to you."

"Can it wait until I come to you, my dear?"

"It's about Gretchen." At that, Madam excused herself from the children and guided Lacey around the corner to the bottom of the stairs. She sat on the stairs while Lacey plopped down cross-legged on the floor. "I'm sorry to take you away from the twins, Madam."

"Don't worry about it, child. Now, tell me. What's wrong?"

"I'm just sad because nobody ever comes for me. Gretchen was only here for five months and she has a home already. Is there something wrong with me?"

"Oh, heavens no!" Madam cupped her face with her hardened palms, caressing her cheeks with her thumbs. "There is nothing wrong with you. Sometimes things happen that we don't want, but it was her time to go. Don't bog down your mind with worries. Besides, don't you like living here with the other children and me?"

"I do! Really, I do. It's just, I miss having a mom sometimes. Besides, Gretchen never even said goodbye...and neither did Damien or Kristin or—"

"Did you finish your book, Lacey?" Madam interrupted. "You'll be quizzed on it tomorrow."

"And Damien never even took his lucky marbles! I still have the blue one. Maybe I could give it back to him and—"

"Enough!" Madam Goodin stated. All of the air froze in the room. Even the dust fragments hung in midair like tiny ghosts. There was an ominous emptiness behind Madam's eyes, like there was something lurking, waiting for a reason to jump out and Lacey didn't want to test it. She jumped to her feet and ran back into the living room to finish her reading. As she rounded the corner, Madam followed her movement with unblinking eyes.

Dinnertime was followed by their baths and their beds. Lacey attempted to actually sleep but her thoughts kept her from sinking into the goose feather pillow. Instead, she kept her eyes closed and thought of the manicured garden that she worked on all morning and her friends who were gone.

Saturday emerged with the singing of blue jays around the house, the crispness of arriving autumn, and blinding light. Lacey stretched awake and glanced across the room at the empty bed, reminding her that Gretchen was no longer here. With a groan, Lacey flipped toward the window and began to think about her parents. She could feel her mouth dragging down, so she swung out of bed and padded her way to the kitchen for juice. As she reached the bottom of the staircase, a movement from the sunroom caught her eye. Normally, the light-laden room was closed; but not that morning.

Lacey crept closer to the open door, drawn in by the sound of clattering paint brushes against marble floors. She rounded the doorframe like a mouse, curiously sniffing out the mystery in the air. That was the first time that she had ever seen Mr. Goodin up close.

He was covered in layers of jackets and sweaters and scarves that made her feel warm. His hair and his exposed skin was caked with dirt and muck. He wiggled his leg as he painted and while Lacey wanted to leave, she also wanted to stay. The way he painted on the canvas reminded her of a waltz: calculated and poised. Though she only saw it for a moment, it appeared to be a water painting of a woman with a yellow scarf and a child walking into an aquamarine light. The color of the woman's scarf and the way her hair seemed to bounce upon her back was uncomfortably familiar to Lacey.

As she began to quietly slink away from the mysterious co-master of the manor, something caught her eye. On the ceiling was a piece of yellowish glass, no bigger than her hand. It looked dirty. No cloudy, like there was an actual lightning storm beyond. There were no thunderclaps or pittering of rain drops against it, but Lacey couldn't shake the feeling. A crack came from the fire and she jumped back, the floorboards creaked. Mr. Goodin spun around, letting his paints fall to the floor; he had wild eyes that softened when he saw her. He staggered towards her like a toddler, arm outstretched.

"No, no, no I'm sorry. Please." He whispered his plea but it was too late. Lacey flew up the stairs and into bed before he'd even reached the door of the sunroom.

She spent the rest of the day trying to avoid Madam in case she'd heard of her interaction with Mr. Goodin. Each child had been told to stay away from the man. "My husband has become ill since his involvement in the Great War," Madam would say harshly. "He's harmless, but better left alone."

The twins appeared to have fallen asleep mid-wrestling, woven in-between sheets, limbs and pillows thrown haphazardly about. Kimberly was humming the same lullaby-like tune that she whistled to almost every day as she braided her hair. Lacey sat on her white-sheeted bed, occasionally side-glancing the empty bed that used to be Gretchen's and many others' before her.

"You haven't been sleeping much, have you?" Kimberly's voice was like a breeze: wispy and musical. Lacey wished sometimes that she sounded like her when she talked. It was as though she was singing, but she'd never tell her that. Compliments were curses to Kimberly—better left unspoken.

"What?"

"I know you haven't been sleeping. You just look out the window and try not to wake us up."

Lacey looked down at the wrinkles on her bed, pushing them into different ranges and forms.

"Have you been having nightmares again?" Kimberly inquired.

"Yeah," Lacey whispered to the linens.

"You need to sleep, though."

"I know."

"Maybe if you think about something happy before you sleep, you won't dream about what happened."

"Maybe."

"You should try it. You really should rest, Lacey."

"Okay. I'll try."

"I'll know if you go to the window again. I can hear you. I can hear everything."

"I will," Lacey said, chuckling with nervousness. "Good night and thank you, Kimberly."

"Don't worry about it."

Kimberly turned off the light switch by the door and returned to bed. Lacey wanted to tell someone about the yellow glass, but knew it sounded ridiculous. She already felt crazy—she didn't need anyone confirming it. Lacey stared at a speck on the ceiling until it started to blur. Her eyelids closed.

Roses. Yellow roses and white roses and red roses.

Roses. A field full of roses. And lilacs. And magnolias.

They make the air smell sweet, as though there was a hint of honey with oxygen. Someone stands, back facing me, in an opening between the clustered cypresses at the end of the meadow. I walk towards her through the grass. On the grass. It's cold. The grass turns to gravel. I'm walking barefoot through gravel and I'm next to her, holding her hand and laughing. Her hand is warm so I hold on tighter and look down and suddenly I'm wearing shoes. Behind me is an empty street with a few parked cars and a rusting street lamp. We keep walking, walking, walking, walking, striding, running, running, sprinting. We're sprinting. I can't keep up with her pace. My shoes are getting dirty and I keep tripping on the hem of my dress. "Mommy! What's wrong?" She picks me up as she starts sprinting, sprinting, sprinting and she tells me to close my eyes. She screams, stops and jerks, dropping me as she starts staggering. Walking, staggering, staggering, falling until she's on the ground. "Run, Lacey! Run!" A faceless man stands above me, casting a colossal shadow over me and over my mom. He clutches a knife in his hand, a dripping knife. He drops it and backs away slowly. He's screaming and crying and I can't move but he's apologizing and it's raining. "Mommy, what do I do?" I pull on her yellow scarf. The rain pounds against my body but I feel nothing and see her lying, face down, under the street light. "Mommy, please." She isn't moving, she isn't moving, she isn't moving so I touch her. But she's still just lying on the dirty concrete as I poke her shoulder and hold her face and look into her blue eyes. She just looks back as if all the residents had left the apartment of her brain so I scream. Her name. With a crackling voice one more time. But she still isn't moving. My hands shift back and forth like hummingbird wings covered in blood...her blood, her blood is on my hands and staining the bottom of my white dress. I look into Mother's blue eyes that glistened this morning while she made me blueberry pancakes with orange juice. Eyes that squinted when we watched television because she was too lazy to look for her glasses. Eyes that cried whenever Father's birthday came along. But her eyes aren't blinking and she isn't moving and she isn't moving so I hit her with my bloody hand but her eyes are open and her mouth is open and the blood won't come off as I scrape it across the gravel and I can see his shadow approaching and—

"Lacey, wake up!" Eden screamed as she shook her awake. Lacey popped up into a seated position, fists at the ready. They almost connected with her and her brother. "What happened?"

"Did you have a bad dream again?" Adam asked.

"Yeah, but it's fine. I'm fine, I promise. I just need to get some orange juice."

"You have to hurry, we have to go to church," Eden said quietly.

"Oh! That's right!" She realized that both Adam and Eden were dressed and ready for service. Sunday was the one day that Madam Goodin let the children sleep in, but they had to be ready when she opened the chapel and started prayers. She sprung off the bed and rummaged through her clothes to find a dress that was still clean. Kimberly was in the bathroom, so she threw it on quickly.

"Oh no, my shoes!" The last time she wore them, they got dirty and she'd taken them to be washed. She bulleted down the stairs into the basement washroom. Her shoes were tucked near the sink, under a pile of clothes that made her pause. Gretchen's favorite yellow blouse was hidden within the pile but there was just enough exposed to see dried blood stains and a long laceration that split the garment in half. She tried to remember the last time that she saw Gretchen wearing it but she couldn't. Though she knew not to touch, she reached for it.

"Lacey! Service is starting!" Madam hollered from the top of the stairwell.

Instinctively, she threw a pair of pants over the bloody shirt and grabbed her shoes. She ran up the stairs and into the room filled with wooden pews, fragile bodies and stained glass windows. Unable to focus on the Madam's sermon on unfailing forgiveness, Lacey thought about the blood in the basement—her friend's blood. Though she tried to convince herself otherwise, every nerve in her told her that something horrible had happened to Gretchen. And more importantly, that Madam knew more than she wanted to admit.

***

After service and after lunch and after activities and after dinner and after wash time and after the children's bedtime, Madam made her way to her husband's chambers. It was on the second floor of the house, in the wing opposite where the children slept. She visited him at least once a day to see if his condition was improving. But there was a noticeable change in his demeanor after Saturday morning. She entered the unlit room, shut the door and followed the shadow cast by the man looking out the window and speaking to himself. She sat next to him on the bed, clutching his hand in hers.

"I'm sorry," he whimpered.

"For what?"

"She saw me yesterday."

"Who?"

Mr. Goodin twitched, scratching his head furiously and then turning away to face the moon.

"Is that what's been bothering you?" she asked.

"I didn't mean to kill that lady. Or any of them. She has to know that. I didn't mean to hurt them. It's just that something happens to me when I see the yellows, I think. They—my brothers—they died in the daffodils. The soldiers knew we were coming. So they attacked while we were sleeping. Peaceful like lighting bugs in the thicket. They killed us all...all of them, except..." A tremble started in his jaw and traveled down to the pinky of his left hand. "Just tell her that I'm sorry. The little girl. The one from the street light."

"It's fine. Calm down, dear." She put her arm around his shoulder and held him tightly. "Everyone makes mistakes. And she told me she's happy here. She doesn't know what happened."

"Maybe if I just tell her that I'm sorry then—"

"Not right now. You need to keep up with your treatments before something that stressful."

"But I really think it will make me feel better. I think if I just tried to explain that she'd—"

"Trust me. Just wait. The time will come when you can tell—" Her lie was interrupted by the resonant *ding* of the doorbell. "I'll be right back."

At the door stood two men in gray suits: one with a small leather bag and one with a large wooden barrel. Madam Goodin opened the door and shushed them. "Don't wake the children."

"Where is it?" The one with the bag inquired.

"It...she's downstairs in the freezer. Does he know where it is?"

"Yes, Billy's been here before." He pointed towards the basement door. The bigger man followed the direction of his finger and disappeared into the darkness. It did not take long for him to return, sturdily holding onto the barrel. A delicate hand swung loosely over the rim—a small, pale hand. A child's hand. It bobbed with each step he took. He whispered something into the other man's ear as he passed. "Inventory is accounted for." Both of them looked at Madam. "The blood type is...?"

"She is, no, was, O negative."

He handed her the bag and told her to count it. She did and he thanked her for her business. "We'll contact you soon," he said and closed the door behind him.

Madam Goodin stood on the "Welcome" mat that ushered in visitors to the manor. She stared at the leather bag for a while in silence. A tear rolled down her face and splashed against the hide, her knuckles whitening around the zipper. After a few minutes of stillness, she closed the case and wiped the weakness from her eyes. With a deep sigh, she turned inside to lock up the Manor's main source of illness. She needed to check on her husband.

***

Long ago, in what feels like another world, there was no Madam. There was no orphanage. There was only the hope of a brilliant and beautiful tomorrow. There was just the miller's daughter in a growing town in upstate New York. And a baker's son. A match made in heaven. They grew up playing tag around the mill, teasing each other at the marketplace, until they fell in love. Three years into their marriage came the war—everything changed. She'd encouraged him to sign up. She thought it would be brave. He could go on an adventure, see the country and write to her every day. So he signed the papers, put on his uniform, and walked into the horizon with the other young townsmen. His letters came every day, in an increasingly desperate tone, until they stopped. He came home, but fractioned, never quite whole. Her husband was scared, confused, rageful. But she knew her gentle baker's boy was still inside him. So she moved them away from the lights and noise—somewhere safe. Or so she thought. They found a little town, not too many people, perfect for a fresh start. So she found work as a headmaster for an orphanage by the lake and he...well... tried to get better.

Until, one night he came home, drenched and iron-scented. He kept muttering, "something bad happened," his hands shaking. She ran, but she couldn't save the crumpled, cold woman who lay drenched and bloody on the cobblestone. Or the next one. Or the children. She couldn't save any of them. Especially not her husband from the madness that made him a monster. The chaos ravaged his brain and there was nothing she could do. All the dreams she had for a peaceful life slipped away.

***

As the echoing of Madam's footprints became increasingly distant, Lacey stopped trying to muffle her sobs. She kept seeing Gretchen's hand hitting the edge of the barrel. The sound of the flesh against the wood was barely distinguishable from the crashing waves of the lake. All she wanted was orange juice.

Instead, Lacey was given a revelation.

As her tears stopped, she wondered about Anna, Bradley, Christian, Allison and Damien. All the others she had been told had found a home.

Lacey knew she had to escape from the Manor. But not without her friends. She and Kimberly could escape if they got the chance, but the twins? They were too small to flee unassisted and too big to be carried by a pair of sixteen year old girls. She needed a plan. A foolproof plan. She'd keep this to herself for right now. The last thing she needed was for Kimberly and the twins to panic. They couldn't alert the Goodins that they knew.

A chill crept through the air, drying her tears. Lacey would do what she needed to do. Her mother had told her to run. So she would get herself and her friends out of the Manor if it was the last thing she did. She ran past the sunroom, not noticing the flash of yellow or the smell of blueberry pancakes that filled the hall.

She was too busy thinking of a plan.

In Mis Own Palabras

K. VICTORIA HERNANDEZ

Isobel sits in her car after the funeral and tries to force herself to cry. Her tears never come on time. Only when it's wrong or inconvenient. Alone in the car, she looks up at the mirror and it looks down at her, saying, "How much did you love her, really?"

Her body betrays her, and her eyes are dry.

After a few minutes of sitting in her guilt, Isobel starts the car and follows the rest of the procession to her grandmother's house. Vicente is playing and someone made Nana's favorite food. It is here, in a corner of the front room next to her mom, when Isobel asks if she can stay.

"Stay? Here? Why would you want to do that?"

"I can help prepare the house, for resale."

Her mom sighs, "Don't get sentimental Isa," then she says, "let me talk to your tios. See if they humor you."

A few hours later all the family is gone except for her. She returns with a duffle, a sleeping bag, and her thoughts.

Her thoughts are awfully mean when they're idle.

Isobel puts her things in the bedroom. It isn't large but there's room for a full bed, wardrobe, full-sized mirror and loveseat. Boxes of memories are stacked against the walls. She looks past them and sees spots in need of shackling, dusting, re-painting. She will work on this room first.

Tomorrow.

She unrolls her sleeping bag on the bed. From its folds comes the ouija board her mama would smack her with if she knew she had it. She traces the letters with her fingers. When she looks up again her eyes go to the open bedroom door. A single small print still hangs next to it. The center frame contains a calligraphic script of the Lord's prayer in Spanish. Isobel reads it in her head, then out loud. She hears all the mistakes, the words she hasn't had to know or say. Or, she does know them, but not in this order. She knows pan y padre y cielo and all of these words, but when she closes her eyes and tries again to repeat the prayer from memory they're gone.

She stops before the "Amen" and takes herself, her board, and a candle from one of the boxes to the front room, closing the door behind her.

Isobel sets a pillow on the floor and the ouija board in front of her. She opens on her phone, "The 10 Most Important Rules for Using a Ouija Board," and skims through the first few rules until she gets what she needs.

"*Rule 3—Do not do it in your own home. One of you will have to leave, eventually, and spirits are awfully good at waiting.*"

It's not her home. It'll be no one's in a week, and then it'll be someone's who does not matter.

"*Rule 4—Like a good restaurant, atmosphere is everything. Keep it dark for your ghoulish date, with just a candle or two to see the board with.*"

The candle she has is one of the velas de altar Nana used to put up as decoration.

"*Rule 5—Assign someone to be the notetaker, another to be the leader. Notetaker writes (as in with pen and paper!) down the message to decipher after the planchette is done moving. Leader asks the questions. Everyone else, hold on and enjoy the ride.*"

Isobel keeps her phone open on the notes app. That should be fine enough.

"Rule 6—Do not leave the planchette on the board. Even if you are leaving the room for just a bit, take it with you. It's bad luck to leave it, and you wouldn't want them to say anything important while you're gone, would you?"

For a planchette, she has a short glass scratched from years of use.

Isobel ignores rules 1 and 2.

"Rule 1—Be sure of what you are getting yourself into. Read the stories. They're all true, yup, every one."

"Rule 2—Do not do this alone, because you won't be alone for long."

She gets herself comfortable, lights the candle, and glances at her phone notes for her pre-written, internet-translated questions.

"Spirits. Espíritus, están—son, bienvenidos aquí." Spanish speaking ghosts need Spanish spoken questions. "Yo llamo al espíritu de Dorotea Molina-Sanchez. Por favor, ven aquí."

"Wait," she thinks, "that's 'come here', what's 'come forward'?"

"Por favor, uh, presentate?"

Isobel waits for a response. She welcomes the spirits a second time, with more confidence and, she thinks, less mistakes. She waits and welcomes them again. Her leg is shaking and she needs to pee. She shouldn't get up, can't stop it now—but what if she pees in the middle of it? What if the stress distresses her too much, they say you can't do this properly if distressed. And distracted. And this and that and, and–

Isobel runs to the bathroom, leaving the planchette alone on the board.

In the bathroom is a window looking out into the backyard. Having left her phone with the board, she opens the blinds for a distraction and sees the orange tree, haloed in the dark by the bathroom light. Isobel notes the cobwebs and dust on the sill. And the smudge. An impression from someone's hand, it looks green-blue in the light.

"It'll only take a second," she reasons.

She is dusting the windowsill when the smell of Clorox is interrupted by oranges. It's sweet, but cloying; it makes her want to vomit. The orange tree stands in the dark, in the yellow light like she caught it lurking and her flashlight is just about out. Then the hand impression between them becomes two.

Isobel remembers what she left alone, drops the rag and runs back to the living room. The planchette is sliding across the wood, hard enough to scratch, fast enough to go flying.

"Wait wait wait! Espera! Esperate!"

Her foot kicks her phone across the room. She scrambles for it and can hear the board scratching secrets behind her. Back on the floor with phone in hand, Isobel discovers she cannot type on her phone without looking at it, and she cannot look at two things at once.

"...osasqueestashacioendogaurdaestoamtesdequespaselklomalonoescomosdituvierasqueusarestodetodosnmodoserresmaslisfoqwueestobasta..."

"Um, are you...estás? Um." Isobel tries to translate in her head and speak but she can't. The desperate, violent sound of the planchette fills her ears. Her breath matches the speed of the glass spelling and she watches and she sees all the scratches forming, and the foggy impression of heat on top of the shaking, board-carving glass. If this is *her*, then this may be the longest one-on-one conversation they've ever had, and even here, Isobel is not a part of it.

Isobel flips the board. The motion of it blows out the candle so when she runs to the bedroom she runs in darkness. All night Isobel cries, overwhelmed, and ashamed. She prepared questions and memorized them in both languages, and imagined this moment so that, even if it didn't work, she could at least say she tried.

She tried, it worked, and she still couldn't do it right.

✳✳✳

Rule 9—Never, ever, ever taunt or goad a spirit into communicating with you. They will.

***

Isobel wakes up in the bedroom feeling like a fool. She leaves the house through the back door, looking down when she passes the open doorway to the front room, and comes back the same way with take-out breakfast. Sitting crossed-legged against the inside of the closed bedroom door, she open-mouth chews too-hot oatmeal and thinks about what to do first.

Her uncles say there were ghosts of past residents in her bisabuelo's home, and that's why her Nana wanted a new house so bad when she came here.

Isobel's grandmother saw monsters, and shadows where there shouldn't be.

"Premonitions run in our family," so says Isobel's mom.

Isobel has never had a premonition, or seen a ghost.

When she leaves the bedroom this second time, Isobel steels herself and enters the front room. The ouija board is still there, glass cracked on its side. She tosses them both in the trash and decides to clean the front room first. It was going to be the bedroom, but now this room feels in need of purging.

The couch and dining table will stay for open houses. The rug too. It could've been just a sweep and a dust, but the way things were arranged, it was all wrong. When Isobel cleans it is like she is looking for a strand of hair that fell between the floorboards. Like if she makes the tile grout white again a door in the floor will reveal itself, open up to a library of family records and secrets no one has told her, all of them easy to read, easy to pack up and take home with her.

The goal is to have a potential buyer walk in and feel like the house was always theirs. Home to house to home again. No room for memories, they make bad roommates.

Isobel eats leftovers from the reception for lunch, goes back to cleaning, then eats them again for early dinner. When she enters the kitchen in the evening she smells gas and notices a cabinet door left open. She had used the microwave to heat up her food, not the stove, but she must have put it on at some point. Flipped the dial with her elbow? And the cabinet door has a bad hinge. All of them do.

She eats at the kitchen breakfast table and, looking at the now closed cabinet, recalls what it used to hold. Canisters of rice and beans and, hidden behind those, little bags of pan dulce, galletas, and forbidden candies.

"Para los niños!" said her most diabetic Nana.

Sometimes, Isobel's mom would walk at sundown to Nana's house, when the light was golden and chilled skin to a light sweat. Isobel didn't often go with her, but when she did all three of them—her, her mother, her grandmother—sat in the kitchen and drank coffee, paired with their favorite pastel. Isobel's was the puerquito.

There is a story, told in one language and paraphrased in another, about her great uncle. They called him "Puerquito" because he was always playing in the mud and had been a little, pale chubby boy. The story ran long when Nana told it, but her mom's translation seemed shorter, like words were being left out. When Nana told the story it occupied their evening; now, Isobel can tell it in two sentences.

She tries not to think about how much of her Nana she's lost in translation.

Isobel double checks the stove before going to bed. There is a crash. She pushes open the bedroom door and at her feet lies the framed prayer. Its glass shards reflect her face like a mirror. She cleans it up quickly.

***

In her sleeping bag, Isobel thinks about premonitions, and why they are so choosy about who gets to see them.

When she sleeps she does so on her side to prevent sleep paralysis, and in this way Isobel knows that even if truth came to her in a dream, she would not take its word. She'd rather call it a condition and find new ways to sleep so as to never dream at all.

The last image she sees before waking are of orchards snapping and leaving their roots in the ground. It is the coldest hour of the night, and Isobel is not sure if it was the chill that brought her back from sleep, or the intruding sound of wood floorboards creaking.

The creaking starts at the front door, the front room, to the right and into the kitchen. The attached backyard door—a flimsy, noisy, metal thing—shakes at its hinges. Twice. Into the yard and back in, then through the tv room where she hears static, before she remembers her uncle disconnected the TV yesterday and it shuts off again. Isobel listens and follows the schematics of the house in her head. Next is the hall, past the bathroom door, past the baby photo gallery, ending here, with her, at the bedroom door.

It must be the wind blowing through unsealed windows. The wood in need of replacing. The pipes rusted over and making a fuss as though the whole house is in a stage of mourning.

Isobel mocks her fear; she gets up to mock the thing outside her door.

"Are you done?" She says, face to face with the inside of the bedroom door. "Because I need to sleep. You know, mimis? Or do you want to keep talking? Go ahead, I'm aaaall ears." Seconds of silence. "Mhm, yeah, cool. Buenos noches, and,"—she knocks the door—"keep it down out there!"

She chuckles to herself, the fear made silly and thus gone.

The house knocks back.

Isobel scrambles into her sleeping bag with her eyes on the door. She waits and there is no other knock, no wood creaking, no vengeful spirit comes to pay her back for her insolence. She waits a little longer, then lays down and prays for no dreams.

✳✳✳

Rule 8—Always, always close the session. A nice, solid goodbye is polite. More "Adios" than "Hasta lluego!" Definitely not "Hasta pronto." You don't want that.

***

The terror of last night washes away with a shower, but the impression remains. Isobel remembers her mistake when she opens the window to let the steam out.

She didn't close the session.

She ran like she runs from everything and, goddamit, of course she forgot.

Isobel grips the edge of the counter, forcing herself to breathe to the rhythm of her throbbing back. In this overwhelmed state, heaving over the sink, this would be the time to cry. Instead she breathes and focuses on the pain from a night spent curled up like a child.

She asks the internet for help.

ouija board forgot to close connection

ouija didn't say goodbye

ouija make spirit leave post seance

ouija cleanse house

ouija make it stop

"If you'd like to get rid of the ouija board completely, bury it in the ground without the planchette. Sprinkle the ground above it with holy water as well as the area where you used it."

In the box where she found the velas is a small bottle of holy water her Nana kept in her nightstand drawer. She takes these, and the board and planchette from the trash. In the garage is a bin full of gardening things no one has touched since the fruit trees were planted. She gets these too.

The soil is dry and full of clay. Or she thinks it's clay? Pale and flaky, it comes off in chunks and falls off weed roots with little reluctance. It's poor soil, but the grass grows well enough and the trees fruit each year without issue. An aguacate tree stands proud in the back corner, a small guava by the wall for the birds, and the orange tree, center of the yard, between the west fence and the plastic playground set full of spiders, only dusted off for holidays when the youngest come around. In another year or two the babies will be too old, but then maybe there will be grandchildren. Or not.

Isobel makes a note to move it to the curb.

The hole she digs is far enough away from any one of these trees, between them and the house. If the board scorches the earth it touches with fiery demonic curses, her Nana's oranges will still be alive and ready to enjoy come next season.

There is a basket of oranges sitting on Isobel's mom's counter at home. Only a few from her Nana remain. There's always too many for the two of them to finish, but this year she vows to do it. She will devour each one and suck on the rinds. She'll swallow seeds in hope of one taking root.

She'll feel it when it grows and thrives inside of her, and even though no one will believe her, she'll say, "I have my nana's orange tree growing against my spine. Everywhere I go, I can smell it. When you kiss me, I taste citrus. And when you tell me 'te quiero,' my throat burns like acid."

Isobel buries the board. She prays three times: once when the hole is filled, once while she sprinkles the holy water, once again after, just in case. She does the same inside the house, praying three times over the spot in the front room. The planchette she wraps in a dish cloth and smashes it in the sink with a hammer, then takes it out to the neighbor's trash.

A lightness washes over her for a brief moment. She takes it to mean it is over, whatever was in the house is gone. No tears of relief come her way. That's okay, hunger does.

In the kitchen she checks the fridge to make sure she really did finish all the food from the reception. One of the first things the family did after Nana's passing was empty the fridge. Her passing wasn't a surprise, so most other things were already in motion and could wait, but no one can plan exactly when and how fast a body will no longer be hungry; when a kitchen will no longer have three generations of family to feed. This is how homes become houses.

In the days before, there had been all sorts of food—sandwich meat and mayo; salchichas and eggs for breakfast, with tortillas, of course; leftover canned salsa covered in cellophane; old salad dressing; soy sauce packets; butter and then the tub that said butter but was actually beans; so many limes; somehow not enough cilantro; chocolates and sodas she wasn't supposed to have "pero es para los niños."

Everything, para los niños, los nietos como Isobel. But Isobel didn't eat the food often. She was never that hungry when she came, and there was never anything she really wanted. Wasn't it impolite to take food from other people's houses? They ask and you say no, no thank you, I'm fine. Nana would ask, "cacajuetes? No? Chocoláte? Soda? Galletas? Duvalín?"—the Duvalín caught Isobel, for a time. They didn't sell that candy in the regular markets. The other sweets were just sweets but this was special, this was a Nana sweet that you could only get here. Nana bought some more for her, until Isobel started to learn that maybe so many sweets wasn't good for her health, and that maybe encouraging her diabetic grandmother to hide away more candies wasn't good for her Nana's health either. Most times Isobel just said thank you when her Nana offered and insisted she really wasn't that hungry.

But she could have been. Isobel could have—*should* have—taken more. Should have found the space. Now there is no food and no one to ask if she'd like a snack. "Do you want this? This? What about this? But you're so skinny. Mija, eat. No? You already ate? Are you sure? Really? Okay, okay. If you're sure, then I'll stop." With grandmothers it's never just about the food.

Maybe being full was always a choice, and she chose not to make room.

The bottom drawer still smells like fruit. Like citrus. Fruit is not supposed to leak its smell, but it's there, in the bottom drawer, where there are no—

An orange, already cut and peeled, so the slices are sitting lightly on their skin but not attached. Like how Isobel used to ask for it. She'd ask for all her fruit snacks peeled, "apples, oranges, aguacates, toast."

Her mom and Nana laughed when she said toast, like the crust was a rind and white bread a sweet fruit. Isobel was too young to know why this was funny but she knew it was her that made her family laugh, and so she said it again, and again. Still, sometimes, she'll say it when she remembers, and her and her mom will laugh and reminisce on the old days when this house was new and there was still so much time to try.

Isobel smiles. Her mom must have taken one of the last oranges from their counter basket at home and put it in the fridge for her ahead of time. Like with the boxes and furniture neatly ordered by "for family" and "for dump", she wipes her hands of dust and packs away her grief.

Isobel picks up the orange and takes it to the backyard to enjoy in the mid-day sun. When she does her eyes fall onto the orange tree, now full of white flowers that weren't there when she re-entered the house.

She blinks.

The flowers are withering.

Blink.

The flowers are gone and now oranges weigh the branches, a failed season, the proof of which covers the ground. Wilted flowers, bodies returned to the earth.

Blink. And there, right there, is a green-blue impression, like the one the sun leaves behind closed eyes but now her eyes are wide open and it's watching her from under the orange tree.

Blink. It has no face but it's looking at her. Blink.

It's still there.

Blink.

She's still here.

Blink. Blink. Blink.

The dripping orange in Isobel's hand burns a cut she didn't know she had. The impression takes a step forward, and Isobel runs.

She grabs the car keys and gets as far as the porch, then a thought stops her: "Running, again?"

Minutes feel like forever. Isobel, in time, turns around and re-hangs the keys in the kitchen. She plates the naked orange still in her hand and washes off its stick, then sits at the breakfast table to eat in full view of the open backdoor. In case they are *her* and still there, wondering how Isobel could leave them alone so easily, why won't she eat and why, even for her, she can't cry.

* * *

Rule 7—The spirit is going to say things. About itself. About you. Just because they say it doesn't mean it's true. Just because it begs, doesn't mean you should let it in.

* * *

The footsteps return at midnight.

Isobel wakes up angry. And scared. And angry because she's scared.

She hears steps coming from the front room, through the kitchen, to the yard and back, the TV room, the hall, until whatever they are stops at the bedroom door.

And what if it's not her?

The handle of the door shakes.

And what if it is and this, what Isobel does now, is exactly the kind of granddaughter she really is.

The loose hinges shake and clack with each knock.

She doesn't want to see it. Tries not to. Chooses not to.

"Por favor,"—it speaks like air brushing skin, and scratching behind the eyes—"déjame entrar. Por favor. Por favor. Por fa—...puh-, po-lees, puh-lease. Please."

Isobel doesn't get up right away. It takes her a long time. An embarrassing, shameful, horribly long time to get up and open the door with a welcome that would never be enough. But, by the time she does, they're gone.

Isobel apologizes to the shadows. Nothing. She slams the door shut and opens it again. Still nothing. She does this over and over again until her body feels as tired as her heart. Isobel has no more words to hate herself with, so she screams into her hands and begs herself to cry.

Instead, she sits on the bed, angry and ashamed of her own dry face.

And she keeps sitting.

And sitting.

Alone with her mean, idle thoughts.

"Will you leave in the morning?" they ask. "And without a proper goodbye?"

***

The soil digs up easier the second time. When her shovel hits wood she bites her lip and tastes citrus.

Isobel does not run but walks back to the bedroom, committing each room to memory. Not as it is then but as it was when this house was home to three generations, and to a woman who did not need a language to show Isobel how much she loved her. Isobel's carries the Ouija board against her chest. She leaves the bedroom door open and sits on her Nana's bed facing the house beyond its frame. This time she will not leave, she will not look away.

The footsteps start their walk.

The front room. The kitchen. The yard—hear the orange tree shake, smell it in the sheets—back in. The TV room and its static. It rounds the hall corner and there they are, a green-blue image in the shape of a small, hunched body. An impression is the mark left when the thing or person who made it is already gone. It is a reminder of things left unsaid and business undone. Its presence reminds Isobel she was too late, then it walks down the hall. At the door frame, where the door should be, the impression raises a fist but does not knock.

"Have you let me in?" Isobel imagines them saying, "Finally? Will you sit with it?"

The fist is lowered again and Isobel is shaking, her body telling her to say no, no, I don't want to deal with this right now, not ever, no.

Her body feels every emotion her mind decided was too inconvenient, too painful, to look at.

But she stays. She will not look away.

They walk in and the ghost—this loud, relentless spirit—passes through the bed and envelopes her.

***

Rule 10—Not all of us got to say goodbye like we wanted. I hope you get yours. I hope you make it count.

***

Isobel sees herself from above in her grandmother's room, cradled by the green-blue presence. In its embrace, they are together, without barrier, or misunderstanding.

The grief remains and the grief is dripping with guilt.

Time rewinds. She sees herself as this body, in this moment, on this mattress, and then she walks backward in someone else's. From the house into the cemetery. Into a coffin. Into the earth. It is dark and it should be cold; instead, the weight of the earth is like being held by the one you love when you can't possibly hold yourself up any longer.

It is rest.

That's all death ever is. Rest.

In this dark space there is a cry. It is herself, Isobel, weeping from above on the surface of the hallowed earth. She feels her own grief as it was felt by her Nana six feet under on that day of her burial. In her car Isobel stares at the street and the procession going by. She begs herself to cry, and is ashamed.

"I'm sorry," she hears herself say. "I'm so sorry. Lo siento. Or, per-doname? I—fuck, I can't even do it right, right now, I can't—I'm sorry. I'm sorry."

Time walks back further. It needs to stop. Isobel sees where this is going and she wants to make it stop.

The two of them are together, in this bedroom and room arranged how it should be. Nana Dorotea lies unresponsive in her bed. This was not how she wished to go. Not how she wished to say goodbye to the world and Isobel knows that.

The Isobel of the past is sitting, holding her dying grandmother's hand and remembering her grandfather's passing so many years before, and her last goodbye to him done through the words of her mother. Not her words, not her goodbye, not her "te quiero mucho, siempre, mucho." Years since then spent learning and re-learning what she could. She tried, she really did. The past Isobel says goodbye to her Nana in her best Spanish and it feels so very much not enough. Her eyes are misty but unrelenting in their desire to run, run far from this pain.

And so time pities her, and moves forward again.

✳✳✳

Present Isobel shakes on a stripped mattress, held in the arms of a memory. She's exhausted. A hand brushes her hair and face against their chest.

"I tried."

"Yo sé."

"I wanted to say goodbye the right way."

"Tú lo hiciste."

"I wanted to tell you, in my words, with my voice, alone, lo mucho que te quiero."

"Mija. Mi más hermosa del mundo. You never stopped."

Isobel brushes at her cheek as the illumination disappears. Her hand comes away wet.

$\{\ 4\ \}$

Carlos and the Immortals

SABRINA PRESTES

Ariana Garibaldi da Silva carried the weight of the world on her back—or at least it felt that way with her heavy cello case. After her morning lesson at the prestigious Colégio dos Mortais, she headed to the front of the school. High windows revealed green hills behind the town, guarded by a giant statue with arms raised toward the sea.

Ariana was the only 16-year-old who still had a backpack on wheels. And today, instead of textbooks, it carried a stack of flyers she'd designed. The music director always did an abysmal job of advertising their shows, and Ariana wasn't one to play to an empty crowd.

One day, she'd perform in the grand orchestras of the empires up north. Surely in the Imperial court of Brazil. Maybe even the Incan empire of the east or the Aztec empire still fighting for control of Mexico. Either way, Ariana knew she was destined to overcome her mortality with the timelessness of music. But her path to fame started here—with the announcement board in front of her.

Several girls already circled it, whispering to each other. Ariana braced herself for battle. But as she approached, she saw what they were actually giggling about—another flyer already pinned to the board. With the words *Autumn 1979: Circus of Wonders* in red.

At the center of the flyer, a teenage boy flashed a perfect white smile. He had brown hair parted in the middle, a few shades darker than his skin. He wore a red nose, a ruffled collar, and the caption below him read: *Win a date with Carlos The Clown!*

"Are you signing up for the raffle?" one girl asked her friend.

"I definitely will," she said. Then noticed Ariana standing nearby. "Ari, you should do it. Or you could get your *mommy* to pay for your win."

Ariana made her face go completely blank. Neutral. She'd learned how to prevent her pink cheeks from turning totally red. "I don't know what you're talking about, Bianca."

These were the same girls that teased her for her rolling backpack and her unibrow, which she'd shaved off for years until she realized it did nothing to make them stop.

But Bianca only gasped. "You've never heard of Carlos The Clown?"

"No."

"He's all over television! They say the circus found him as an orphan juggling on the street in Paraguay. He's the only human, but he does the most dangerous things even though he's not immortal like the others! He can do quadruple somersaults on the trapeze; he rides a motorcycle on a tightrope over a pool of flesh-eating mermaids... Can you imagine that?"

"If he's the only human, how is it possible the circus is coming *here*?" Ariana asked.

How had she not heard about this? Her mother was the mayor, and surely they'd need her approval first.

"I don't know, but I'm excited," Bianca squeaked as her friends gave her side-eyed glances. "And it's happening right here on our field!"

And then Ariana noticed the dates for their shows. The first was on a Thursday in two weeks... the same time as her orchestra performance.

After the girls left—with no teasing this time, shockingly—Ariana put up one of her own flyers. But now she found her design bland compared to the circus' promises of dangerous wonder. She yanked their ad from the board and took a closer look.

In the corner, she saw a cage with a blacked-out shape inside and a question mark on top. The caption read: *For the first time, see the legendary monster boy live!*

***

A camp was pitched throughout the large field beside Ariana's school—a camp she hadn't seen on her way to class this morning. A huge circus tent laid crumpled on the grass while a few people—*immortals*—worked to set it up. A trio of gray-skinned children, their shadows dancing behind them. A towering, skeletal woman with sharp fangs. A nymph with pointed ears who made the grass wilt at his feet.

What would Ariana's mother make of this? She'd based her last election campaign on the promise of keeping their town safe from "outsiders". Which, Ariana had to admit, didn't mean much with the surge of crime *within* their small republic's borders.

Ariana watched the immortals, lost in her thoughts and confusion until one of the federal officers guarding the field approached her. "Good evening, Ariana. Are you here for Carlos The Clown?"

"I suppose I am," she said. "Can you please call my mother and tell her that I'll be home late today? Tell her I'll get a taxi, and she can give the chauffeur the evening off."

"As you wish. The line starts over there."

Carlos himself stood behind a table with a colorful box on top. A crowd assembled in a line in front of it. One at a time, each person filled out a ticket and slipped it into the box. Carlos juggled six—or was it eight?—red balls in the air, dancing and cheering with the crowd. In a swift movement, he caught all the balls in both hands. Then, in a typical magic trick, he pretended to pull out a flower from behind one boy's ear, and the boy smiled, bashful.

Maybe Ariana was biased, but she felt more comfortable approaching a human. Thus, she waited in line as the sun set, watching the gray-skinned children chase each other's shadows on the field. Eventually, she came face to face with a juggling Carlos, who was shorter than her and wore a polka-dot suit. He paused for a moment, staring at her cello case—and probably her unibrow—before giving her a perfect white smile.

"Read," she said. She took one of her flyers and slapped it on the table. Then she did the same with the stolen circus ad. Carlos, startled, dropped all the red balls on his head, earning several laughs.

"Do you see my problem?" Ariana asked.

He scrambled to catch the balls. Then he did a silly little jump, hands on his hips as he leaned over the papers. He smiled at his own picture, then moved to her orchestra flyer. After a long moment, he looked up, smile gone.

"Do you see my problem?" she repeated.

He spoke slowly but with full conviction: "You're slowing down my line."

"My orchestra will be playing at the same time as your show. I would like to kindly ask that the time be moved. Or else, I'm afraid we'll have to shut down your circus."

Carlos looked her up and down, from her sandals to her white dress to her shaggy blonde hair.

"Shut down my circus!" he cackled. He opened his arms wide, turning to the others in line and the stoic officers nearby. "The mayor's daughter thinks she can... shut down my circus!"

Laughter erupted around her. How did he know who she was? Her cheeks turned bright red, but she didn't look away. Like always, she stared blankly until the laughter—and her blush—faded.

"Not my fault no one likes classical music," Carlos said, and she strained to understand his accent, half his words coming out in Spanish. "But if you want to perform with me..." He squeezed his clown nose. "Do you like to swallow swords?"

More like he could swallow her bow, and she'd play him like a cello.

She glared at him, and he let out an exasperated sigh and threw the balls in the air. "Okay, okay; over, over. It's Carlos' break time." He waved at a police officer, who came to take his place. Then he jerked his head in the direction of the tents, motioning for Ariana to follow.

***

Following Carlos into the camp at twilight might've been a bad idea—especially when it was filled with beings that were, to Ariana, still more legend than real.

Carlos greeted everyone they passed, speaking in a quick Spanish Ariana only understood due to her lessons at the Colégio dos Mortais. The nymph she'd seen earlier sat on the grass and played a wooden flute. He looked no more than thirty, but his eyes revealed centuries of life—and Ariana had no idea how she could tell. He smiled as Carlos did a little dance to the pleasant tune.

Ariana nearly jumped at the sight of a man with slit-shaped pupils, leading a jaguar on a metal leash. Could she use her cello as a weapon if someone attacked? What happened to those flesh-eating mermaids Bianca mentioned?

"Finally found your lucky date?" the man asked Carlos, his Spanish accent unfamiliar. European, maybe? Could he be one of those refugees she'd heard about on the news, fleeing nuclear disaster?

Carlos stopped in his tracks, arms straight at his sides. "Not yet, sir."

The man raised an eyebrow at Ariana before walking away. The jaguar let out a low growl, and Ariana actually jumped this time, her cello case bumping against Carlos' head.

"Ay!"

She was quick to say, "Sorry."

He rubbed his head. "First time seeing a big cat?"

"More like my first time seeing anyone who isn't human."

He gave her a slow grin, almost eerie in the orange lamplight. "Scared?"

"I should be."

He laughed and led her into the circus tent, now standing tall with little flags on top. Inside, uniformed city workers adjusted lights and stood on ladders to secure the trapeze. They worked alongside the immortals of the circus—the type of inter-species partnership Ariana knew was normal in much of the world, but the decades-long segregation of the República Juliana made it so she'd only seen it in films. And what did the city workers feel? Were they afraid? Or were they old enough to remember a time *before* the immortals were cast out?

After putting his hand above his eyes, looking around to make sure no one saw them come in, Carlos took Ariana underneath the benches.

"Get down," he said. "And... quiet."

She took off her case and dragged it under the benches with them. Her rolling backpack fell and made a loud *clack*. Carlos put his finger to his lips and shushed her—also loudly.

What would the officers outside do if they found her here? What would they say to her mother?

"Now what?" Ariana asked, trying not to sneeze at the dusty air. Her cheeks warmed not with embarrassment, but an unfamiliar, jittery curiosity. It'd been so long since she even had dreams as wild as this.

Away from the crowd, without his tricks, the clown looked weary in the dim light.

"Why do I need to help you?" he asked. "You're a rich girl. If you only play that thing—" he motioned to her cello case "—I think you have a good life."

She crossed her arms over her chest. "You brought me all the way here. Would it be so difficult to reschedule?"

His whole body slumped as he sighed. "You know Spanish?"

She nodded.

He rubbed his face, smearing the white makeup around his lips. Was he ashamed or relieved? Either way, Ariana didn't judge him. With circus shows scheduled back to back, Portuguese lessons were surely not his top priority.

"I don't make the schedules," he said, taking off his red nose. "The circus master sets the rules. The man with the cat. Big old reptilian."

Definitely not a refugee then. What if he was part of the Nazis who set off the bombs that destroyed Europe in the first place? Now they wanted to make their home here—in the Americas.

"I don't understand why the circus is allowed to come to a human-only republic," she said, "especially if the reptilians are running the show."

"The first secret you need to know," Carlos began in a low hush, and she brought her head closer, "is that your little republic only won independence *because* of them. Tiny state in the south of Brazil. Wasn't powerful enough for a revolution against the crown. But with reptile money from what they called the... Old World? The game changes."

"Why would they want to fund the independence?"

"Divide and conquer. The Empire of Brazil was too strong. Powerful immortal families... more immortal than the reptiles, hah! That's their second secret. They can't live forever. All they can do is keep their bloodline going. And they think: break the big countries up, and the power stays with them. Investing their gold in drugs and trafficking...it's their new underground empire of blood."

"Why are you telling me this, Carlos?"

"I like to meet people in each city. Learn new things every day. I love my *Maravilla* family, but sometimes I feel alone." He shook his head. "I can talk to the circus master. I'll ask him to change the date, but... I want to know what secrets you can tell me."

The weight of the world beyond the República Juliana's borders weighed on Ariana's back. Carlos didn't *seem* like a threat, and he'd told her more than her mother had. So, for the sake of a fair exchange, she returned his honesty with the only secret she knew: "The republic is dying. Each day, more people leave. My mother says it's dangerous to let immortals in. But that's not what our independence was about. My ancestor Anita fought in the revolution. You can find her statue in the city square. She wanted as many people as possible free from the monarchy. And this... separation of species. It's like it came out of nowhere."

Carlos' mischievous grin returned as if he was getting ready to ride his motorcycle across a tightrope as Bianca said. He rubbed his hands together and got closer to Ariana, his ruffled collar brushing her neck.

"Ever heard the legends?" he asked, and she tried to ignore how being this close to him made her steady heart race. "What happens when humans have babies with vampires? With monsters? With mermaids? What happens when mermaids and vampires have babies? But with the scientists from Brazil... anything is possible now. That's the third secret. The reptilians are afraid."

"Then why would they want a circus of immortals to come here?" Ariana asked.

"I haven't figured it out yet." He shrugged. "And you? Do you ever think of leaving this place?"

"I will do my best with my show on Thursday," she said, blinking at him. "But I have dreams to tour the world."

"Like me." He pulled away, throwing his clown nose in the air before catching it effortlessly. "I didn't think a poor boy would live a rich girl's dream."

A rare smile spread through Ariana's cheeks. She hated to admit it, but she understood why Bianca thought he was so dreamy—mischief and danger paired with a sweet smile and warm eyes.

She turned away from Carlos, unzipped her backpack, and handed him a few flyers for her show. "Can you take me back now?"

He held out his hand. "I'll be here tomorrow so you can sign up for the raffle. Deal?"

Ariana rolled her eyes. "I could get a date with you regardless of whether or not I won."

Still, she shook his hand. He must've been sixteen at most, but his palm was rough and calloused.

And with that, Carlos and Ariana snuck out of the empty circus. As they crossed the camp, they passed a small tent—the only one not lit, guarded by officers with assault rifles in tow.

In the darkness, Ariana glimpsed glowing white orbs behind the bars of a cage.

***

The following week, the city of Laguna bristled with sand, sunshine, and excitement—but not for Ariana's orchestra. Carlos' perfect smile spread all the way to tabloids at corner stores: *Raffle for a date with human daredevil Carlos closes after thousands of entries; How this Paraguayan orphan broke 12 world records!*

Television crews became the local pests. Headlines on news stations read: *Crowds flood into Laguna, driving largest tourism demand of the decade; Is the Circus of Wonders the start of an era of integration?*

Each day, Ariana checked the school announcement board for an updated circus flyer, hoping Carlos worked a magic trick to change the date. But maybe he forgot about their promise because it remained the same. Along with the caption that made her nauseous every time she read it: *For the first time, see the legendary monster boy live!* The only act who drew as many headlines as Carlos. No pictures of the monster boy existed, but reporters called him an abomination. A perversion of all the laws of nature. A genetically-engineered fusion of four different species.

The legend went that a mad scientist tried to create a demigod, and the monster boy was his failed attempt. He'd escaped into the forests of the Mata Atlântica, where he was raised by white-eyed monsters, existing only in rumored sightings and urban legends until now.

On her mother's rare day off, a chauffeur drove her and Ariana around the city. They put up flyers on every corner, even as Ariana remembered a certain clown's words: *Not my fault no one likes classical music.*

Would her cello ever be anything but bland? Her conversation with Carlos under the benches felt like a distant dream. In the news, the circus master with the snake-like eyes announced the "lucky winner" of the date with Carlos—none other than Bianca Machado.

Ariana stared at her last flyer. Maybe no one would come to her show, but at least she spent the day with her mother. She clung to the thought as tears welled in her brown eyes.

The woman mirrored Ariana—blonde hair on her head but dark hair on her limbs, back, and, of course, her signature unibrow. She always reassured Ariana with stories about how she, too, received rude comments in her school days. "Silly things like hair don't matter when you have the blood of the revolution in your veins," she used to say.

Later, as the two sat for dinner, alone in their grand table that could seat at least twelve, Ariana finally asked: "Why did you authorize the circus to come here anyway?"

Her mother looked up from her notebook, where she'd jotted down notes for her next interview. The reporters hadn't spared *her* from their mobbing, and they'd even stopped Ariana a few times, who gladly took any opportunity to promote her orchestra show. Although tempted, she didn't dare tell them the secrets she'd heard from Carlos.

"It wasn't my decision," her mother admitted. "This was the president's orders. But part of me thinks they're trying to fuel inter-species tensions."

"Isn't there enough tension?"

"I know I have kept things from you, but you see how the republic is at risk. I fear they are trying to make us wage war against the Empire of Brazil. And I think that monster boy is at the center of their plan."

"Whose plan?"

But she already knew. How predictable. The shapeshifting reptilians who, since their spaceships first crashed into Spain four centuries before, now had their hands in everything.

With a sigh, Ariana asked, "Can you at least tell them to change the date?"

***

A crowd waited outside the circus for the sold-out show. Flute music sounded from large speakers. Lanterns cast the field in warm light. Ariana avoided the commotion and made her way into the Colégio dos Mortais, enveloping herself in darkness.

She'd spent the afternoon crying in the bathroom. Her busy mother wouldn't watch her play the cello tonight. But it didn't matter when the music director announced that their orchestra performance was officially canceled.

Ariana turned on the lights in the silent auditorium. Wiping her eyes, she crept slowly to the stage, where she set up her cello and played by heart—empty without the buzz of the clarinet or the rumbling crescendo of the drums. She even missed the squeaky violins. Still, she felt their phantom music notes echo through her in the spotlight, pretending a grand crowd filled the hollow room.

From the corner of her eye, a shadow flickered along the circular walls. And then something materialized from thin air, perched on top of an empty seat. A boy with gray skin covered in black veins, curly brown hair, and glowing white orbs for eyes.

With her hand trembling around her bow, Ariana finished the tune. Then she stood to face the monster boy, almost flattered he'd come to watch.

But even he didn't have time for the rest of her music. Black shadows trailed in all directions from his bare feet, across the floor, and up the walls. And then he disappeared, not making a single sound.

***

"Miss Garibaldi, is everything alright?"

Ariana ran toward the officers, her dress billowing behind her. "I saw him! The monster boy escaped; he was in the auditorium over there—"

The officers exchanged looks, adjusted their rifles, and ran toward the school without another word.

Loud drumming and cheering sounded nearby. Colorful lights flashed within the circus. Without the officers on guard, Ariana slipped under the tent. Finally, she caught her breath. Until...

On the stage, she saw the famed globe of death. Motorcycles zoomed sideways and upside-down inside a metal mesh sphere. Carlos kneeled at its center, blindfolded, surrounded by four swords wedged into the mesh.

He smirked and squeezed his clown nose. Picked up a sword that would surely cut his short frame in half. But he raised his head and swallowed it effortlessly, the revving of the motorcycles as loud as the roaring crowd.

Carlos stood. Head inclined to the skies, he did his silly little dance, so close to getting run over Ariana couldn't bear to watch. He picked up another sword, threw it in the air, and caught the handle blindfolded. The move earned the loudest applause yet. Then he did the same with the next sword. And the next. And soon, he juggled three swords with the fourth still in his throat, the blades so close to slicing the motorcyclists riding faster and faster around the globe.

"And that's your first taste of Carlos The Clown, everyone!" shouted the circus master. His rumbling voice boomed through the speakers, followed by the roll of drums. "Let's give a big round of applause to Roy and the Xavina triplets on the motorcycles!"

Applause, applause, applause. The globe of death was nothing but a colorful blur.

An officer ran through the entrance. He shouted something unheard over the noise. The circus master positioned his microphone to say something else, but the white-eyed monster boy materialized in the shadows behind him.

And didn't hesitate before tearing the man to shreds.

Screams, screams, screams. A stampede of feet down the benches. Sporadic clapping from those who still thought this was part of the act.

Carlos carefully regurgitated his sword. He ripped off his blindfold. And he and the motorcyclists, frozen in the metal sphere, watched their mutilated circus master bleed out on the ground.

A crowd of humans helped pull the metal sphere apart, releasing those inside. One of the motorcyclists abandoned their bike, and Carlos hopped on, still holding one sword. His eyes caught Ariana's in the commotion. And his wide, painted mouth contorted in a grin.

"Ariana!"

Without thinking, she ran to climb on the motorcycle behind him. Carlos revved the engine and blasted out of the circus faster than anyone could run. He even tore through the tent with his sword. By the time Ariana realized she still held her bow, it was too late to help Carlos through the red and white fabric. She had no choice but to wrap her arms around him and clutch his polka-dot suit for dear life.

Outside, a black cloud appeared on the field, several meters above the ground. The stampede of people erupted in shouts as the monster boy somehow stood atop the swirling shadows. But he did not wound. He did not kill. He only watched as the circus tent collapsed in a *poof*.

"I knew he'd escape," Carlos said, then charged toward the school. He drove the motorcycle through the open door of the auditorium, and then they went airborne, headed straight at the cello Ariana had left on the stage.

"Not my cello!" she begged.

He crashed into the stage, dodging her cello while miraculously landing on both wheels. This would surely make one of those *Top 10 Deadliest Carlos The Clown Stunts* lists, the impact alone was enough to give Ariana a concussion. But he continued along the empty, dark hallways of the Colégio dos Mortais. The only sounds were the crackling engine of the motorcycle, the crowd's distant screams, and the racing of Carlos and Ariana's fragile, mortal hearts.

Even as the monster boy appeared right in front of them.

"Let's go!" Carlos hooted—and almost ran him over until he disappeared into the darkness. Carlos let out a cheerful laugh, then glanced back at Ariana. "Best first date ever?"

"What does he want?" she breathed. But before Carlos answered, she found herself in the absence of light. Softly, her cello played as the background music to the void, rising to a symphony with all the instruments that never were.

***

Ariana Garibaldi da Silva woke atop a desk in an empty classroom. Her neck: scratched. Her mind: spinning. Carlos: gone. And the monster boy? Standing in front of her. Casting no shadow in the dim emergency lights.

She held out her bow in front of her like a sword. How she'd kept it through the void, she had no idea. But the monster boy did not wound. He did not kill. He only... watched.

"Can you understand me?" Ariana asked.

Somehow, his blank, glowing eyes told her yes. Here was not only an immortal, but a supposed failed demigod within arm's length. Calculating. Intelligent. Restrained. Wielding powers she'd previously thought impossible.

She took a step closer. "What's your name?"

In a low growl, he said, "Jásper."

His mouth was filled with perfect, razor-sharp teeth.

"What do you want?"

A map of the continent was pinned to the classroom wall. He pointed a clawed finger at Rio de Janeiro. The capital of the empire. He made a black, wispy crown emerge from his hands and put it on his head, upon which it dissipated into nothing.

Carlos' shouts echoed down the hallway. Then came the increasing crackling of a motorcycle engine—and a very loud *crash*.

"Ariana! Ariana, are you dead?" he called out in Spanish.

"I'm in here!"

The monster boy vanished as Carlos clumsily stormed through the classroom door.

Ariana collapsed against the clown in an exhausted, dizzy hug. "His name is Jásper. And I think he wants to take the throne."

***

The story of that night made global headlines as the massacre that wasn't: *Genetic abominations may pose humanity's greatest threat; Empress of Brazil vows to search for missing killer.*

They made it seem like he'd murdered hundreds when the death toll was just one—the circus master who'd probably trapped him in that metal cage in the first place. In the weeks before he escaped, had he really pretended to be contained by it?

Monster boy back to legend.

Still, the Circo das Maravilhas continued its historic success in the seaside city of Laguna. They stayed for two more weeks, and in their next sold-out show, Ariana played her cello in the center of the globe of death.

And Carlos and the immortals whirred around her on their motorcycles in a colorful, brilliant blur.

***

After her stunt in the globe of death, people swarmed Ariana for pictures and autographs everywhere she went. The tabloids at corner stores read: *Carlos The Clown and cello star...dating? Carlos fans send Laguna mayor's daughter death threats.*

Ariana would be lying if she said she hated the attention. The only bad part was her mother's scathing disapproval—"What were you thinking? You're not going to run away with that clown, are you?" She'd made Ariana swear on her life she'd finish her studies. And at least school wasn't so bad anymore. Even the girls who once made fun of Ariana's unibrow suddenly decided to become her best friends. And maybe she didn't totally hate Bianca anymore after hearing how well she played the clarinet...

On Carlos' last day in town, Ariana took him on a small ferry across a thin strip of sea to the deserted side of Laguna. She led him into lush hills and an overgrown path, pleased to show the daredevil something he'd never seen before. At the end of the path, they stepped onto a beach with huge boulders, rocky cliff sides, and no one in sight. She'd never seen Carlos this excited—not even in the stunt clips she'd seen on television. And all they did was simply jump into the waves and lounge on the warm sand.

"Come with me," said Carlos as he rolled over to tan his back.

"Where?" Ariana asked.

"Curitiba," he said. "That's where my *Maravilla* family is going next." He traced a sad face into the sand. "You could teach me Portuguese. I'll teach you Guaraní."

"I don't know," Ariana said, not meeting his gaze. "My mother was angry enough about me performing in the globe of death without telling her first."

Carlos sighed. "It's not so bad out there."

"I suppose not, if you've survived this long."

He grinned and adjusted his sunglasses over his nose. "*I'm* the one they should be afraid of."

Ariana held her hand to her mouth, stifling a laugh. This was the first time she'd seen him not only shirtless, but without his clown attire. Carlos on his day off, his silliness not as exaggerated for the sake of a show. No, today he made jokes only meant for her.

And in addition to the jokes, they now shared another secret no one else knew: one day, Jásper would return to claim the throne. He definitely had the mythical powers to do so. And the day he did, she figured the world was bound for chaos. But would Jásper only be playing into the reptilians' warmongering goals? How could anyone know what to fight for when every rebellion benefitted them?

"What if you left the circus?" Ariana asked. "I can ask my mother to get you a spot in my school. What if you learned to read?"

"I can't," Carlos mumbled.

"Why not?"

"My little sister. She's on the other side of the continent. I think...New England? They sent her to work for that elite reptilian family. The Nacrours."

Ariana's face fell. Everyone on the planet knew what that meant. In addition to the drug trade, the formerly-royal Nacrour family dominated the illegal sex trafficking market. There wasn't a single high-end escort not under their control. Only street prostitutes had the chance at freedom, which put them in far more danger than the Nacrours' pampered, traumatized girls.

"If I break my contract," Carlos continued, "they'll kill her."

Impulsively, Ariana wrapped her arms around him, the sunscreen on her cheeks smearing onto his. Surprise rushed through her when he hugged her back tightly. His freedom came at a steep price. Was it one Ariana could convince her mother to pay for? Would she even care?

"I'm sorry," Ariana whispered.

"It's okay," Carlos said into her hair. "Maybe my *Maravilla* family will be back next year."

{ 5 }

The Ivory Brush

K.C. AMIRA

Two coffins sat heavy in the center of the room, both deep oxblood red and shimmering in the light from the stained-glass decor. I peered through the crack in the heavy wooden doors. The smell of oak and mold was comforting. I loved these doors, the small etchings on the frame marking each inch I'd grown from the day I could stand. I'd never known another house and each creaking floorboard was as familiar as the lines on my own hands. The room was quiet as I imagined I could hear the dust in the sunbeams streaming through the window. I poked my head in, hoping no one would see me sneaking between the labyrinth of chairs lined up, but a familiar hand on my shoulder gave me pause.

"You know you are not allowed in there, Sylvie. You are not yet ready to see such things."

My mother's hair, black like a raven's wings, fell loosely over her shoulders. She had that sad look in her eyes she'd had for days—darkness no light could break through. I stepped back into the foyer and pushed the doors shut.

"Lo siento, mamá."

She knelt down in front of me, tucking a loose lock behind my ear.

"It's alright, amorcita. It just isn't time yet. Paciencia."

I nervously ran my hands over the pleats in my skirt. I felt as though I had been born in this high-necked white dress, but its stiffness reminded me that I had only put it on that morning. Mama grabbed my hand and led me into the sitting room. I glanced back at the large oak doors—whispers calling through the keyhole, calling me back to the coffins. I'd only started hearing them three days before, a night tainted by violent sweating beneath my sheets that I could not fully remember. The only thing that stuck with me was the warm, wetness of my bed. When I woke, everything was strange, but beautiful somehow.

The day after, the coffins appeared and the whispers followed me from room to room. They called a name I did not recognize, but somehow remembered. A name long dead but filled with life.

"Vamonos, mi amor, let's brush your beautiful hair."

Mama sat me on the sofa, the one adorned with intricate white and red floral patterns that mimicked the garden outside. I felt the pull of the ivory brush on my scalp and the sounds of the bristles sliding through my hair drowned out the whispers. They always grew louder the farther away from the room I got. The overwhelming swirl of voices grew raucous as I climbed toward my bedroom. In the attic, they screamed, so I stopped trying to escape the living room where papa would sit by the fire and cry, never looking at Mama or me. It's as if he did not know we were even in the room. He only stared into the flames, whiskey in one hand and a cigar in the other, muttering to himself.

"All I wanted was a son. Why couldn't you have given me a son."

He was drunk and lonely, eyes glazed over. I did not want to be near him, but there were no whispers when he was around me. So I found myself stealing away to sit behind the lush, blood-red armchair he so loved, drowning in the silence save for the rustling of the ivory brush through my hair. Mama would stand in the doorway, giving me a sad smile, until she vanished into the darkness of the hall.

The night that the coffins appeared, I watched my father lean into the fire and pull a few scraps of paper out of his coat pocket, the chain of his watch glinting in the firelight. He stood slowly, as if he bore the weight of the world on his shoulders, and tossed the scraps into the flame. As he exited the room and vanished into the shadowy hallway, the voices rose, engulfing me like a swarm of cicadas in the summer heat.

This time, it was only two distinct voices—young girls, dripping with fearful innocence.

"Hermana, come find us."

I scrambled to the fire and grabbed the scraps of paper from the kindling. I thought the flame would burn, but it felt like an evening breeze, my skin untouched by heat. I stretched the ashen-edged paper out before me on the rug. Two young women looked back at me, their cheeks rosy, hair auburn just like mine, wearing the same pleated dress as me. The whispers came again, this time from the stairs.

The hairs on my neck stood up to meet the smoky room and I knew that this time, I could not run.

I followed the voices.

The whispers coiled around the banister of the winding staircase, bouncing between the framed photos of Papa and his brothers. The somber eyes of my tios followed me up each step, my tias looking on with encouragement. I was careful to be silent. I couldn't wake Mama who had already taken to bed, or disturb Papa, a starving lion in his unknown grief. The whispers continued to dance through the archway and I paused as they fluttered amongst the shapeless off-white sheets that covered my family's old furniture. I could smell that each piece was made from the same oak as the doors that separated me from the coffins. The same moldy smell as I stopped at the doors to Papa's office, a forbidden place. The whispers danced behind it, calling to me to enter, begging me to chase them deeper into danger.

I could not feel the cold of the doorknob as I twisted it open, careful to not make a sound louder than the rain outside. Papa knew love, but he also knew violence, and I was risking body and mind for these voices. He was as swift with his belt as he was with his embrace; I preferred the latter.

Papa's office was a mystery to me. I had imagined it in both nightmares and dreams, where monsters lurked and magic hid—unopened Christmas presents stashed away behind hanging coats made from the finest wool, and letters and documents meant only for his eyes. In the moonlight, I could see bits of paper scattered on his desk, but these bore no images of girls I had never met. Instead, they were adorned with scrolling letters I could barely make out, recognizing only Papa's handwriting:

"Un hombre que no puede engendrar un hijo no es un hombre en absoluto..."
"Padre, perdoname mis pecados..."

I knew there were secrets in the fire.

I could not make sense of the words. Was I reading them wrong? Maybe they weren't Papa's at all, but a letter from some estranged businessman with whom he had severed ties. I had heard stories of Papa's employees and business partners falling victim to opium dens and the poisons of whiskey and tequila. I had even overheard hushed voices saying they had taken their own lives because the war between Mexico and Spain had brought hard times upon their homes. With nothing in their pockets, they could no longer face their wives and fathers and chose to leave the living world by looking down the barrel of a gun. I was told that I was too young to know such things, but the walls in our house were thin, every vent a channel for gossip and family secrets.

The whispers started once more, softly and then growing louder from the drawers of his writing bureau. I had watched two men carry it into our home when I was nine. It was the middle of summer; they smelled like pollen and sweat. I had seen men like them in the marketplace, selling aguacates and queso fresco in their colorful stalls, their skin pricked a deep brown by the sun. Papa called them a word Mama chastised him for; she called them our brothers and sisters. She let me play with the girls who braided each other's hair by the fountain until our driver took us home. The bureau brought back memories of a time without the terrors of suitors or blossoming into a young woman.

As if they could sense that my mind was elsewhere, the whispers swelled around me, returning my gaze to the drawers of the bureau. One drawer seemed to glimmer in the light, revealing to me that within it was the secret that had drawn me in. I peered through the keyhole, praying that the magic that was happening around me would find a way for me to gain access to the drawer. Whispers rose again, but this time they rumbled down the stairs, to the heavy oak doors and the coffins. They waited patiently for me to lay my fingers on their latches and look upon those laying in wilted silk and lace.

The whispers were silenced by a single footstep in the hallway. It was not Mama's soft gait; it was the muffled thud of Papa's opera slippers. Lightning cracked outside the window and I felt as though I had been catapulted into one of the ghost stories my cousins told me to keep me up at night, tales of mad men and their monsters. I went to flee but my ruffled sleeve caught fast on the handle of the drawer, emanating a sinister glow through its brass keyhole. I pulled, but the drawer wouldn't give. Falling to my knees, I wept as thunder clapped and lightning struck, illuminating the ghostly faces of the two young women whose whispers I had been following all night. They floated outside the window, wind-swept and soaked by the storm. My chest heaving, I tugged, trying to free myself. Let the fabric tear. Let me ruin my good dress. I would take any shame over the shame of facing my father. The doorknob to the office slowly turned and I gave my sleeve a final yank. The fabric tore and the drawer came tumbling out of its slot. I gathered the contents to my chest and scrambled behind the curtains in a futile attempt to hide from my father.

He entered the room, slow and sluggish, the soles of his slippers muffled across the russet, gold-trimmed rug. Was he really so drunk that he didn't hear my cries or the clank of the drawer? I tried to catch my breath as he walked past the bureau, a glass of whiskey in his hand. He didn't notice the missing drawer or the ink pots that had fallen from the writing table; instead, he meandered to the fireplace, running his finger through the dust that had collected. He traced the picture frames—one of me at the zoo, my favorite parasol hanging by my side; a photo of my First Communion, white fluffy dress covering my shoes; and a Christmas portrait from many years ago, my cheeks plump, Mama's rosy, his eyes stern. He stopped at a photo of me, ten years old and grinning in my school uniform, ice cream dripping down my top as I stood in front of an aviary teeming with parrots—my first trip to the zoo. Bringing the photograph to the armchair, he leaned forward to light the fire, stoking the kindling and sipping his whiskey simultaneously. As he stared at the fire, his eyes changed from amber to black, swallowing the light from the flames like a void. He pulled my photo from the frame and began to tear it to pieces, tossing each shred into the fire with the same deliberation I saw on his face when he gave betting advice to my tios. I wanted to scream, to grab him, to stop him from destroying one of the only good memories I had from the Catholic school I hated so much. Yet my hands were bound to the drawer and its contents. I lowered it slowly to my lap and looked within. Glinting in the firelight was my ivory brush, its paddle flecked with, was that blood? It was caked onto the bristles. I felt bile rise in my throat as I picked it up. Beneath it sat a pile of my hair, neatly bound with a blue silk ribbon.

The whispers rose again, frantic and chaotic, creating electricity in the air that stung my skin. Two more bundles of unfamiliar hair were in the drawer and an old photo of Mama I had never seen before. In her arms were two young toddlers, round and bouncing in linen summer dresses. Mama looked so happy, but Papa had that same stern, empty look in his eyes. I flipped the image over and read the faded ink on the back—

"Jose y Maria con sus hijas, Guadalupe y Marisol, 1811"

I felt my heart turn to dust, emptiness swallowing me whole. Stuck to the back was an image of another child—an infant, lying peacefully in a basket surrounded by flowers, eyes gazing at the ceiling.

"Jose Fuentes Jr. 1809 – 1810. El hijo de Maria y Jose Fuentes. Descansa en paz."

....the son of Jose and Maria Fuentes. Rest in peace...

My ears began to ring, quietly at first as the room around me began to spin. I looked up, desperate to find something to anchor me. I dropped the hair and the photos and ran to the doorway, only to stop right in front of Papa. He stared down at me, but it was like he did not truly see me. Instead, his gaze passed straight through me and out the window at the specters of Guadalupe and Marisol, their hair floating around their heads in the wind like hundreds of wriggling newborn snakes. Both girls held ivory brushes in their hands, each covered in flecks of blood. If they were made of flesh and bone, you would have seen their knuckles go white with how tightly they gripped the brushes' handles. With both fiery rage and gentle grace, one of the girls threw her brush at the window, but the ghostly object merely flew through the glass. Papa, as if breaking out of a trance, dragged his slippers down the hallway and climbed the banister, balancing precariously on the ornamented railing. I felt something warm trickling down my ears and the back of my neck. I reached up to touch the stickiness, but before I could look to see what it was, the coffins began to scream. They screamed for me to come to them and free whoever lay inside.

I bolted down the hallway, past Papa atop the banister, past the sitting room where Mama always brushed my hair, and through the giant moldy oak doors.

The coffins vibrated, buzzing with the whispers of my dead twin sisters who lay inside these coffins. I could feel them calling to me, crying out to me that they had died by Papa's hand. How could Mama never have told me she had had children before me? How could she deny me the joy of learning about my sisters? Or maybe she was sparing me the pain of knowing I had sisters that had been snatched away from me before ever being able to know them. Maybe she was afraid she would have to explain what happened to them. Maybe this is why they were telling me themselves, even if it was too late.

I grabbed the latches on the coffin on the left, fighting to open it, tears streaming down my face.

"No se preocupen, mis hermanas. Estoy aquí para salvarte!"

My body vibrated in tune with the humming of the coffin, the ringing in my ears excruciating, my eyes seeing nothing but blinding white light. I was the peak of chaos, the wind shattering the stained-glass windows, the rain beating against the house. I felt neither heat nor cold. The lid of the coffin flew open and everything went still.

Quiet.

A deafening silence. Inside of the coffin lay a young girl, her hair cut short in chunks, bits of her scalp raw. She had the same almond eyes as my sisters and me, the same glowing cheeks muted in death. The hair on her head, however, was not Guadalupe or Marisol's. I recognized it as my own chestnut hair, wet and matted against my skull. My breath hitched as a familiar hand landed on my shoulder.

"Mama, who is she?"

I asked even though I knew that the girl in the silks of the coffin, in the dress that I had known my whole life, with the tattered sleeve intact was me.

I looked up at Mama. Her once shiny locks were tousled and caked with blood like my own. In her hand, she held the ivory brush which had been used for such violence.

"Who's in the other coffin?"

Mama bent over to wipe a tear from my cheek.

"The place you are going, mija, I am going too."

She glanced at the coffin with a knowing look in her eyes and took my hand in hers.

"For some of us," she said, "being a woman is a curse. We are not always wanted in the places we are born into. We cannot choose the arms into which our writhing naked bodies are placed when we come screaming from our mothers' wombs. But you and I, we are strong, and we will be reborn stronger than before, for now we know what pain this world can offer. In another world, mijita, there will not be such great pain."

As we started walking away from the coffins, I heard a sickening thud come from the stairwell where Papa had teetered atop the railing only moments before. Something in my heart stirred, but after that, I felt nothing, maybe only that my sisters had gotten the justice they had been longing for, even if it did not come by their hand. I felt a sense of peace for them, and myself and Mama. Mama paused, locked eyes with me and said, "Not to fear. He will not be joining us. That, I can promise you."

The great oak doors stood open, no longer smelling of mold. The sun was shining brightly, illuminating our coffins once more. I gave myself one last look in my deathbed and a parting well wish before meeting Guadalupe and Marisol. They sat waiting, their expectant smiles bringing new warmth to the dark. Their curls bounced as they stood to welcome us, full and intact, not wild and distressed like before. I noticed that my own curls shone brightly once more.

"Come, mijitas," Mama said to all of us. "Let's brush your hair, and I will tell you all about your brother."

$\{\,6\,\}$

L.A. Llorona

JAELIN ST. CLAIR

But fix thine eyes beneath: the river of blood

Approaches, in the which all those are steep'd,

Who have by violence injured.

Canto XII, Dante's Inferno

The water slowly drifts by and spray paint echoes across the river bed. The sound of the band *War* blasts in my eardrums, muffling the silence around me. The spray can clicks, clacks, and releases hues of red. The paint drips, leaving a trail that covers the neon-pink graffiti. It was a turf war of sorts: the kind that children play and yuppies pay good money to display in some museum. Art, some would call it. Vandalism, others would say. For me, it's a Tuesday.

"That will teach them," I say, my hands shaking after taking a long drag of my joint. It glows white-hot then ashen as the oxygen burns out. I am alone with *War* as the ashes scatter into the wind. Flicking the nub into the L.A. River, I continue my Tuesday routine. My hand is still shaking, the music still playing, as time itself unwinds.

Morning

"D'ante, wake up!" my mom shouted. I can smell breakfast–a tempting offer. I wonder if it's grits or chilaquiles in the oven. My bed is warm and safe compared to the early crisp summer morning. However, as light slips between the slits of the curtains, I feel the day calling to me against my wishes. I want that warmth, that safety, to stay by my side. Its presence lingers around my body, but I need to piss. And between wanting to keep sleeping and pissing, the urgency won the battle. My eyes open, adjusting to the mess in my room that I swore I would clean. Throwing my covers off, I tip-toe around the dirty clothes that I was organizing for the lavandería. Our machine broke, and our landlord, as usual, refuses to fix it. I keep telling my mom to sue or withhold the rent or some shit, but she always says we have to stay in our lane.

"I'm up!" I look down; my hands are shaky. I forgot to eat last night as usual. I slip on some basketball shorts and head out of my room. There is the familiar groan as the water pipe under my bed roars to life. I noticed my laundry basket had my favorite jeans. Unwashed still from...that night. It didn't feel suitable to wear jeans in the on-coming weather. As I close the door, the hallway is dim, but the smell of breakfast is stronger than when I first woke up. I can smell the tomatillos, serranos, and garlic roasting on the cast iron flat top—the smoke rising into the vents and out into the city. You would think with the way my mom cooks, she would be running a restaurant.

"Morning, mijito," my grandma says, plopping a wet kiss on my cheek. I am surprised by her, or maybe I just didn't get enough sleep. She has coffee in her hand and chews on some bacon she most likely stole from the basket of cooked breakfast meat.

"Morning, Abuelita." I wipe the sloppy kiss from my cheek like I was eight years old and head towards the fridge.

"Are you eating with us or are you gonna run out in the streets," my mom asks curtly, her eyes not looking up from the flat top.

"I can spare the time," I say, opening the fridge to grab some milk for the coffee. "Besides, it seems like you're making chilaquiles."

"That's good. I heard the door open last night, and I thought it was your father, but he was already in bed." I hear the tomatillos sizzle as she turns them over.

"I was—" I hesitated.

"Ay, Mariella, he was home. That was me going out to feed the gatitos." My grandma came in with the cover story.

"Oh," my mom says. She has her hands on her hips, her hair running neatly in a braid along her back. She was only a few inches shorter than me, but her presence could still melt mountains. It was the fierce accusation gaze that only mothers could give. Even at 18, I felt its intensity.

"Yeah." My Abuelita sips her coffee and nibbles on the piece of bacon that she stole.

"Stop taking the bacon!" my mom chides my Abuelita.

"Then cook a little faster! We are hungry," she laughs.

I stifle a giggle as I pull up to the table.

"I saw on the news that another shooting happened over some graffiti. Some gang violence." My mom's eyebrows start forming a furrow —her worry lines have grown more pronounced as the years have gone by. And maybe I could be called a street artist; I go and draw on places where other people draw. But I'm no gangster—I do it because I am bored. I want to get better at designing. And art school is only for yuppies with the money and connections.

"Uh, mom, the tomatillos," I say.

"Dios mío!" she screams, rushing to grab them off the flat top.

"Making salsa?" I ask, trying to change the subject, my right hand hiding in my pocket.

"Yes, your father got a promotion so I'm making enchiladas," she replied, cutting some corn tortillas into strips and frying them—

multitasking between breakfast and dinner. My dad worked in one of Ralph's warehouses, fulfilling orders for grocery stores. He started there just when I was born. It is good money but some days, it isn't enough. My mom often prays for him to get home safe. It's dangerous to be Black these days, just as it is dangerous as it is to be Mexican. The police see you one way; the gangs see you the other way. You are lazy to one party; a menace to the other. Sometimes you can't tell the difference within yourself. So you simply try and hold on to both worlds in order to sow some identity. Even if your Spanish is broken, even when your dialect is odd. You just hold on to both worlds in order to find the beauty in both.

I close the fridge, milk in hand, and head towards the coffee to wait on breakfast. Today is a good day to take the bus and paint the L.A. Bridge before they destroy it. The one bridge that's been in a ton of movies—especially car scenes. Most folks see L.A. through movie screens, car chases, and the misshapen lens of Instagram filters. Some try to gatekeep its beauty. For me, I just want to tag it.

Afternoon

The summer months were usually filled with water balloons, children screaming as the guy who sells raspados would come by. Today, the birds are chirping, cars honking in the distance as the traffic grows louder by the minute. I moved to L.A. when I was three years old. While I hate how expensive it's getting, the bustling cultures make it home. The street food isn't half bad either. On the other hand, the cops, the gangs, the fear of it all. It just makes no sense to me how violent this place can be. Making my way to the bus stop, I noticed the sun is shining, but everyone's inside.

I'm waiting, one ear listening to *Earth Wind and Fire*, the other listening to the heavy traffic. "One ear in, one ear out," my mom used to yell at me, grabbing a rag to clean up my bruised face and knuckles. The cars pass on by, some red, some blue, old minivans filled with junk. They head Downtown or the opposite way, always trying to escape something. I pull out my pen and take a long hit, letting the smoke dance in my lungs.

"She weeps," a deranged voice shouts. I turn as a cart rustles by, pushed by an unhoused man, sunburned and missing a shoe. He has a grin on his face and tears in his eyes as he pushes his belongings toward the shade, chanting to the street. *Earth-Wind and Fire's* song fades. Replacing the track is the sound of a slow squeaking tire, its wheels pressing heavily into the hot asphalt. Like a shark from the corner of my eye, I spot a black and white car rolling by.

She weeps, she weeps

She weeps, she weeps

Its mortal engine rumbles, creeping ever slowly as my world becomes muffled and slow.

***

"Yo, Dee, you good, my nigga?" Eric, with a mouthful of burger, asked me. I was chewing away slowly as we sat in front of the Snack Shack. It was nighttime. The smell of grease and smoke blended well with the evening's entrance.

"Yeah," I hesitated, taking a sip of my strawberry soda. "I'm good, just tired."

"Man, you look like you've seen a ghost." He paused, taking a sip from his soda can. "Don't tell me you're still on that shit."

"What shit, Eric? I can't stop thinking about it. I've been smoking more than usual just to cope."

We ate because there was nothing more to say. We sat there in silence as cars passed by. It was violent, the kind of silence that pulls at you until it makes something come out of your mouth. "I still have that video, Eric."

Eric and I met in the back of a cop car as teenagers. We always say it was circumstance: wrong time, wrong place. We've looked out for each other since then—compatriots in the art scene.

"Nigga, what?" he said in a quiet whisper. "Why the fuck do you have that video?"

"Because it ain't fucking right," I whispered back. My eyes shifted to the streets, then back to Eric, who's only trying to help. Guilt weighed heavy on my body, sleep escaping me at night. I was paralyzed by it.

"Right, shit, it's L.A., my nigga." Eric stood there for a moment before reaching for his phone. "Shit, I gotta go. Ay, Dee, do us both a favor and get rid of it. Nothing good comes from that shit."

"Sure." Shoving the last of my burger in my mouth, I grabbed my skateboard and headed to the bus stop. I knew my mom didn't like me out this late but there were errands to run and streets to paint. It was then that I saw her—a shadow in jeans and a t-shirt, wearing his face. My chest began to tighten as I knew all too well that walk.

"D'ante? It's good to see you." Her smile looked aged; no amount of foundation could hide the deep cracks of her grief.

"Hey, Mrs. Rose," I smiled back. Her son was killed recently. I knew Alex from high school. He was going places, man, trying to be a lawyer. I remember when he would argue with my mom as to why I shouldn't be grounded. Honestly, it almost worked when he threw a gap-toothed smile at her. My heart broke as she sat down at the bus stop. Yet everyone knew what happened. No one could do much about it. Not even me. "Where's your car?"

"I had to sell it to cover the funeral costs." She grasped her hands; you could see the fact that she had to pawn off her rings as well.

"Wow, I'm so sorry," I replied.

"It's okay," she said, looking off into the traffic. "It ain't right that they took him from me."

"I know." I choked up a bit.

The façade couldn't be maintained any longer, as tears streamed down her face, ruining the foundation she had meticulously applied. She stood there crumbling, the echoes of the destruction of her world, her joy ripped from her. I just held her. I didn't know what else to do.

"I want justice, D'ante. I know my baby didn't just die for that." Flashes of those innocent childhood memories came to me. Riding bikes and dancing to wacky music. Those sweet memories felt like bitter ashes on my heart.

"I have to go. I'll stop by tomorrow. My mom's got some food for you to try." I smiled as the bus rolled up. It was the last time that I saw her.

I turned around, staring at what might be the last thing I ever see. If I twitch, I'll die. If I say the wrong thing, I'll die. If I reach for my wallet too fast, I'll die. The car rolled down its window slowly, a white face appearing out of the beast.

"Hey, young man, do you know a Darell?" it asked me.

"No...no sir." Just like my father taught me.

"Really," it pondered.

"Yeah," I stammered.

"I just got the wrong person then." It rolled its windows. And slowly, the beast drove off.

"Jesus Christ.." I exhaled. Time crawled back to its average pace. The bus rolled up, I got on. The last thing I saw was the man in the shade, sleeping. The weeping must've stopped for him.

"She weeps, she weeps," I whispered.

The bus, the unhoused man, everything drifts into the distance as if it didn't matter.

Dusk

There's something methodical about smoking a blunt, spray painting, and listening to funk music. The last of my joint floats down the river as the day ends. I look at my phone, thinking about the video. I could delete it, forget what I saw and chuck it up to being in L.A. Or, I could send it to the local news. I ponder the right thing for what seems like an eternity as the bluish-orange sky turns its famous red. The fiery heat of the day cools down, only the concrete keeping its remnant heat. The violence, the indifference, the isolating feelings well up inside me.

"Well, D'ante, at the end of the day, you have to make sure you can sleep," I say to myself as I look towards the horizon. It's calm on the outskirts of the city. But as I look out, my eyes are drawn toward the river again. A shadowy figure, small as an ant, lingers in the distance. It grows steadily, and I can hear moaning and crying. I take out my headphones. No, it's not my music. The sound of despair and sadness crawls on my skin.

"Mi Ijo, Mi Ijo, donde?" the voice wailed.

I've heard stories about a woman crying near the river. And I'm not sure if it's anxiety or maybe my tolerance isn't as high as I thought it was, but the sound weaves around my skin.

"Donde, donde." The noise drags itself. Between the cars passing by, between the paces of my heartbeats, it intertwines. The shadow grows closer, walking along the riverside. I assume it's the woman, bringing the night with her. My feet are planted firmly and I'm frozen in place.

***

It was a routine traffic stop. You'd think that a broken tail light would be just a ticket. But not tonight. My biggest fear isn't death by cops or being jumped for tagging the wrong sign. It's the inability to do anything but watch. Watch as a life is taken.

"Are you giving me attitude, boy?" it screamed.

"No, officer, I'm not. I just want to go home."

His name was Alex. He liked peanut butter and jelly sandwiches. He sang in his church choir and had a smile that could light up a room. He wanted to be a lawyer. He saw there was work to be done. I looked up to him as a big brother. His mom made smores whenever I'd spend the night at his place. We'd watch scary movies or anime with Spanish dubs.

He didn't deserve this.

"Step out of the fucking car." It screamed, drawing its gun and aiming it at Alex. He was a mixed kid like me. We were children of colonization and

trauma, not belonging to a world that was hostile to us. Alex wasn't white; he was dark-skinned. That alone was a crime in itself.

Alex knew the game, my Abuelita knew the game. Yet the violence, the indignity, the fear, never changed. The onlookers were too frozen to move, except for me. My hands shook as I began to record.

"Please, officer," Alex said. "My mom's waiting for me at home. I'm just trying to get home—"

"Hands in the air," it commanded.

"This is some bullshit—"

The gun rang out death, 9mm fangs biting into Alex's chest. They would say he raised his hands too fast, too aggressive. They'll say the officer "was afraid for its life." They'll find an aggressive photo of Alex. Violent, they'll call him. They'll say he didn't have a father. But those of us who knew Alex, knew his mom, knew the truth: that they got away from all that. But violence finds its instruments. It always finds a way.

"Momma..." Alex whispered as the blood from his body pooled. Shock as his body registered his unbecoming. I felt like his blood was on my hands that day. The stickiness as my phone caught his life slipping away. I should've thrown a paint can at the officer. I should've shouted and jeered. But, like everyone else, I was frozen. The officer turned around, noticing my phone. Nose flared like a demon, it marched towards me and I ran. I always wondered if its body camera caught my face.

Evening

The shade grew more significant as the sunset drew to a close. The being came closer. Its wailing and walk was unfamiliar and yet familiar.

"Donde?" she repeated. As she approached, recognition washed over me.

"Ms. Rose?"

My mouth was dry, hands clammy and sore from clenching my hands. She stopped in her tracks. She wore a white dress, so dirty and frayed at the edges it was almost gray. Dripping wet, she smelled of mildew and earth. I recognized her look of despair. Her hands reach out, and I feel a gentle pull like rushing water. As she grows closer, it turns from a brook to a river.

They call them the Wailing Women—ghosts of themselves after experiencing tragedy and inflicting harm on their children. Who knows, maybe they got in an argument and the last thing she said to him was horrible. That guilt is something no priest or therapist could reconcile. They die by drowning themselves.

I try to move, try to run. My heart is beating faster and faster.

"Mijo," she moans.

And something kicks within me; I take off. Fighting the invisible current lapping at my ankles, I run for my life. Maybe it wasn't real. Maybe it was the blunt. But I run, either way I run. I climb a fence, remembering the stories my grandma would tell me about her days in Jalisco. How the sound of wind would sound like weeping. How her cousin disappeared when he was only four. How all they found were his shoes, soaking wet. So I ran. Dazed and confused, I ran. I ran until I heard a command.

"Get on the fucking ground!"

Looking to my left, I see them, hands on their holsters. Behind me, I notice that the river is far.

I comply—anything to get that wailing woman away from me. My choices are drown or get shot. I decided to take my chances with them. At least I know the rules to the game we play.

"Officer, please, someone is after me," I plead with them. I change my voice to a higher tone to sound non-threatening.

"Sure," it said. "You look fucking high." It wasn't working. That voice was familiar though.

"You gotta believe me." I turn my head to get a look at the officer. I remember. It walked towards me over a storm drain. "Shit," I whisper.

"Well, tonight's my lucky night." Hands grab my shoulders. "Get up, boy." With momentum, he swings me onto the hood of his car, my head hitting the beast. My ears ring as laughter fills the air.

"Careful, you're on thin ice already." One officer chuckles.

"Oh please, this little shit right here recorded me. That video could put me out of a job." The officer was bigger than me, at least 6ft. It gripped my arms tighter. "Say, boy, do you have that phone on ya? I mean, if you did post the video, I'd be on paid leave and shit, so maybe I am lucky?"

"Yes... yes, I do," I wince, trying to maintain civility. Between the waves of pain, I noticed her current pulling me towards her. "If you let me go, I'll... delete it."

"Let you go?" it whispered, hot breath on the back of my neck. "Now, why would I do that? I'll just say we found another body in the river. Some strung-out junkie huffing paint or maybe drugs."

The pulling sensation grows intense. I can feel it flowing underneath us. I can't help but wonder—can anything truly confine a river? Or grief?

"Michael, just get the phone so we can go," one of the other officers says, shivering suddenly. I noticed it too, how cold it got all of a sudden. It's freezing, way beyond L.A. standards. And the current pulls towards me, growing vigorous and violent. It's overwhelming.

"Shut the fuck up, I got this," it shouts. Tracing its hand up my thigh, it inches toward my pocket. I feel the shame, the violation as it comes closer.

"Donde," she whispers in its ear. The officer's hand stops mere inches from my phone. The current stills as L.A. Llorona appears behind the officers. One drops to the floor. White-faced. Dead.

"Victor," it shouts, releasing me to grab its gun. She releases me from her pull and I run again. I flee toward my neighborhood, looking back over my shoulder once. The woman stands in front of Officer Michael, gun raised right at me. I hear the shot, a single discharge.

But then I'm on the bus, heading home. My hands shake, nausea flooding me as I get off and approach my front door. Everyone's asleep. I take my clothes off, noticing the bruises on my forearms where the officer grabbed me. I stand in the bathroom, waiting for the water to warm up. Once it does, I step in, the water baptizing me in fire, washing away the filth. I stand there for an hour, trying to process. I change into my pajamas and get in bed. Pulling out my phone, I open Facebook to upload the entire video. The warmth of my bed can't shake her presence. I look down and see her at the foot of my bed. She stands, weeping softly. I edit the caption and upload before turning over to get some sleep.

She weeps.

She weeps.

She weeps.

{Romance}

{ 7 }

Calle Verde 4 O'clock

MARIEL JUNGKUNZ

Growing up, my grandmother's dogs all looked alike. Light brown, sandy-colored mutts (*Puerto Rican sato*) with warm, fat bellies like un tanque. They were solid and tough from the giant platefuls of food Abuela fed them straight from her saucepan. Their smallish heads, with floppy triangle-shaped ears, seemed out of proportion with their big bodies. They had curling tails that looked oddly cat-like to me.

My first dog was one of Abuela's signature mutts. I was 10 when we left Bitsy, *my* dog, behind in Puerto Rico. My mom said I had been too young for a dog so she lived with my grandparents. I dressed her in doll bonnets and carried her like a baby. When we moved to Florida, that's where she stayed. And where, without our supervising eyes, she gained those rice-and-bean pounds in a hurry.

I don't know why I think of Bitsy so much now, since I also left behind my best friends, family, school, and a house I loved. But it was practically impossible to grasp the magnitude of it all, and sometimes all I could focus on was the little dog. Maybe because she wasn't expecting anything from me—I couldn't write, couldn't call, couldn't send her pictures, and so she'd remained happy to see me, and always ready to resume our friendship when I returned.

Not everyone was as forgiving. My aunts, for example. Some called at first, but none visited—it was like we'd moved to another planet. We were people who traversed an unforgiving wildland and set roots in a New World. No one could understand why we'd *do* such a thing. Like, what were we needing that we could leave—so very dramatically and personally—them? So even though they were our familia, they started dropping slowly out of my life, no matter how much we'd loved each other once.

So it's not a surprise that Bitsy greets me for the first time in five years like I'm still ten-years-old and live just down the road.

I mean—does Bitsy remember me? Does she know who I am as Tía Nina and I walk in through the front door reserved for fancy visits on a scorching day in June? Who knows, because I'm pretty sure that waddling butt-waggle of a greeting and that happily snuffling snout aimed at my hands is offered to everyone who sets foot in the house. It's her own version of the SUPER HAPPY Puerto Rican kiss-and-hug hello at the door that grown-ups offer up to each other no matter how much time has passed. (*I just went to get toilet paper, but I'm still your hero!*) As a kid, I'd always gotten some pretty squishy hugs and extra wet kisses. Although I've perfected my own air kiss by now.

***

I should note that my Abuela is happy to see me, yeah, but she's also suspicious right away.

"I don't know why you're here," she shrugs me off with a hug. "I told them that I was fine."

I'm not expecting the frustrated look she gives me or the rebellious head shake. But I'm not her tiny granddaughter now. I'm just like them— another meddling relative bent on changing her.

"Well, Estela's here to visit you from Florida, and she's staying, and you know what you can and can't do— the doctor already told you," Tía Nina says as she drops my old Hello Kitty suitcase in the guest room just past the living room. She's Abuela's exact opposite when it comes to looks: tall, athletic, lean, and muscular; she teaches some high-intensity kind of yoga. When she pops over to where we're standing by the '70s plastic couch, she helps Abuela untangle her house dress. The giant cast on her arm is making it difficult for her to get dressed.

"Qué? Oh, it's nothing." Abuela swats her away like a bug. She walks away to putter around the kitchen where she's most comfortable. Her slippy-slappy slippers take her as fast as she can.

Tía and I look at each other—that tenuous familia connection making us instant best friends in this situation. *She is so stubborn*, our look said.

This time, Abuela broke her arm. She's always having emergency after emergency and insists on living alone. But that's not only it. Abuela has refused to follow her doctor's orders for years.

It was just two weeks ago Mamá called on me—I was the granddaughter tasked with taking care of her. Even though I was on summer vacation, I couldn't believe that Mamá was roping ME into this. Why me? The one with a crippling fear of flying? The one who can no longer speak Spanish naturally? It was surprising even to me how quickly my dreams had become a generic American film adaptation of my life.

Yes, I adore my Abuela. I was practically raised by her before The Move: that trademarked Puerto Rican coming-of-age situation my parents introduced into my life around year 10. I could go on and on about her house, her squishy hugs, and her mysterious parakeets and lemon tree. And Mom, knowing this, motioned for me to join the family conference call about two weeks ago. I'd been completely engrossed in a book when she barged into my room.

"Come here!" she hissed at me. She motioned for me to follow her. She sat on her bed and put her phone on speaker.

"Okay, I've got Estela here," she said, her voice suddenly all sing-songy.

"Estela—it's Tío Raul. ¿Cómo estás, mija? Oye..." He launched into the story about how Abuela had been alone and slipped in a puddle while mopping her marquesina (the carport that doubles as a room). "Thank god for the nosy vecinas, because they heard her right away."

"Yeah, it was Myrta who heard her first," my mom explained. "She couldn't get in the house, but she called the ambulance, and Rogelio showed up with the keys ..."

The tias were chorusing "ay, bendito" and "pobrecita" in the background.

"Oh no," I said softly. Abuela is a tough cookie of a woman. She's 62 years old, round and sweet, with dark cinnamon wrinkled skin. Her hair is black, jet black, never dyed—yet no gray anywhere. She laughs when she's nervous. As a kid, I made her nervous with my wild imagination and what-ifs. But as much as she is soft and pillowy, she is *unsinkable*. But she rarely heeds advice, especially from doctors. She once "prescribed" her own pills to a neighbor who "needed them more than her." This was especially problematic because she's prone to depression and mood swings—something easily managed with this once-daily pill she seldom takes.

And when something like a broken arm derails her, it has the potential to click dominos down all the way to a massive revolú. There's no translation for this word; it just means a general ruckus, tumult, but without the old-fashioned connotations. All in all, it's just a way better word in Spanish.

"I would go see her every day," Tía Nina said. "But I can't spend the night, and that's when she needs help too. You just don't know what she's going to get into."

"But that's why I asked Estela to join us!" Mamá smiled at me encouragingly. "Estela is on summer break—*tell them, tell them*—and would love to spend a few weeks with her Abuelita."

I know my face must have registered the surprise.

"Oohhhhh," I said. It perfectly captured how I felt in both Spanish and English. "Bueno..."

Mamá gave me a pleading look. I thought about my summer: guys and my art class. I sighed.

On some level, it made sense for me to go—and when my mom makes up her mind, well...

"Ay, Estela! That would be perfect." They all started chattering in Spanish, talking about how they'd all bring me meals, pick me up at the airport, and take me to the beach. Tía Yoli offered to get the guest room ready so Abuela didn't have to, and Mamá hugged me, her whole body sinking into me.

There was still Fernando to contend with.

***

While Abuela makes her one-handed coffee and listens to the morning news, Bitsy and I cuddle on the couch right by the tiny kitchen. Abuela's house was decorated back when yellow and orange were fashionable colors. It covers the tile, linoleum, appliances—whew, it's a whole circus in here.

I notice Abuela still has a picture of 7-year-old me on her record player. My grin reveals missing teeth and short curly hair, back when I thought I was going to be the next kid to reach stardom as Annie. My curls are longer now, but the humidity is creating more of a giant cloud than slick ringlets.

I sneak a quick glance in the direction of Fernando's house—his family lives right next door. When we were kids, we could see inside each other's houses if we stood on our doorsteps just so.

"You can't expect to cook and clean like you always do, Mami," Tía says sweetly. "You know that. So Estela is here to help you *just* a little bit."

Un poquito is what she says, and doesn't the word sound friendly?

Abuela glances at me and mumbles to herself while she warms up the water for her Yaucono. I watch as she strains the coffee through the colador, and she methodically adds a little condensed milk. I feel like an archeologist, unearthing relics of each unfamiliar moment that would have been a regular part of my life five years ago. She's clearly upset I'm here as she thinks she doesn't need help. Her normal tic is going to be mumbling to herself as she goes about her day. I sigh. Bitsy looks up at me to make sure I'm okay and wags her little tail; I pat her rump.

"Do you walk Bitsy?" I ask Abuela.

She bursts out laughing. "No, no. Esa mangansona? No. She wouldn't last three steps."

"That's not true! She used to run up and down that hill in the backyard, didn't she? She might surprise you."

"No, I'm too old. Can you imagine? The neighbors would laugh at me. We don't walk dogs."

"Well, I'm walking Bitsy."

"She's not some fancy walking dog," she says, shaking her head.

From my seat, I spot someone leaving Fernando's house next door and getting in an old silver car. It must be Fernando. He has a little sister, but this person leaving is about my age. From where I'm sitting, I can watch without anyone knowing I'm watching.

"All dogs like walks!" I say a little too cheerfully.

***

Before The Move, I was la madre de la manzana. I was the queen bee, fellow Americanos. My grandmother has a double-lot, the only one in her neighborhood. So, her house sits next to a giant, empty field where another house should be. That made me the default boss of the kids since I was not only one of the oldest, but I also had what, for lack of an official park, was our only neighborhood park. The fact that Abuela's house also sat on a cul-de-sac helped seal my reputation, as we could also play in the road and seldom worried about traffic. There was a perfect tree in the center of the cul-de-sac island, and that was also a key player in our afternoon adventures.

Fernando was my best friend and his sister was our constant shadow. We used to read my uncle's old comic books, chugging Sunny-D, and build forts from my grandmother's vinyl, Technicolor couches. We divvied everything up like a brother and sister would, devouring Batman, Superman, and Fantastic Four stories, then acting them out. Fernando teased me for reading Archie comics and my mom's old Periquita comics, about a girl I would have to describe as having some sort of strange porcupine hair on her head.

Fernando was the only person who'd ever seen the comics I drew or knew how much I cared about art. We would compete to be the best in class, the other boys refusing to take me seriously or believe I could one day be a good artist. But he believed in me. He'd always ask to see what I was drawing even when the others ignored me. We'd tease each other at school, playing pranks, and then we'd spend hours after school playing with the neighborhood kids or drawing together.

When I moved, even though Fernando had been a very enthusiastic pen pal, I stopped writing.

After seeing Tía off and unpacking my bags, I offer to fix Abuela's lunch. There are a couple of rice dishes in the fridge that the neighbors have brought her. I reheat them, hoping she won't be picky. But I'm wrong. She complains about the recipe her neighbor used. I think it smells delicious as I heat it up in a saucepan but I don't say anything out loud. This Puerto Rican food smells like a dream.

I sat around this kitchen for so many years, avoiding Abuela's food. What an idiot. I make a plate for myself and I'm sadly reminded that I won't get to taste her legendary cooking on this trip.

We sit and eat, her fake fruit centerpiece between us. She notices my eyes glance at Fernando's house next door and she starts to grill me about my American life; she's not satisfied with my answers.

"Are you here to see Fernando too?" she asks bluntly.

I'm not prepared to talk about him, and I'd hoped no one remembered him like I did.

I'll never forget the last messages we exchanged when we were 11. He emailed me a few times in a row, ending with "Hey, just wondering how you're doing." And finally, "What's wrong? What villain trapped you in a silent spell?"

I carried his words around with me for months, then more casually for years because I felt so guilty that I didn't respond. *Was* I trapped? *Was* I spelled? But then the longer I waited, the more it seemed weird to write back without getting into the specifics of what had happened, and why I didn't.

With every year, the chances of my apologizing and reaching out got slimmer and slimmer. My advice-column quoting best friend Chelsea begged me not to do anything about it. She proclaimed that we'd clearly all moved on and that a few years of silence was a *lifetime* in teen years.

But Chelsea didn't have to deal with the fact that his casa was next to my casa, and we might see each other again. Fear of flying, all that, was a barrier—but for how long? And now here we are.

Abuela watches me with the same eager look I once reserved for the tiny, beloved ramekins of flan she'd keep in her fridge. She's excited.

"Oh, how is he?" I brighten, trying to match her mood, hoping she doesn't suspect I'd rather avoid the subject. I'm expecting some small talk about school or his mom so I can just nod and redirect.

"Hecho todo un hombre," she starts out and then goes on to gossip like we're living some telenovela. Which, when you've known everyone for decades, it kind of is. Apparently, the girl from up the street stops by his house all the time, but Abuela can tell he doesn't like her. No one in the vecindario does, really. He bought a car, but she's worried he's not responsible enough, and she wonders if I'm driving yet.

I tell her that I got my permit at school, but I'm still stuck on the fact that she's basically telling me that a) Fernando's a snack, and b) he might have a girlfriend.

"Pero es todo un caballero," she adds smiling.

A manly, perfect gentleman. Thanks a lot, Abuela.

I don't have a poker face, so I'm sure she sees my reaction to each word play out on my face. *Yes! No! Boo evil girlfriend!* Etc. And the final blow to my heart:

"Are you still writing to him?"

"No, we stopped a long time ago."

And all the heartbreak of the ages oozes out as she says, "Ay, que pena."

Yes, I agree. It's the greatest pena of all. *Ay, que pena.* They're just everyday words we say all the time, but at their core, they are telenovela, sprawl-out-on-the-bed-crying sad.

***

I have a boyfriend. Maybe? Bradley's a friend of Chelsea's cousin and the bass player in a band. We were in the same physics class last year, and I sat behind him, staring at his lightly freckled neck. I wasted a lot of hours that way. Don't worry, I still aced the class. His neck wasn't there to interfere with my GPA.

Chelsea and I had lunch with the upperclassmen because of that advanced science class. It messed up our schedule. So we stuck together the first few weeks of school, then started tagging along with her cousin, his skater friend, and Bradley. Bradley tried to ask Chelsea out, and she said no, and then he asked me out via Chelsea's cousin, and we all hung out at a football game, sneaking away to get fast food and then wandering the hallways of our school at night.

I texted Bradley before I left, and he seemed confused by me. He didn't ask about Puerto Rico. "I don't know if I can wait," he wrote. "but I hope your gramma is ok." I think about his response as I give Abuela her medication. Maybe I've got it all wrong? Maybe he's just afraid to say he likes me?

"Abuela, take your medicine," I coax her. I serve her the pills with a tall glass of guava juice.

"Ay, mija," she exhales with exhaustion. "I don't want to. I'm tired of it. And I'm all by myself. And your Abuelo never believed in it."

"He didn't want you taking your medications?"

"No, he thought they were fake."

"They help you, Abuela."

I look at her face and smile at the happy, crinkly eyes she can't hide even when she's sighing.

After her pills, I clean the kitchen. She gives me directions, and I wash just like she asks.

"Nina brings her own cleaners, and I don't trust them. Smells like no lemon I ever smelled!"

The whole house reeks of her cheap cleaner and I'm practically gagging at the fumes.

"Abuela, it's your house, I'll clean however you want."

"Go take Bitsy for your walk," she hugs me. "I'm going to take a nap."

I'm not naive, so I wait long enough to confirm she is sleeping and not secretly cooking some giant asopao with her way-too-heavy cauldron. I grab what looks like Bitsy's new and never-used collar and leash and put it on her.

She spins around trying to get a look at it. This is a dog with no neck. She's just a little roll. A little burrito with a sweet face.

I test out the leash, pulling her around the room. She takes a few steps, then lays down and refuses to budge.

She just needs practice.

20 minutes later, I set out with Bitsy in tow, giving her some little tugs to keep her going.

I decide to follow the neighborhood sidewalks instead of heading toward the little business district nearby. Abuela's street quickly gives way to unfamiliar houses and I take it all in—I'm a TV character stepping off a familiar set and into another story. I remember everything about Abuela's street, but nothing about these other places, even though we must have driven these streets constantly on our way over to Abuela's house from our own, about 10 minutes and three neighbor-hoods over.

I get a few "Buenas!" from the neighbors who are out in the yard, though I don't pass a single person out for exercise or a leisurely walk.

As I round the corner of the church where I was baptized, and where my parents were married, I hear a strange sound.

It's a high-pitched bark; it's getting closer and closer. In the split second that it takes this over-frenzied beast to reach us, Bitsy panics. I pick her up to keep her safe, clearly not thinking about the implica-tions of carrying a dog the hefty size of a full duffel bag in my arms while I fend off an attacking mop. I'm calling the dog Yappy.

Bitsy is whining and yelping like she's in pain when in reality it's my own legs that are on fire. The dog has pulled a hole in my pants with her nails.

I'm about to make a run for it when Yappy gets her claws tangled in my pants' drawstring.

To loosen her claws, I turn in a circle, first one way, then another, and qué lio. Bitsy is starting to perk up and bark back instead of whining.

I'm spinning around and around with my pet sausage roll in my arms and another howling in fear at my waist because it can't get its nail loose when I hear a voice behind me. I don't look; I'm just trying to keep my pants on.

"Ok, stop, for a second and I can help you."

I hesitate and turn the other way to see *his* face. The face I've thought of for years now.

I yelp and try to grab at my pants while still holding Bitsy. I almost fall but he grabs her from my arms and I untangle the terrified dog at my waist. It lets out a giant bark and runs off to hide.

"Are you okay?" he says, laughing. Bitsy is kissing his face as if they're long-lost best friends.

"Whoa whoa," I warn her. She pants and smiles obliviously. Dogs. I shake my head. This whole thing is ridiculous. He sets Bitsy down gently.

"Bolín is nuts," he gestures in the direction the other dog ran. "She's tough one second, and then she'll get scared of her own shadow, literally. I'm Fernando," he adds, sticking out a hand in greeting. "You're walking Bitsy?" he looks confused.

"Oh, yes," I smooth down my curls instinctively. *I remember you! Do you remember me?* His green eyes scan my face, and I take a breath. "She's a little new to walking. Well, new to being walked."

"Yeah, I wouldn't have thought it possible."

"She was doing okay until Bolín came along."

He laughs. "She has four sisters. All terrors."

I let out a loud laugh and his face shifts.

"Oh my god, Estela!" He crosses his arms and looks at me with a playful smile. Growing up, Fernando had been the serious scholar type, and it doesn't seem like he's changed much. He's polished, and he's got a nice watch on his wrist, so he looks older than he is. He has the same perfect smile—I suffered through retainers when I was 9, he didn't—and his lashes are ridiculously long and dark.

"Are you visiting?"

"Well, yes, staying with my grandmother. Until her arm heals."

"You've been in Florida all this time."

"Yeah."

"Well, welcome." Where we might say "welcome back" in English, here it's enough to say bienvenida. *Welcome.*

Since Bitsy doesn't know what to do with herself on a leash, we walk her back as we talk politely about my Abuela and his grandmother's health. So many malaises between the two of them. But of course, his family lives with his abuelita, so they all help her. I wonder if Abuela wishes we did.

"We look after her too, you know," Fernando says. "We are neighbors. Your Tía Nina is here a lot but maybe it's not enough?"

I feel like a time traveler. Yesterday he was a kid, today he's a tall stranger. He's dressed in a button-up shirt with rolled-up sleeves–was he at work? But he's also got chunky sneakers on.

"So how is Florida?"

"Well, I don't live anywhere near Mickey Mouse, if that's what you're wondering."

"That's all we know," he said, laughing. "Can you blame us? Well, that and Miami."

"Yeah, it couldn't be any more different. I live in the Panhandle."

"Not the pan itself, too bad."

"It's hot and boring in the suburbs, and we don't have any lizards. Or beaches."

"Aw, what? Everyone loves Florida!"

"Yeah, right."

I wonder what's happened in this neighborhood over the past five years. I can ask. I can catch up. I can find out. It's hard to imagine all my friends grown up, driving, and going through dating drama.

"So did you like 'Into the Spiderverse'?" Fernando asks as if it's a seamless transition from casual banter into movies.

Are we still doing this?

Didn't I grow up, painting acrylic black-and-whites from photos in vintage magazines, making ceramic pots, and sketching the giant leaves from El Yunque from memory? Didn't I win a couple of fancy awards for my watercolors? My parents, my brother, and I dressed up to go to a fancy gallery opening where I represented my school in a holiday exhibit. At my teacher's encouragement, I'd added glass shards as snow to my gloomy, dreamy watercolor landscape. "Window to Winter," I'd called it.

Would I rather be sketching comic books in the cul-de-sac club?

I eye him suspiciously.

"I think you forgot to write back," he says, shrugging, to break the silence.

Even Bitsy is quiet. She's actually sitting down and panting happily. I don't know what to say. My phone beeps with a text. *"How is your grandma???!!!!!"*- Chelsea.

I don't even think she knows her name. She's not my *Grandma*.

Why had I ever called her *Grandma*? Why had I changed her name to spare some monolingual half-friend the embarrassment of not being able to pronounce ABUELA?

Mi abuela.

I'd practically been raised by her. For years, I'd lived here.

"Oh, that reminds me!" he says, snapping his fingers as if he suddenly remembers it. "Your Abuela has something for you at home. From me."

Was he absolving me? Is it possible we could just pick up where we left off?

Bitsy needs water so we say some awkward goodbyes. I know we will seek each other out again soon to maybe sort it all out.

When I get inside, I ask Abuela what she has from Fernando. She smiles softly and after she comes back from her room, hands me a comic. It was a Miles Morales issue, dated from five years ago. It was from the week I left PR. A post-it note was slapped on the front:

Nos vemos! Come over the minute you get back. Your Fernando.

For Every Flower, A Bird

KIARA MEDINA

The coquíes were frantic.

On any other night, their rhythmic calls would have been a comfort, their sound a crescendo amongst other nighttime noises. *Coquí. Coquí. Coquí.* It was the sound of her childhood, the sound she would fall asleep to every night, as steady as her own heartbeat.

Tonight, their desperate cries made Alida uneasy.

By the time she reached the cave, she was coated in a thick layer of sweat. She was sticky and no matter how much she swiped at her forehead, the sweat remained. Here, she couldn't hear the coquíes anymore. It was quiet for the first time all night, but the unease in Alida's stomach hadn't gone away.

Taroo wasn't here.

She knew there was no need to worry. He was most likely still making his way to the cave. She tried to ignore her negative thoughts.

At the center of the cave, a pool of water stirred. It was fed from the ocean through a small opening at the back of the cave. Alida had explored it once and found the opening barely big enough for a child to squeeze through. When she had gotten lost the year before, she had bent down to drink some of its water, hoping it was unsalted. When she reached into the water, it lit up, glowing blue. She didn't drink, just watching in wonder.

She sat by the pool, legs pulled to her chest. The water was clear enough that she could see the bottom. She had never tried swimming in the pool, but she figured it must be shallow. There was something about disturbing the water that made her hesitate. The glow was beautiful—it didn't need her to intrude with her whole body. Her hands were enough.

"Alida?"

She looked up at the sound of her name. Taroo walked in and she felt the weight of her worries dissipate. He reached for her, tenderly, until his calloused fingers found her waist and pulled her close.

It had been months of stolen moments and secret meetings. Any moment their romance might be discovered by their tribes. The Tainos believed Taroo's Carib tribe were savages, only wanting to destroy. If either knew what was happening in this cave, Alida and Taroo's lives would be in danger.

It was worth the risk to Alida.

She'd met Taroo when he had gotten a vine tangled around his ankle. He was hopping on one foot as he tried to unwrap it. His dark hair covered his face as he desperately tried to keep his balance. As he pulled at the vine, it tangled further. As Taroo gave one last pull, the vine snapped tight around his ankle, knocking him to the ground with a thump. Alida couldn't help the laugh that escaped her.

He had seen her then. Their eyes met and she knew something had changed, even though he was a Carib and she was a Taina. They spoke for a bit before going their separate ways and agreed to meet again the next night. He was different—the word 'Taina' hadn't fallen from his lips with disdain.

She had lost count of how many nights they had met in this cave, the times they stayed up talking until finally dozing off on the hard ground. It wasn't comfortable, but she wouldn't trade a single moment of it for all the comforts in the world.

Taroo pulled away slightly to put his hand on her cheek. His expression was unguarded, and in it, she could see the love he had for her. He showed her his true self, keeping nothing hidden. She knew his deepest fears, his struggles, his desires. And he knew hers. Alone together, they were vulnerable.

But even now, Alida knew she wasn't truly alone with Taroo. She could feel the weight of her ancestors on her shoulders, previous caciques watching her, watching her fall in love with the enemy. She came from a long list of powerful people who fought and died doing what they could to protect her tribe from the Carib. She should be one of them. But she couldn't deny what she felt for Taroo. If they could find love despite their differences, maybe their tribes could, too.

She thought of her father and knew that it could never be true.

"Alida?" Taroo asked. "What's wrong?"

Her face must have shown what she was thinking. The stolen moments were everything to her, but she couldn't help but wish they didn't have to be stolen.

She sat down by the pool again, Taroo following her. He held her hand as he waited for her to speak. Alida knew from experience that he would wait as long as it took for her to find the words.

But how could she capture all the love and fear she's feeling?

"Are we destined for ruin?" she asked.

Taroo looked away from her and at the pool, as if the magic water would somehow have an answer. His eyebrows furrowed, lips pressed into a line before he let out a breath and smiled.

"No," he said finally. "We are destined to change the world."

She laughed. His words were simply a hopeful fantasy. There would be no changing the Carib's minds, or the Taino's, or her father's. The hatred ran too deep. There was too much hurt on both sides.

"Laugh all you want," Taroo said. "But, we will be together forever. We'll start a life together, even if it means leaving and going some-where new. Borinquen is a big island. We'll start a new life. More will join us, others who think the way we do, others who don't see tribes, only others like them."

She rested her head on his chest, relishing his warm body. His hand pulled her close.

"The hope you have is beautiful," she said.

"You think it's misguided," Taroo said.

She nodded. "There's still too much hate between our people. If your tribe found out the truth, they'd execute both of us. If my father found out..."

She could imagine him torturing Taroo in front of her, to teach her a lesson. Caciques needed to lead with strength. Not fall in love.

"We risk so much every night to be here," Alida continued. "For stolen moments that no one can know about. Last night my mother almost caught me. It was only by the gods that she didn't."

"But don't you see?" Taroo asked. "The gods protected you. They are in favor of us."

"If they were, we wouldn't have to hide," she said.

Taroo was quiet, his fingers absentmindedly trailing her arm. He looked at the pool again.

"Someday, we won't have to," he said.

He sounded so sure. She wanted him to be right. She wanted his optimism to be rewarded and not destroyed, but she had seen too much evil in the world. She couldn't quite let herself believe there would be no consequences to their meetings.

"For now, this is enough. Isn't it?" he asked.

"For now," she agreed. She couldn't help but smile, settling his hand on her heart.

They talked about lighter things. They told stories about people the other had never met and never would. As they talked, the world belonged to them. No one else existed besides Alida and Taroo.

The sun made its appearance too soon, casting the cave in hazy yellow light. Alida and Taroo barely slept, spending the night using their fingers to memorize the other's face. They knew they had to return home, but neither made a move to pull away. They did not want to stop touching.

"Taroo," Alida said.

"Alida."

He said her name as if it was the answer to every question he had ever had. She teared up.

Taroo's expression changed. In an instant, he looked worried. He reached out to her.

"It won't be like this forever," he said.

Pulling away, she stood. She always pulled away first, always faced reality the soonest. Taroo dreamt of impossible futures. She could only see the future that had been laid out for her.

They walked to the mouth of the cave in silence. Taroo's hand found hers and he gave it a squeeze.

"I'll see you tonight," he said.

She nodded. She at least had that to look forward to. All that would happen in between—her father's rantings, her chores—wouldn't matter after the sun set and she was back with Taroo.

That was all she ever needed to do—find her way back to him.

The walk to her village was quiet. The coquis were silent, but their frantic cries still echoed in her ears. She couldn't help but feel that something was about to happen.

As she neared the first row of bohíos, Alida heard footsteps coming from behind. The first thought that crossed her mind was that Taroo had followed her, despite the danger. But he wouldn't. He wouldn't tempt fate like that.

She turned, her heart sinking. She kept her face expressionless, gaze unwavering at her father.

Had he seen? Did he know about Taroo?

"What are you doing, sneaking out in the middle of the night for hours?" her father yelled.

"I went for a walk," she lied. She was shaking, even as she tried to hide it. "I couldn't sleep."

Her father looked at her as if he knew she was lying, but he didn't say anything. She refused to flinch at his gaze, even though every muscle in her body wanted her to run, far away, back to Taroo.

"This will be the last time you challenge my authority by doing whatever pleases you," her father stated. "I've told you not to go out into the forest. Have I not?"

Alida swallowed hard. "Yes, but—"

"No. Tomorrow you shall wed Tiburon and then you will no longer be my problem."

"No!" Alida gasped.

Her father grabbed her shoulder and dragged her back into the circle of bohíos, bustling with morning activity.

She couldn't marry Tiburon, even if she wasn't in love with Taroo. Tiburon was violent and cold. He showed no mercy, killing countless Carib without remorse. He had looked at her for far too long too many times. The thought of his hands on her body made her want to vomit.

Her father shoved her into their bohío and she landed on her side, swallowing dirt.

"You will stay here. If you so much as look out, I will have you tied up. Do you understand?"

A million responses danced on her tongue, but she forced herself to only nod. Her father left without another word.

Once he was gone, she couldn't hold back her tears. She had no idea how she would get back to Taroo.

She knew she couldn't escape tonight; her father would be watching, waiting for her to leave. He would probably follow her in an attempt to figure out what she was doing every night. If she tried to get out, she might lead her father to Taroo.

Taroo had been wrong. There was no future for them. There would never be a way to change their people's minds. All they knew was hate. And now Taroo and Alida's future was gone.

She cried until everything in her was withered and dying. All she could do was lie on the ground and hope for escape. From the window of her bohío, she could see the full moon, shining in her beautiful glory. She sat up quickly. For a moment, she began to hope.

"Please," she whispered, almost afraid to say the words out loud. "Help me."

She wasn't sure if any of the gods would be listening to her. But the moon looked bright as if it was listening.

When nothing happened, Alida felt all hope leave. She wouldn't get her happy ending.

Suddenly, a bright light filled the room. So bright that for a moment Alida worried people would rush in to investigate, or that her father might think she was escaping. The light burned her eyes until they adjusted and she saw the Moon Goddess standing in the middle of the room.

She had a stout body, her head the crescent shape of the half-moon on its side, an almost illusion of a grin with a body. Her dark skin glowed the way the moon lit up the night sky late at night when even the stars weren't visible. The goddess looked at Alida without expression.

Alida wasn't sure what to do. Should she speak first? Should she wait for the goddess?

"I have heard your cries and I am here to answer them." If the Moon Goddess knew of her love for Taroo, of her wish to escape, perhaps she could help. "I can offer you a way to leave everything behind," the Moon Goddess said. "I can turn you into a flower."

This wasn't what she expected. It would stop her marriage to Tiburon from happening, but it would also keep her away from Taroo. The goddess had to know of her love for him and the reason why the idea of marriage to Tiburon was all the more repulsive to her.

"You'll be away from all the problems that plague you," the Moon Goddess said.

"But what about Taroo?" Alida asked.

"What about him?"

He was everything to her. She wanted to believe she could start a new life with him and change everyone's mind. But if she went through with this, would their hope for a future still exist? Did the goddess not know how they felt for each other?

"I don't want to lose him," Alida whispered. "I love him."

The Moon Goddess looked at her carefully. Alida couldn't tell what the goddess saw in her expression, but eventually, she nodded.

"I will give Taroo the opportunity to find you," the Moon Goddess said. "I will place you somewhere where you are sure he will be able to find you—but it cannot be the cave."

Alida's heart sank at the thought. The cave was where they spent most of their time, where he would be looking for her right at this moment.

Where else would he look to find her? He didn't know anything about her village, and she didn't know anything about his. There was no other place they had shared a moment.

Except...

"I'll do it," Alida said. "I know where he will find me."

***

Taroo waited by the water. His hopes had flickered into nothingness, his stomach in knots. It wasn't like Alida to be away for so long. There had been times when she hadn't been able to make it out of her village, but those had been few and far in between and never lasted for more than a day or two. He had lost track of how many days it had been since her last visit.

Something must have happened to her.

But Taroo had no way of finding her. He knew everything about Alida: her favorite foods, her secret desires, what made her laugh the most. But all he knew of her tribe was that they hated his. He didn't know where it was located. Their cave was enough. Now, he didn't know where to look and to wander aimlessly would be madness. He would be killed before he had any chance of reaching her.

The cave was damp because it had been raining for days. The cave smelled of a dead animal. Even the pool was faded. Taroo wondered if it would glow. Maybe the pool and Alida were linked.

He approached it, kneeling down. He skimmed his fingers lightly over the surface, the water rippling in response. The glow was faint, but it was there.

But still no Alida.

He had never felt so helpless. He had found a new life when he met Alida, and imagining a world without her seemed impossible.

The last night he had seen her she had been worried about being caught, about what their families would do to each other if they knew the truth. He had seen in her eyes how scared she was. His words had not reassured her. Even though he could imagine a better world for them, she couldn't.

Maybe it had been too much. Maybe she had decided that the sneaking around wasn't worth the risk. That it was better for her to deny her feelings. Even though the thought stung, he couldn't blame her if that was the case. She had risked everything to be here with him.

But no, that wasn't right. Alida loved him, truly and deeply. She wouldn't leave like this.

Which meant something had happened.

He needed to know the truth. Even if it meant that he might lose his life trying to find out. It was better than remaining in this cycle of unknowing.

He stood, ready to begin his search when the pool caught his attention. The water was glowing brighter, forming an image. At first, he couldn't make it out—it looked like a small body with a semi-circle attached. But once the image became clearer, he realized it was the Moon Goddess.

Taroo couldn't tear his eyes from the water. If only Alida were here to see it too.

The Moon Goddess stared at him, and for a moment Taroo didn't know what to do. Should he kneel before her? Should he speak first?

"Taroo," the Moon Goddess said, her voice quiet. "I know of the love you have for Alida."

His heart came to a complete stop. The Moon Goddess knew their names. She might know what had happened to Alida.

"You wait in vain," the Moon Goddess continued. "She will not be returning to this cave."

A sharp pain shot across his chest at her words. Was Alida gone? He didn't want to ask.

"What happened?" he asked.

"Her father," the Moon Goddess said. "He found her after spending the night with you. He was furious, arranging her marriage to one of his warriors. Alida did not want this marriage."

Taroo swallowed hard. Had she taken her own life to avoid it? He had plans for their future, but maybe Alida couldn't see them through this complication.

"She pleaded with me, asking for a way out of this marriage. For a way to regain her freedom," the Moon Goddess explained. "She forwent her human body and became a flower. She is away from those who thought to use and harm her."

Taroo wanted to shout with joy. But just as soon as he felt the joy, it disappeared. If she had become a flower, how would they be together?

"Where can I find her? How do I restore her body?" he asked.

The Moon Goddess's image rippled in the water as if she might fade away. But Taroo had too many questions, too many things he needed to know to be able to be with Alida.

"I helped her to escape from the clutches of the men who would abuse her," the Moon Goddess said.

"I am not one of those men," he stated. "I love her, and she loves me."

He could see the Moon Goddess' disbelief. How could he make her understand their devotion to one another? Alida was within his grasp again. He could not let her be lost to him.

"I'll take her place," he pleaded. "I will forgo speech and sound if she and I can be together."

"You would forgo your life for her?" the Moon Goddess asked.

"Without hesitation."

She considered it for a moment. His heart raced as he waited for her to make a decision. Finally, the Moon Goddess nodded.

"Alida's flower is in the woods, in a place she said was important for both of you. You will forgo your human body and take that of a hummingbird. Only once you find her and she accepts your presence, will your bodies be restored to you."

"I will find her."

"You will not regain your body if you do not find her. You will spend the rest of your life as a hummingbird."

"I understand."

The goddess looked at him for a moment longer, before whispering words he could not hear.

Within moments, Taroo's human body faded away, replaced with the body of a tiny hummingbird. He was weightless, his wings flapping at speeds he couldn't begin to process. The world seemed so much bigger. The glowing pool was now an ocean.

The Moon Goddess was gone. Taroo tried to say thank you but it came out as a chirp. He knew she would understand him anyway.

He needed to find Alida. The Moon Goddess said that she was in a place that was important to them. This cave is where they had spent most of their time, but the goddess said she was in the woods.

It occurred to him that he hadn't asked what kind of flower she had become, or what color. He knew nothing else, nothing to help his search.

They had mostly stayed in the cave in order to not be caught. It was too risky to venture anywhere else for too long. Taroo didn't know of any place Alida would have considered special to them that wasn't the cave.

He flew out and into the woods. Everything seemed covered in a gray shadow, the light from the moon barely illuminating the night. Maybe it would be best to wait until morning. How was he supposed to find a flower in the dark?

He traveled in between trees and plants, moving so fast he was dizzy. With every branch he landed on, every random flower he saw, he felt more at home in his new body but more overwhelmed at the task before him. The world was so big and he was so small.

He landed on a massive tree covered in vines. The area seemed familiar, but he couldn't place it.

For a brief moment, he considered begging the Moon Goddess for help, but he knew she wouldn't give any. She had already done what she set out to do. It was up to him now.

"Alida! Alida, where are you?" he asked.

His words came out in birdsong. The sky began to lighten as the sun rose. After hours of searching, he still hadn't found her.

Maybe he didn't love her as much as he thought he did. After all, he should have figured this out immediately. Now she was lost to him, and he had no idea where to look.

He had fallen in love with her the day he met her, the day when he first heard her laugh, despite it revealing where she was standing. Maybe she knew he wouldn't have been able to chase her while being tangled in a vine. After hearing her, there had been no other choice. He knew he was to spend the rest of his life with her. The memory was as vivid to him now as it was when it had happened.

The sun illuminated the world as it began to wake up. The trees and flowers looked vibrant again. The vines on the tree began to move. Taroo's heart leaped in his chest. He knew where to look.

He knew where Alida was.

He flew from his perch, traveling faster than he thought possible. The world around him was a blur but he knew exactly where he was going. He didn't stop until he made it.

The clearing looked the way it had the first night. He could even see the vine he had gotten tangled in was somehow still on the ground. And in the midst of it, a small, red flower.

He slowed his approach. His heart in his throat. What if he was wrong? What if this flower was a mere coincidence? But no, it had to be her. This was where everything had started.

This is where their new lives would start, too.

He flew towards her, his long beak reaching into the flower. He nudged her petals. The Moon Goddess had said Alida must accept his presence before they would return to their human forms. He didn't know what it meant, but he hovered over her. She fluttered in the wind. So delicate and small. Even in this state, she was the most beautiful thing he had ever seen.

"Alida. I'm here," he said. "I'm here. We're together. We can be together."

He didn't know if she understood him, or if she could hear him, but he didn't know what else to do to let her know he was there.

One of the petals brushed his cheek gently and within a matter of seconds, Alida stood before Taroo, both in their human forms.

They looked at each other for a moment, almost unsure of what just happened. He reached forward first, wrapping her in his arms, as she buried her face in his chest.

"You're here," he whispered. "We're here."

She nodded. "My father—"

"The Moon Goddess explained," he said. "I'm sorry I didn't do anything before—"

"It's all right," she said. "You're here now."

"We're here now," he said. "And we are starting anew."

He took her hand as they began to walk away, from their old lives, from everything that kept them apart, and toward a future all their own with moonlight illuminating their path.

{ 9 }

Besitos

ASHLEY JEAN GRANILLO

8 PM

When the clock strikes midnight, Lupe will be fifteen and her lips will (hopefully) be obliterated by her long-time crush, Joaquin de la Rosa. After all, it is tradition for a quince's chambelan to whisk her off into the darkest corner of the ballroom, or to a balcony that overlooks the city, so that he can gift her with her first romantic kiss. But to get there, Lupe has to escape the familia—the chismosa tías and the too-tough tíos. Never mind the gawks of her primas and primos. Those little tattletales—even the older ones! They're the worst with their connections to the adult world and their fake wisdom. Thankfully, Lupe's best friend, Teresa, agreed to be a decoy.

Lupe puckers up in the ballroom's mirror, her lips frosted in a thick layer of hot pink lipstick like a miniature cupcake. Her tiara, all swirling loops of cubic zirconia, catches the dim light from the ballroom's dressing lounge and makes the highlighter along Lupe's cheek shimmer—a galaxy of wishes of and for Joaquin.

***

8:15 PM

The door slams behind Teresa. It catches the tail end of her tulle and pulls her back toward the ballroom where Lupe's primas await to question her. *Which one is Joaquin? Is he cute?*

"I have a plan," Teresa announces.

Teresa rests her head on Lupe's shoulder. In her reflection, Lupe wears two heads. Teresa details the layout of the ballroom, the dance floor, and where all of the tías have gathered to judge their mutual friends. Lupe hears them already, a cluster of hens clucking their disapproval. *Young women should not show so much chi-chi, mija.* The tíos are by the stage with the band, drinks glued to their palms. They'll be too busy reminiscing on their low-rider days and getting glares from their wives to notice their niece slipping away. But the primas...they are relentless.

"I'm not worried about them," Lupe says. Worrying takes up too much of her headspace. She'll lose her concentration. All she pictures is Joaquin's lips, full and round like a plum. Of all her friends, Lupe is the only one who has never been kissed by someone she's in love with.

"You should worry about enjoying your party, Lupe." Teresa sounds like some extension of her consciousness—the good one with the fluffy wings and a halo.

"I will. Once I get my kiss."

"We went over this."

A chilly blast from the air conditioning whips over them. Lupe imagines herself transforming into some kind of ice queen—unbothered and ready to conquer in the name of love. Teresa has been kissed (with tongue!), but even she doesn't understand what it means to be in love.

"It needs to be perfect, Teresa."

"But you have been kissed a dozen times before."

Lupe shakes her head. Not in the way that fireworks erupt behind her eyelids, and her irises form into the shapes of ruby, emoji hearts.

"None of those were real. I'm not changing my mind; I'm going in." Lupe doesn't wait for Teresa to protest, to feed her more lies about her past. So what if Teresa's been kissed with tongue? That doesn't give her the ability to read her mind or feel her feelings.

***

8:35 PM

Joaquin enters the ballroom, bringing what's left of the light outside in with him. Lupe gravitates toward him, her heels no longer gripping her pinky toe. But Carlita wraps her arms around Lupe's neck the moment she hits the ballroom and holds her in what most would assume to be a cousinly embrace, but is more like a warning.

She presses her red-rose lips, the kiss of death, close to Lupe's ear. "Show him to me so I can stick my heel up his ass. You may be a quince, but you're too young for all of this love crap."

Lupe wipes the side of her face without flinching. "You're the one who got married and had kids as soon as you graduated high school. You made your choice, let me make mine." Lupe smiles at her own comeback. It feels que adult. She can see her crown reflected in Carlita's eyes as her prima digests the request. The dangling number fifteen charm in the center of Lupe's crown pulsates, ready to unleash fifteen years of secrets between them, of all the travesia things Carlita did that Lupe swore not to mention—or else.

Carlita won't stop her now that Lupe is old enough to be considered a credible witness. "Don't get pregnant." It's the oldest warning in the Mexican mom handbook.

Lupe tosses her head back in mock laughter. At least Lupe has six years before she becomes one of them.

Carlita releases Lupe into the wild amongst friends and family. There are the neighborhood kids she used to play handball with late into the evening when June bugs clung to the screen doors and mosquitos nipped at their ankles. They liked to climb the rickety and rusting swing sets to new worlds, somewhere far beyond the cinder block homes.

Cesar—the one boy with the light brown, almost yellow eyes—slides into her view like an old photo fallen from a shelf. The scent of sweat and dirt fills her nostrils, back when two kids liked to pretend and play house. Make believe husband and wife.

"Guadalupe," Cesar says, his voice textured with maturity. It no longer crackles like static.

"It's Lupe," she says. It offends her that Cesar would have the nerve to say something stupid like that.

Before either of them can part ways in awkwardness, Lupe's amá forces them together for a photo. Joaquin walks behind amá with one of his friends, completely unaware that she is smooshed up against her past.

Their arms touch—the slightest zilch of a spark. She looks up at him briefly. Cesar used to be short with a shaved head, a little fuzzy egg. Now he's a mile above her height with a tiny mustache, follicles spread far apart like the distance between states. Still, she can see the crust of his fresa respado in the corners of his mouth.

Crap.

Cesar *had* kissed her. They were six. He lingered longer than their other friends. Crickets chirped their song as they sat in the grass under a full moon in the middle of the summer. The raspado man made their ices extra sweet.

"Lupe, look at my red lips," Cesar said.

And she turned her head, he pecked her on the lips.

Lupe felt nothing. Not embarrassment, not even a hint of affection for Cesar. Still, she held his hand that night as though she would never let go.

And now, once the flash goes off, she disappears—colorful orbs bouncing in her view as she blinks. A red dot covers Joaquin's face, but just by the way he walks, she knows it's him.

***

9 PM

Outside, the garden cools in the soft breeze. The wind kicks up droplets from the koi pond and sprinkles Lupe's feet. Joaquin stands alone, a plastic wine cup filled with crisp apple-raspberry cider in his hand. He reeks of sophistication and grace in his gray suit like a Mexican spy.

Lupe takes a cautious step forward, more afraid of scaring the fish Joaquin seems to be so keen on. The fish pucker up when they reach the surface. It appears they also want to be kissed. *Joaquin is mine*, Lupe recites, a mantra that she's told herself since the ninth grade when they first met in Ms. Bio's physics class. Everyone could see that what was between Lupe and Joaquin was kinetic energy. It's precisely why Ms. Bio moved her to the opposite side of the room, to avoid the inevitable romance. Que cute it would have been to kiss for science.

The fish scramble with the appearance of a shadow. It startles Joaquin. For the first time, he locks eyes with Lupe. But he takes a quick swig of the cider, tossing it back as men do with their tequila, and pads his way back to the ballroom as though he were late for something. Lupe tries to chase after him, but a warm hand wraps around her wrist.

This better not be Lucy, Lupe's older sister. She pivots on her heels, and tips slightly to the side, not quite balanced in her shoes. Her amá said to wear her pink Chucks until the ceremony, but no. She didn't want to waste time on those traditions. A dance, Lupe could manage that much, but no dolls or shoes or dances with her Daddy. Joaquin would bring her into her adulthood instead.

"Gabriel. Hi." Lupe tugs her arm away from his. This kid always follows her. They had homeroom together since the sixth grade, and their lockers were never out of sight from one another.

"Hi." Gabriel hasn't grown in two years, except for his booming voice. He's short, and Lupe is sure she'll tower over him even without her heels. His freckles dust the bridge of his nose and bloom across his cheeks.

There's an awkward silence between them, but the music from the ballroom and the laughter fill up the remainder of the space.

"I just wanted to say feliz cumple, Lupe," Gabriel says softly as if he knows Lupe wants to accuse him of something. Of what—stalking?

The notes in her locker were a little obsessive. He left one daily. She never bothered to write back. Most of Gabriel's scribblings were made up of small talk. *Como estas? I'm good. Just reading some boring ass shit in English...* And that was as romantic as Gabriel got. If he had any intentions of being her suitor, he should have made that known.

"Thank you," Lupe says. She waits for another letter, but this time, to be hand-delivered. But Gabriel stands there in his shiny zapatos and button-up as if his clothing delivers the message.

Gabriel shifts his weight from one foot to the next and slicks back his too-gelled hair. "You look beautiful, girl."

And now Lupe remembers. In fourth period world history, the kids got restless. The substitute was too busy writing a worksheet by hand, he didn't realize the kids had started a game of truth or dare. When he looked away, someone leaned over their desk, stretching their lips across the aisle for a mack.

By the time the dare reached Lupe, the bell rang. But Cynthia, the class badass, held her accountable.

"I dare you to kiss Gabriel."

Everyone waited for this show. They gathered around the pair, creating a cloud of hormones. Kissing Gabriel was the distance between Lupe and the pizza for lunch.

"Fine," Lupe said.

Gabriel leaned in, and Lupe felt herself start to lean away. But his lips were magnets; they did not repel. It was Lupe who pulled away from the force and ran toward the cafeteria, not looking back.

Damn it. She *had* been kissed. Again! But did it count if she didn't actually feel anything?

"I have to go," Lupe tells Gabriel. The memory is too much, and Joaquin—there he goes again into the ballroom.

Alone.

***

9:15 PM

Lupe's amá makes her stand in the center of the dance floor. She knew she shouldn't have chased Joaquin in; the risks were far too great. Now she has to dance with her tíos who smell all sour of beer and jolt her arms up and down like the way they always make babies dance to the song El Chinguililingui.

She gets traded from one man to the next, old and young. The youngest is her nephew, Julio. He's eight and already knows he's the best dancer in their familia. And this would all be fun and que cute if only Papa were here. Lupe scans the room to find him and knows that's one of the stupidest things she can do because he isn't there. They buried him last winter just before Spring. One last death for the season after the trees and the sunshine, and then, life bloomed around the family again. Sort of.

The music stops for a second. Julio bows and then steps away to get some punch for his good work. A piece of pan dulce, too. Lupe watches him grab two—one for his mouth and one for his free hand. Aye niño.

She remains standing in the center of the dance floor, hoping for Joaquin to swing by and drag her into his arms. But she can't find him.

Teresa, however, is standing at the other end of the dance floor, her tiptoes on the edge like she is afraid to jump into the pool of bodies, a worried look on her face.

***

9:20 PM

Joaquin has to be messin' with her. He's making her chase him so that, when the time comes, the kiss will be more than eager lips. Maybe he'll use his tongue. The thought makes her shiver, but not in a way Lupe is sure she's comfortable with. She wants her jacket, something to hold her together. Is that how she should be feeling, though?

Lupe and Teresa are back in the lounge. Teresa closes the door, then checks the stalls for patas. There are no feet or the hems of skirts dusting the ground.

"What happened?" Lupe asks.

Teresa clicks her acrylics together. She scratches her eyebrows with the end. Her mouth opens, but no sound comes out. Lupe adjusts her crown, not sure what she should be doing with her hands, or what to ask.

Finally, Teresa steps in closer and takes Lupe's hands in a tender way. A way that does not signal friendship. The way Teresa laces her fingers with Lupe's feels so much more intimate than locking elbows as they walk to class.

"I have been thinking about you and Joaquin. Even if he kisses you, it won't be your first Lupe. We already had *it* together."

Lupe sucks in a breath like the air is her first illegal cigarette behind the bungalows on the PE field. She holds it until her lungs burn. "You said it was just an experiment, that it would help me practice."

"I did want to help you practice. But I didn't know I'd like it. That I loved you." Teresa remains close. Hopeful. Lupe can tell. It's that look she gets when she listens to her favorite song or eats Hot Cheetos with extra chili sauce.

In the girl's bathroom at lunch, Lupe remembers the coolness of the tile against her arm. She leaned into it to extract the heat from the harsh Southern California autumns. The leaves were crunchy because they were burning, not simply dying of old age. Her hairline was sticky with sweat, and her lips had a small crack down the length of her bottom lip.

"I had to practice before today. For Joaquin." Lupe said. "You know I love him, right?"

Lupe didn't know where to find a boy on such short notice. It was hell trying to make her own list of guys for her quinces court. But Teresa had already made up her mind. She cupped Lupe's face and leaned in, tongue pushed up against her lower lip.

It was squishy, wet. Not in the sexy sort of way women kissing women make it look in rap videos. It was just empty. The literal act of kissing.

But how did Lupe tell Teresa, standing all mas pretty in her spaghetti strap dress that she didn't have any feelings for her beyond what they were in that moment? It was just a kiss. Like Gabriel and everyone before her.

A kiss.

Un besito.

***

9:35 PM

Lupe pulls away. "I love you, Teresa."

There's more Lupe wants to say. That it isn't that kind of friendly love that gets equated with the friendzone. It's not punitive. What she feels for Teresa is the only love she knows—extreme loyalty. She can see a future with her. Of them growing older together, little viejitas who make their tortillas in the early mornings like their abuelitas for their family.

Yet, the look on Teresa's face says otherwise. For her, love is kisses, hugs, and whatever is supposed to happen on prom night. "But you aren't in love with me."

Lupe's amá storms into the lounge, her eyes accusatory. Yes, everyone knows about all of the kisses, except for Teresa's. That doesn't mean that the chisme hasn't traveled yet. The scent of coffee lingering in the air means someone has talked.

Damn Carlita.

"The dance! If you do anything tonight, Guadalupe, you should be dancing. Right now."

Teresa doesn't wait for Lupe to redeem herself. She disappears into the cafecito hour.

***

10 PM

The tías gawk in the corner with the swaying tíos. They pass drinks in a line, then turn to one another, not even bothering to cover their mouths. It's like her family wants Guadalupe to know that they know about her plethora of besitos.

Lupe stands in the middle of the circle of fake suitors and friends of friends, who her amá hired to be in the court since Lupe only had Teresa. Now Teresa is not even here, leaving one dude out of the ring. Lucky him. How she wishes he can take her place and dance with Joaquin.

Joaquin, the guy Lupe has waited for all evening. He's finally in his rehearsed place, lips pursed in a grin. They lock eyes, and she knows that he never wanted her alone. Their kiss was meant to be public. But of course. Joaquin adores the attention and admiration of his parents and friends and the boys on his soccer team—how Suavecito. The theatrics of the kiss will be the talk in all of his inner circles. It won't be about Lupe.

But isn't that what tonight should be? Lupe's transition into adulthood?

This shit sucks because adulthood sucks. People leave you, and men, all they want to do is kiss you. Your tías and tíos like to shame you as much as your primas y primos love to invade your life. Your parents make you feel obligated to be grateful. It's not a natural feeling. Just like love...or sex...or whatever people are supposed to discover before they reach the dance floor.

Joaquin moves through the suitors as they twirl and twist, hands clasped behind his back, unassuming. As he approaches Lupe, he outstretches one hand for her to take.

She stares at it for one too many beats and they miss their cue. There goes the first spin, but Joaquin is unmoved. He waits. He's patient. A true prince. Lupe takes his hand and they're spinning like tops on the sidewalk. The ones from the paletero carts in the summer.

Lupe keeps her eyes half-lidded, blocking out the faces in the crowd. She catches a glimpse of Teresa's shoes, but by the time she makes the second revolution, Teresa is lost in the sea of her family.

Joaquin pulls Lupe upright and close to him. The music pauses, and now she knows he has planned it to happen like this. He knew about the break in the music and used it to his advantage. And she lets him kiss her.

There's a collective sigh before there's an uproar of applause. By now, Lupe expects to smile, to feel compelled to marry Joaquin and declare her love. But that never comes. Instead, what infiltrates her mind is a chasm of emptiness. A literal ditch filled with her hopes and fantasies because kissing Joaquin is a lot like kissing Cesar, Gabriel, and Teresa.

This is a total nightmare. Lupe's eyes pour hot water down the sides of her face and run under her jaw. Joaquin, the prince he is, wipes them away. He kisses her again. Everyone falls in love with the idea of them.

Everyone except for Lupe.

****

10:30 PM

How could so many kisses bring so much sadness? Kisses were the ultimate displays of affection, of human contact. You're literally swapping DNA with another human. But for Lupe, kisses were the equivalent to stars—untouchable. From a distance, they bring comfort, but up close, they burn.

Lupe keeps her arms around herself at the quinces' table. She watches her familia dance in front of her, all unaware of how much she wants this night to be over. But there's more.

Carlita is at the back of the hall tinkering with a computer, which is hooked up to a projector. A translucent sheet covers one wall, acting as a drive-in movie theatre screen.

Suddenly, the house lights dim, and the projector quietly plays images on the screen. There's music—the kind you hear playing over commercials with serene guitars. Guitars are so emotional.

The familia stops dancing. They point at the screen and clasp their hands over their mouths to stifle their laughter as they reminisce over chiquita Lupe.

"Que bonita," Lupe hears in the echoes around the hall. Yet, her tías don't say that directly to her anymore.

Lupe grazes her fingertips over her lips. She needs mas lip gloss to hide how dry they are. But then someone else will want to kiss her, or remind her of all the ones she's had before.

A voice bellows over the speakers.

"Mija." It's fragile. A piece of pottery cracked and glued, and cracked and reglued again.

When Lupe looks up, her abuelo's deep brown eyes twinkle. The hall goes silent, save for the occasional sniffle.

"You look muy bonita, very beautiful." He laughs with his last bit of strength. "I wish I could kiss you on your big day, but I am sure you have a boyfriend to do that for you, now. You don't need me."

Lupe swears she can hear her heart breaking, but it's just the sound of ice crackling in a lukewarm soda in a plastic red cup nearby. Still, she clutches her chest, just in case her heart bursts out.

She has not seen her abuelo for two years. Cancer took him during one chaotic morning during first-period eighth grade English. As an honors student, Lupe couldn't miss a class. But she had planned to sneak off during second period. She would feign her own illness, catch a ride from one of her tíos—who rarely gave a shit about school—and hold her abuelo in his hospital bed.

The camera stays on her abuelo as he recalls his favorite memory—their breakfasts together before school.

In his hospital bed, Lupe would have held him away from Death, clinging to him while they watched cartoons. A plate of huevos con papas wrapped in a fresh flour tortilla from her abuela's kitchen would have filled their bellies. They'd laugh and laugh, just like they used to before school. And before she left, she would have been sure to give him a kiss on his bald head, feel his waxy skin brush her lips once more.

But that was the kiss she never got. The one she remembers is cold and draped in blue light.

Lupe wipes her cheeks, warm and sticky with mascara. Abuelo says adios. Te quiero mucho, mija. He blows her a kiss.

The hall goes black, and in those few seconds of darkness, Lupe's right cheek sinks inward. Her cheek touches the outsides of her teeth, the besitos abuelo used to give her when she was little.

She turns over her shoulder, hopeful that she didn't remember that day correctly. Maybe cancer never took abuelo at all. Maybe...

Joaquin. Teresa. Cesar. Gabriel.

They stand in the light, their arms all outstretched to her.

***

11:45 PM

Lupe sits on a bench by the koi pond sandwiched between Teresa and Joaquin. They all giggle awkwardly at how massive her dress is; it covers Joaquin and Teresa's legs like a light blanket. Cesar and Gabriel sit across from them, each with a plate of cake, arguably just as, if not larger, than Lupe's dress.

The tíos and tías walk out of the ballroom laughing so hard they wheeze. The Santa Ana winds can't even compete with the breeze flowing out of their lungs.

Lupe waves to them, though, thankful that they have air in their chests. That she can still give them hugs, hold their bodies instead of their memories.

Carlita steps out, takes a survey of the gathering with a tilt of her head. "Did you get your kiss, nína?"

Lupe refrains from rolling her eyes. "I'm a woman today, and I have had many kisses. Except for one..." When she says it, the wind that her familia breathed into her spills out onto the concrete. It stirs the fish.

Carlita drops her gaze to her toes and nods. "I wish I could give you the one he gave me."

Lupe can't remember the last time Carlita kissed her, or when Lupe kissed Carlita. They had to have been young, unconcerned about rivalries and being cool. Too long ago.

"How about just one from you?" Lupe asks.

Carlita doesn't hesitate and grabs Lupe's arms, pulling her from between Joaquin and Teresa. They clap. Gabriel and Ceaser spit cake out from between their lips as they whoop. Carlita flips them off with a manicured nail.

The kiss is no longer than a second. Twice on either cheek. It unleashes something between them, an energy they didn't know was present—love.

Carlita pats Lupe's cheek when she pulls away, the place where the shadow of mascara still hovers over the phantom touch of abuelo's kiss from beyond.

***

12 AM

Lupe lingers behind as Joaquin, Teresa, Gabriel, and Cesar get picked up. She gives them all besitos as a parting gift. Just one for each, on the cheek. It feels like she gives them a blessing on their ride home, a little bit of her and her grief.

In the quiet, without the music and the laughter, she listens to the trickling of the water in the koi pond. It never ebbs but flows back in and out of itself, providing a home.

Water is a lot like love, Lupe thinks. It takes many forms and fills in those empty spaces, like a raspado on a hot day, a dare in the middle of a science class, a best friend, and a dream. They are all shapes of love, whether or not they lead to a fairytale ending.

She steps onto the edge of the pond and stares down at her nose, a direct replica of her abuelos.

"Te amo," Lupe tells the day or anyone in need of love. It doesn't have to start or end with a kiss for it to be real.

{ 10 }

Under A Sea of Stars

JARRARD RAJU

The sea was a symphony of life that typically danced in opulence, but for Prince Theoki right now, she was a murderer bathed in dark teals and murky pools of crimson blood. He watched human bodies flail about as the currents slapped them around until their bodies no longer moved. Theoki lunged his body upward, streaming through the violent tides until his head broke just above the surface. Theoki's green eyes dilated at the horrid sight of a large, rustic pirate ship being torn like tiny seashells.

Theoki tasted remorse like citrus pangs in the knot of his stomach. He understood his father's rampage was only because he had believed the crew onboard kidnapped his only child. Theoki fled because he dreamed of the stars and he knew he would never be able to accomplish it if he remained underwater. He couldn't keep doing what was told to him by his father. He knew Triton would roam every sea until Theoki returned, but he didn't want a life of solitude and meetings and royal duties. His heart pumped for more—for a romantic dance with the constellations that winked overhead.

Theoki sank back under the thrashing dark blue and frothy white tides. The prince glided through the churning water, the thrill of leaving his home warming his flesh and scales against the cold currents. He swam until the floor beneath him gradually raised, jagged brown rocks greeting the prince as the tides rose. Theoki pushed himself up, peeking his head above the surface. The stars still played hide and seek; Theoki's dream was nothing more than a fairytale. But anything was better than Triton's demands for a seventeen-year-old prince. So he pushed on toward the lights ahead on the shore.

He felt the rocks underneath him as his purple and teal ombre tail transformed into a pair of feet. He hadn't used his legs in years. Moonlight danced over his dark brown skin as he reached the break in the waves. The water kissed at his bare feet, reminding Theoki that the sea would always be there for him. He paused as he heard a splash and then a gurgle behind him.

It was a familiar skeleton swathed in heavy navy and rustic pirate gear. He still had a thick auburn beard and sapphire-blue irises. "Ye shouldn't be out here," the pirate said, sparse teeth revealing a flash of gold. The deep lilt of his voice was comforting to Theoki.

"Save it, Bane," he said, furrowing his brows as he turned to the lights on the shore. "I refuse to continue being Triton's puppet. You should understand that—you're nothing to him without me."

"That be the reason I came a lookin' for ye," Bane huffed. "This land is full of humans. If ye cross paths, you'll need my company lad." Theoki watched as Bane shifted forms, bright lights sparkling around his bones to reveal a brown dog with blue eyes.

The corners of Theoki's mouth tugged up as Bane ran down the beach, barking and weaving back and forth. As Theoki stepped out of the surf, he realized he had no clue where the stars would hide—but surely the humans that lived in the village did.

He stared at the golden lanterns strung from building to building, casting purple light along the cobblestone pathway. Were these the stars Theoki was told before his mother's disappearance? He inspected the old buildings. They held more character than his own city bubbled under the surface of the sea. This town cascaded in assortments of emeralds and burgandys and crimsons, while ornamental gold melted into the rooftops. Theoki clumsily marched on further into the quaint village, looking about as he rounded a corner. Until he found himself on the ground.

When Theoki picked himself up from the dirt, his eyes locked on the boy in front of him. His skin reflected the gold light of the lanterns, his hair ashy blonde in the moonlight. Theoki noticed how much his dark brown skin and amethyst hair contrasted. The boy inspected him, his cheeks flushing pink before he let out a low, uncomfortable whistle. Theoki looked down and realized that shifting into this newer form required him to be blanketed by a few pieces of fabric. When one had scales, clothing wasn't needed.

"Are you lost?" the boy said, his warm brown eyes flashing sympathetically in Theoki's direction. His voice was raspy and yet soft. "Or...um...the better question I guess, are you cold?"

Theoki hadn't thought about it. The sea was not a warm place, especially the further down one dove, so he was used to cooler temperatures. Theoki didn't say that though, simply nodding at the human.

"It's quite late here in Fuego Dorado, why don't you come with me?" Brushing the nape of his neck, his cheeks flushed in fiery crimson again. The boy reached his hand out. "That is, if you'd like."

Theoki cupped his palm in the boy's left hand and they started walking.

"I apologize," the boy said. "I never did catch your name?"

"Oh, they call me Theoki. And you?"

"Miguel Javier," he gulped. Theoki could feel the human's grip tighten as the boy stopped.

The prince followed the boy's gaze to an overlook. Gold and reds streamed below, the sea a dark cerulean shadow cast along the shore where the land and waters met. But that wasn't what the boy was looking at. Miguel's clammy hand tightened. Theoki released his hand and stepped in front of him.

Bane could've easily been any dog except for the glowing red eye in the middle of his forehead.

"Enough, Bane." Theoki said. Bane sat back and stopped growling. "You are not to harm any of the citizens that live in this town."

"Ye already be risking these folks lives simply by fraternizing with them."

"He is providing me with clothing. Nothing else."

"Theoki, where exactly are you from?" Miguel backed away slowly. He could see the fear on his face, fear cloaking his bronzed features, turning him pale. He wanted nothing more to do with him.

"I am from the sea beyond this town—the underwater Kingdom of Callisto."

He watched Miguel's eyes shoot up, horror encompassing their hazel glow. "Are you here to drag me under? Am I going to be a meal to your kind or something?" He tripped over himself, landing on his backside as he glared at Theoki.

"Miguel, absolutely not! Merfolk are nothing like that." Theoki glanced at Bane, who sighed. "Well, my father is not very nice, but the rest of us are not like him. Trust me, I fled Callisto for reasons."

"So, our legends in this village are true?" Miguel got up and stepped closer to Theoki. He looked down at him as he was a few inches taller. "If I am to trust you, you are to behave like a human."

"I will if you can promise me the stars." Theoki edged closer, the space between the two boys almost nonexistent. "The main reason I left Callisto behind was to fulfill my dream of seeing the stars."

Miguel nodded and that was enough. "My home is right up this path and my mother is at work for the night. It's small but quiet. You may have my bed." Miguel reached out and grabbed Theoki's hand, guiding him along the rocky path to a ranch-style home. Bane slunk away as the boys slipped inside.

***

Their hands were still laced together as Miguel led him through the house. He pushed open a door at the end of a long hallway and Theoki realized his dream had come true. Everywhere he looked, there were stars. In the center of the room was a bright candle. A glass cage with metal shapes sitting atop of the glow, throwing stars around the room. Everything else was bathed in indigo, large windows in a dome allowing the dark veil of night in.

"This is where you shall rest," Miguel turned on his heels, ready to exit.

Theoki grabbed the cuff of his sleeve. "Please, do not leave me."

"You wish for me to remain in my room while you sleep in my bed?" Miguel questioned.

Theoki could tell that he was tired. His dark eyes shaped like crescent moons appeared to flutter closed. Pain? Exhaustion? Or something else he was trying to hide? Theoki broke his intense staring with a small smile. "Tell me, human, do your people all house the stars in your homes?"

"No, no Theoki," Miguel laughed, low and hummed. "This is just a projector to decorate my room. The stars are not around us, but in the sky above." Miguel stared intently at the prince until he moved to a chair. He dug through a pile of clothes and threw a pair of linen pants at Theoki. Pants on, Theoki climbed into bed, his eyes eagerly dancing around at the illuminated stars.

"Also," Miguel inched closer, taking a seat on the edge of his bed, "about my comments earlier." He rubbed at his arm. "My sincerest apologies about what I said about you. For decades, possibly even centuries, stories have been told about your father, Triton. That's not to say you're the same."

Theoki eyed Miguel. His apology rang true, bringing a wide smile to Theoki's face. He peered up at the projected constellations. "I suppose I should also apologize."

"What no, you—"

"I may be innocent," Theoki interrupted. "But my father has clearly brought great pain to your village for far too long, and for that, I am sorry." They both jumped at the sound of loud barking. Theoki throws a shirt on from the floor and dashes outside. Bane in his dog form greets them.

"Ye be in for it now." His red eye flashed with regret. "We need to get thee home lad."

"No, Bane," Theoki released a deep breath from his chest. "My father's a tyrant. I refuse to go back to Callisto until I can see the stars. Unless Triton steps down, there's no way in hell I'll return."

"Triton is too powerful," Bane sighed. "And who would replace him on the throne? Ye not old enough." Wild colors of white and crimson swirled around the dog in an iridescent glow, inches away from turning back into his pirate form.

"Maybe you could," Theoki said. "You're kind, you care about the citizens of the Kingdom way more than Triton ever did."

"Matey, I am not kin—I is no merperson," Bane stated matter-of-factly.

"You are to me!" Theoki yelled and then went silent. The wind gusted past a silent Miguel. "Theoki, what's going on? Are the villagers of Fuego Dorado gonna be okay?"

Dread filled Theoki. He furrowed his brows and clenched his fists. And when he answered, it was as a prince. "I'm going to make sure of it."

***

The shore where the tides glide against the lands were crowded with villagers, similar in height and complexion to Miguel. Theoki had never seen so many humans at once. He followed Bane, Miguel in tow, as the residents of Fuego Dorado glared and whispered.

"Listen everyone, our town is in grave danger, but we have a plan to save it," Miguel tried simmering down the crowd. "Here with me is the prince of Callisto, the underwater kingdom."

Their glares had turned to terror; Theoki could feel it flowing from them. He knew if he spoke, his voice would crack. The water bubbled behind him and a woman in fuschia and teal appeared.

She removed the helmet to her scuba suit, her skin as fuchsia as her suit. Her shiny black hair barely brushed her neck. "Hello, my prince." Her vocals were soothing, like a calm ocean lapping the shore. "The king has been looking for you in other territories. You must return; Triton is angry. These land dwellers are not safe with you."

"No." The word came out harsher than intended, but Theoki was tired of backing down. He meant no malice to Luciana, after all she was part of the royal family, despite her rarely being in mermaid form. "These humans did nothing wrong, and I tire of my father. He has hurt mortals and sea beings alike for far too long." He turned quickly to face the crowd. "I know you are concerned by my presence here. But for now, you must flee this place. When it's over, you won't have to deal with Triton ever again."

"You heard them, c'mon, clear out." Miguel waved his arms animatedly.

"Please, everyone heed our warning," the mistress of the sea spoke softly. "You all need to find shelter and safety immediately." Then she turned around and returned to the stormy depths.

Miguel grabbed Theoki's hand. "There's something I want to show you before Triton arrives. Fuego Dorado's people will do as you say; they may not understand your world, but they are wise."

"Bane, come find us once the citizens have cleared out and are safe." And then he let Miguel whisk him away. They went back up the mountainside, to a slightly hidden path to the left.

From there, the village lights looked how the stars had always been described to Theoki. Maybe the stories his vanished mother told him were just about this town. They took many turns around the rocky terrain until the village was out of sight. But Theoki saw a glare of golden orbs up ahead. It was a single royal palm tree, dripping with radiant flecks of gold. It was in an open plot with a few random decayed pillars above the teal cerulean seas overhead.

"Welcome," Miguel said quietly.

A smile lingered on his face, his eyes brighter than the lights flickering above. "Miguel, what is this place?" Theoki couldn't take his eyes off any of it. Up here above the clouds, it felt like heaven.

"My Abuela used to come here when she was our age. Not many people in my village know of its existence. Apparently, she was gonna run off with some pirate, but he failed to return for her."

"That's so sad."

"Yeah, but my Abuela believed that he was murdered at the hands of your father, so it's not like the promise was technically broken."

The corners of Theoki's mouth tugged downward. "I've only known you for one night and somehow you are the broodiest human I have ever encountered."

"Have you *met* other humans before?"

The prince didn't remember much from when he was young, but he did remember that his mother used to sneak them ashore to chat with the locals. "Yeah, although most of them were much older, and not nearly as charming as you."

His comment made Miguel snicker lowly. He rolled his eyes, stepping closer to Theoki until there was just a breath's worth of space between the two. "I wanted you to see the stars." He sighed. "The skies here are rarely clear during nightfall, so when I made my promise to you, this spot came to mind. And now your father is on his way to tear my village apart and—"

Theoki leaned in and brushed his lips against Miguel's. He wasn't sure why he did it, but he didn't care. When his eyes opened, he pulled back. The kiss brief, yet tender. They stood silent, the only noise around were the whistling winds. He had never felt braver than he had in that moment, despite leaving home and trying to dethrone his father. "Thank you."

"...for?" Miguel went red. Words were nonexistent as he tried his hardest to breathe properly.

"You gave me the stars, even if they weren't necessarily the ones I had hoped for." Theoki smiled wider than he had in quite some time. If he really thought about it, he hadn't smiled like this since before his mother disappeared. Rumbles sat in the pit of his stomach, knots twisted in his chest. There was so much to say, but not enough time. The ground tremored, his father was nearing.

"Lads, follow me!" Bane yelled. They followed his dog form as he scampered down the stairs.

While they cautiously trudged steps down the eroded pathway, the prince thought about Miguel's family story: a pirate who sailed away to find a treasure so rare. "Bane, what was the rarest treasure you used to tell me about when I was younger?"

"Ye ask me such a question while we make haste down a steep path to fight yer father?"

He didn't pause his descent, but his tired sigh gave Theoki the answer he was looking for. "Cecelia. She was the most beautiful woman I'd ever seen. Dark locs. Freckles. Beautiful brown skin."

"Wait, that was my abuela!" Miguel said. "She was your partner all those decades ago! She really loved you. Never stopped—even when she married the man who became my grandpa."

Bane picked up his speed, paws pounding the ground. "Now not be the time for this lads."

"Bane, when this is all over, I wish to return to Fuego Dorado." Theoki felt a sharp pang in his chest. Something was calling to him about this particular village. There were ties here to his own kingdom. Maybe, if he stayed long enough, he could find the answers about his mother.

The ocean was silent. The wind didn't whistle, and the waves were still. The teal of the water was settled without the normal sea foam. A small distance away from shore, fizzling bubbles erupted. The low tide pulled in, caving in on itself as a dark figure towered over even the largest of pirate ships.

Triton in his kingly form. He was a beast straight out of nightmares. His eyes were crimson and soulless, octopi tentacles hanging from his salty sea green scales. They were rough and aged, not like Theoki. The king looked like a former figure of himself. The prince was sure his disappearance caused much stress on Triton, breaking the king beyond his limits.

"Leave my people alone!" Miguel shouted from the beach. He waved a steady flame on a branch. Miguel gestured toward Theoki, whose heart sank. "And you leave my novio alone too!"

"Are you the human who stole my son from our home?!" Triton's vocals thundered through the air, stretching to the shore. "First, I shall kill your entire village and force you to watch as this pathetic seaside town burns to the ground. Then I'll keep you as my personal pet until I decide a death fitting for you!"

Miguel threw the flame at Triton's face, then he took off running.

Triton ignored Theoki and pulled himself out of the waters in pursuit of Miguel. Triton's form shifted once out of the water into a tall skeletal body bathed in ashy blue with a crown made of bones adorning the top of his skull.

Theoki fell to the sand, watching his father chase after the boy who tried to give him the stars. His sadness was cut short as Bane nestled aggressively against his side, all three eyes staring menacingly.

"Lad, go help ye love. When I scoured these lands, I saw an airship that could put an end to yer dad's tyranny."

"Thank you," Theoki said, picking himself off the ground to rush after his father's large footsteps. When he felt he had enough speed, Theoki lunged forward. With outstretched arms, he grabbed hold of

Triton's dry, exposed legs. The king toppled over in a heap of boney debris.

"Father, you are not to harm this human—ever!"

Triton slowly pulled himself together, his glare locked on Theoki. "You traitorous little guppy!"

Theoki didn't spare him a look. He just grabbed Miguel and yanked him further up the hill away from the village. The further they ran, the closer the sea above the lands appeared. Theoki recalled stories of a being so beautiful, she shined like the crystals found near his kingdom underwater. When the clouds pushed back, Theoki gazed at who he believed to be the moon in all her glory. Crescent-shaped, she bled in an elegant blood-orange over the lands. His glancing was cut short as Theoki was tugged to the ground by a worn-out Miguel.

"Up ahead is a cliff's edge." Miguel turned to face the prince. "Any further and we would have fallen to our deaths."

"I wouldn't want that—especially not for you."

"I wouldn't want that for you either, fish boy—I'm kinda crazy about you now."

The ground beneath them shook violently. Theoki peered over his shoulder, taking note of the top of his father's crown in the distance.

"Lads!" Theoki looked up to see Bane on an airship. His father would never forgive him for treason, but some things were more important to Theoki than living a life ruled by somebody else. He got up, hoisting Miguel alongside him. "I know you said we shouldn't jump over the cliff's edge but it's the only way we can defeat my father." He placed both hands around Miguel's shoulders rather tightly, his pleading too loud to realize Miguel was backing him near the cliff. "Do you trust me?"

"Yes, let's do it."

Their fingers laced like vines, Theoki led them over the edge. He prayed that they landed safely on the giant silvery machine with a large wicker basket attached to its bottom. His weight shifted and the landing wasn't as effortless as diving into the ocean. It was rough and painful, his body ached a little.

"Glad you boys are here now, but Triton shan't rest until he sees us punished."

The gentle glide of the air soothed Theoki momentarily. He knew Bane was right. Before he could speak, Miguel wrapped an arm around his waist, pointing out to the sky in front of them.

"Theoki, do you see all of those flickering white and gold lights up there?"

Theoki nodded.

"Those are stars, my dear prince," Miguel whispered near the shell of his ear. "Your dreams are all around you."

Theoki choked down a sob. The stars were brilliant, glistening and winked effervescently. His whole childhood, his mother had told him stories of the great sea above the lands where stars watched over everyone. He looked below the airship into the water and then back to Miguel and Bane. "You have made me the luckiest boy in all of the seas." He kissed him, quickly, trying to keep the tears back. He dropped Miguel's hand and then ran to the edge of the basket. Without hesitation, he dove.

Ignoring the cries from above, his body soared through the air. Theoki sunk his fingers into the dried bone crown of Triton, confident the impact was enough to drag them both off the cliff's edge. He took a moment while clinging to bone to remember what it was like when the merciless king held his son like love still existed. But it had been years since his father had that emotion in his heart. Triton let out a bellow. Theoki noticed various hues of blues and purples swirling the rushing tides of the ocean around them. The creatures of the sea swam past the father and son quickly. Theoki felt his hands release from the bones of his father and the world went black, static fading to nothing.

***

Theoki opened his eyes to the crowd as he sat in the middle of a crater in the ground. Miguel and Bane pushed through the horde of villagers. There was a small orb beside him. It was filled with rioting waves and the sound of ravenous screams.

"Yer father," said Bane sadly. "He'll be there unless you choose to release him." Theoki squinted at the minty foam raging within the sphere. "Ye saved both yer kingdom and this village."

Theoki was attacked by a tongue full of drool, the pirate in dog form happier than the people from the town who broke out in cheers. Pride and sadness warred in his chest. Theoki knew he had to return home. With the king encased in a magical bubble prison, someone had to take to the throne.

No matter how much he wanted nothing to do with political affairs, the citizens of Callisto needed him. Theoki and Bane approached the shoreline as the night faded away to reveal the crisp morning sunlight. One foot above the waning tide, Theoki felt a pair of hands keep him at bay.

"Will I ever see you again?" Miguel asked, brokenhearted and defeated.

The prince pulled him in, closing the space between them. This kiss was everything he wanted it to be: longer, tender, and loving. "You gifted me something even more than the stars tonight," Theoki said, pulling away. He placed his left foot in the water. "You gifted me your heart, and in return I am gifting you mine. Do not think I will never see you again Miguel. This is not a goodbye."

Theoki turned from Miguel and the others as he let the cooling tides drag him under. With Bane in tow, his legs turned back into scales. He flicked his tail, leaving purple and teal in his wake. A sunbeam shone down on him and he smiled, looking up. His fate had now been forever sealed with Miguel's and his father couldn't do anything about it. They'd meet again under the stars, that he was sure of.

{ **11** }

The Larimar Experiment

JUDY FERNANDEZ DIAZ

My abuela's room was dark, all the shutters drawn, even in the middle of the afternoon. Perfect for sleeping in. Except there was no sleeping in at my abuela's. If the 5:00 a.m. rooster's crow didn't wake me, my abuela praying the rosary at 6:00 a.m. while bathing her legs in a combination of Vic's Vapor Rub and Bengay muscle rub would do the trick. If she saw me so much as move a hair, she would pass me her large rosary to join her. If by some miracle, I slept through all of that, the street vendor started his portion of the daily morning Santiago concert at 7:00 a.m. sharp. Though I buried my head farther under my pillow, I still heard him clearly.

"Llevo aguacate. Llevo plátanos maduro y verde. Llevo habichuelas, rojas y negras. Llevo los guaaaaaaaaaanduuuuuuuuuuleeeeees."

By then, the room smelled less of a medicine cabinet and more of the Café Santo Domingo Abuela brewed daily as she enjoyed her café con leche with pan tostado and mantequilla. One of the million things I missed from being home in Providence was sleeping in on a Saturday. Thankfully, the summer was almost over, and my brother and I were going home soon.

"Mi amor, are you going to sleep all day? We have so much to do."

It was 7:05 a.m.

"What about Alex?" I looked over at the other twin bed in our room to see my brother snoring. He could sleep through ten earthquakes.

"Isabelita, let that boy sleep," she said with a smile. She put her arm around me and ushered me out of the room, closing the door behind her. "Come help me peel the yautía for breakfast y no le lleves toda la masa this time."

"Two more days," I whispered to myself under my breath as I walked to my abuela's small kitchen. I placed a large pot of water on the stove and salted it. The summer had been long, and I was ready to go home. I missed my best friends, Yesenia and Maribel, who I hadn't seen since our 8th grade graduation two months ago. I missed lazy Saturdays sleeping in while Mami picked up extra shifts at the nursing home and Papi slept, exhausted from working late Friday nights en la factoría. I missed walking to Olneyville with Yesenia and Maribel and eating pizza while making up stories for the cute boys that came in to get a slice. Afterwards, I usually took the bus to my mom's job and played bingo with the viejitos. My favorite part of the day was the bus ride back home with Mami. She is a CNA but studying at night to be a nurse. I created flashcards for her and quizzed her on the ride home.

"You're going to be a great teacher, Isa," Mami told me the last time we rode the bus before Alex and I flew to DR for the summer. She scooted close and put her arm around me. I miss her.

"Mi amor, we need more aguacate. Try to catch up with Wellington. He has the best prices for the biggest ones," Abuela interrupted my daydream.

"It's been over twenty minutes. I don't know where he is by now."

"You're fast. Aren't you a runner con trofeos y todo? Here's a hundred pesos. Bring me the change. I'll fry up cheese and make your favorite jugo de chinola."

As my stomach rumbled, I put the pesos in my pocket, my hair in a high bun, laced up my kicks, and started scouring the streets of El Embrujo looking for Wellington.

It wasn't even eight o'clock and sweat dripped down my forehead—my baby hairs drenched.

"Morena, who's chasing you?"

The voice came from Wellington's truck, but it wasn't him.

"Where's Wellington?" I asked, looking at this boy driving slowly. He looked about my age. He was caramel complected with brown eyes. He wore a tattered Boston Red Sox T-shirt and baseball cap.

"Dímelo, linda. I'm Wellington. How can I help you?"

"My name isn't morena or linda." I rolled my eyes. "Also, you're not Wellington. He's a grown man and you're a kid."

"Excuuuuse me. I forgot how uppity girls from Santiago are." He opened the car door and stepped out. "Privona."

"I'm not conceited."

"You are a popi."

"A what?"

"Hija de mami y papi. Riquita. Una niña con cuarto."

I rolled my eyes. "Where is Wellington? Do you work for him? Just give me two of your best avocados. I've gotta go."

"Wellington is my dad and it's also my name." He walked to the flatbed and picked two avocados. "My dad is in Barahona taking care of some business, popi."

"Don't call me that."

"Why not, popi? Tu viajas. I can tell you've got that Nueba Yol glow." When he stood next to me, he towered over me. I didn't realize he was so tall when he was inside the truck.

I reached out my hand and gave him 100 pesos.

"You're not better than me just because you're from New York," he said.

"I'm not saying that I am. I'm also not from New York. I'm from Rhode Island."

"I know girls like you. Born with a silver spoon, looking down on people like me."

"You don't know me. Give me my aguacates."

I grabbed my avocados and walked back to my abuela's house. How dare he! I'm no rich girl. My parents work and I do too. The minute I turned fourteen last month, I started volunteering at my mom's nursing home after school. If kitchen staff called in sick, Mami's boss let me wash dishes for tips. The extra money is going to help Mami and Papi with my quinceañera. Popi my ass!

***

"What's wrong, corazón?" Abuela asked me later that night at dinner after we finished all the weekend chores: cleaning the house, washing the backyard concrete floors, using the hose to wash the outside of the house, and scrubbing all of the pots and pans with Brillo pads until they were shiny.

"Why doesn't Alex have to help?" I asked.

"He's little, mi amor," she answered and walked to the kitchen to get dessert.

"He's literally only one year younger than me," I whispered under my breath.

"He's outside playing baseball with other boys his age. He's made so many friends on this street. Why haven't you made any friends, cariño?"

"I have friends back home," I said as Abuela sat back down at the table and the scent of baked coconut and pineapple dulce filled the air. "Mami said we were coming here for two weeks, and that turned into two months."

"Haven't you had fun playing with your primas this summer?"

"It's been fun, but I miss Mami and Papi and all of my friends."

"I made dulce de coco con piña, mi amor. Your favorite." She smiled, but averted her gaze as she served me a piece.

"I want to go home."

"Isabel, we need to enroll you in primero de bachillerato here in Santiago."

"Ninth grade? Why, Abuela?" I asked, my heart racing, praying that my biggest fear was not about to come true. "I'm already enrolled in Classical High School for the fall. It's back home in Providence. I passed the test and everything."

"Es complicado, mi amor. You are the oldest and you need to understand that so that Alex is okay with it. He's always watching you."

"But I don't want to stay here," I said, feeling the tears running hot on my cheeks.

"Don't you love me?" Abuela asked with a disapproving look as she stood up. I followed her to the kitchen.

"Of course, I love you, Abuela, but this is not my life. Why isn't Mami or Papi coming for us?"

"It's complicated."

"What is so complicated about coming to get us? Wait. Is it money? Is that what's going on?"

Abuela served herself and started eating her slice of dulce.

"Have faith in God, mi amor. Everything will be fine."

"Nothing will be fine. I hate this place! The mosquitos are eating me alive. It's hot all the time. Apagones in the middle of the night with no electricity to power my rinky-dink fan. I'm bored out of my mind most days, because you won't let me ride the concho or the bus, because it's too 'dangerous' or whatever. I want to go home!"

I ran outside and sat in my favorite spot between my abuela's mango and guayabas trees, wiping my tears with the back of my hand. Who leaves their kids stranded in a terrible country and doesn't come back for them? As I sat in the backyard, I could hear kids playing on the street squealing with laughter. Cars passed by with Dembow music playing so loudly the ground underneath me shook. Faintly, I heard a conversation in the distance. It was my abuela talking low on the phone in Spanish. I stood up and walked toward the kitchen door, hovering on the other side so she couldn't see me.

"Yes, I told her. No, she didn't take it well. My son is devastated because Altagracia lost the baby."

Baby? What baby?

"Si, comadre, le entró una depression tremenda. She won't eat, stopped going to work, hasn't slept in days... Exactly, I told him to leave them here. He needs to focus on getting her help."

I tried to inch closer to the door to hear better, but tripped over a guayaba that had fallen on the ground. *Ouch!* I stood up and looked at my scraped knee. My fall distracted Abuela from her conversation and she came out to check on me.

"You okay, mi amor?"

"Who is depressed? Who lost a baby?"

My abuela's frown deepened and she fiddled with her hands.

"I didn't want you to find out this way, pero que vamos a hacer? Let's go talk. At fourteen, you're old enough to know what's going on."

We walked to her porch and sat on her big wicker rocking chairs.

"Your mom was pregnant and she lost the baby."

"What?!" My eyes widened, filling with tears. "That's not possible. She would have told me."

"She found out after you were already here."

"I don't understand. She didn't look pregnant at all. How can this be real?"

"Babies at that stage are tiny."

"I need to leave, Abuela. Mami needs me." I stood up from the rocking chair and walked back to the living room and picked up the house phone.

I called Mami's cell phone. No answer.

I called Papi's cell phone. Straight to voicemail.

Abuela walked quietly to her room and picked up her rosary. That night, we prayed in silence.

* * *

The next morning, I was awakened by Wellington's megaphone.

"Llevo aguacate. Llevo habichuela. Llevo los guanduuuuuuuuuuu-uules."

"Mi amor, can you get another aguacate? I'm making an asopao today after church."

He was the last person I wanted to see right now, but I brushed my teeth, put my hair in two Dutch braids, and walked outside.

"Two avocados, please," I said looking at the boxes of produce.

"Good morning, popi. Aren't you going to ask how my day is going?"

"Not really," I said without looking up.

"Why not?"

"Because I don't care. Here's the money," I extended my hand.

"Wait. Why are you looking so sad, popi?" his voice softened.

"I don't want to talk about it." I looked down at my hands.

"You don't like it here?" He seemed surprised.

"What's to like?"

"What's not to like?"

"I want to go home," I said, finally looking up at him.

"To Long Island."

"Rhode Island. I need to go home as soon as possible."

"Did something happen?"

"My mom..."

"What happened to her?"

"Can you help me find a job? I need enough money to buy a plane ticket."

"A job?" Wellington laughed. I noticed the cutest dimples I hadn't the day before. "Chica popis don't work. They spend their daddy's money."

"For the last time, I am not a 'chica popi' or whatever. Stop being so annoying!"

"Seriously though. Nobody will hire you."

"Because of my age?"

"How old are you?"

"Fourteen. How old are you?"

"Fifteen and I've been working since I was nine. So that's not it."

"Then why won't they hire me?"

"Just trust me," he said, looking off into the distance. "If you don't believe me, go to any of the businesses in this neighborhood and ask for a job."

"Maybe I will." I grabbed my avocados and walked back to my abuela's house.

"You're not going to say goodbye?" I heard him say in the distance. I didn't respond.

That afternoon after mass and a big bowl of asopao, I walked to a cafeteria style restaurant down the street. An older, balding man with glasses was tallying receipts at the cash register.

"Buenas tardes. I saw the sign that says you're hiring a waitress. I'd like to apply."

"Saludos. Wait, aren't you Doña Esterbina's granddaughter?"

"Yes."

"How's your dad? We played basketball together growing up. Doña Esterbina is like a second mother to me."

"He's okay. I guess."

"Does la Doña know you're here?"

"No."

"Look, you seem sweet, but I can't hire you," he said, returning to his receipts.

"Why?"

"I hire employees that need a job."

"I need a job."

"You want a job. There's a difference."

I looked at him, confused.

"Have you been here during the week? Met Mercedes or Ramona?"

"No."

"They're women with lots of kids. Mercedes has five; Ramona has three. They *need* this job. They're not going to quit when a customer is rude or if there's too much work one day. Know why?"

I stared at him blankly. I went to his cafeteria looking for a job and now I had to deal with a stupid lecture. Could my day get any worse?

"Because they have kids to feed. They have to put their pride aside and do what has to be done. Clean the toilet, mop vomit from a drunk customer. Go home and tell la Doña I send my saludos."

I didn't have any luck at the cafeteria, but I don't give up so easily.

Heladeria Bon Ice cream shop? No. Every colmado in the neighborhood with an open cashier position? Thanks, but also no. Every banka seeking a person to sell lottery tickets? No.

After an afternoon of rejections, I had enough. I needed my best friend.

"Girl! I'm so glad you called!" Yesenia's voice came through the computer. "Where are you?"

"I'm at an internet café. My abuela's WiFi has been down since June and I'm dying. How are you and Maribel doing? I miss you guys so much."

"We're good, but we miss you too! Only one more day!"

I exhaled heavily.

"Oh. No. That doesn't sound good. Spill the beans."

"Mami isn't doing good. Papi needs to help her. I have to stay with my abuela a little longer."

"First, I hope your mom's okay. But second, school's starting in a few days!"

"I know. We've been planning freshman year forever! My abuela isn't being too clear with me and I can't reach either of my parents. I'm thinking there's no money for plane tickets."

"Dang. You know if I had any money, I'd send it to you."

"I know! I've been trying all day to get a job and it's frustrating as hell. Wellington was right. No one will hire me. My abuela won't let me take the public conchos cause supposedly they kill you for a cell phone. I miss Providence and being able to take the bus and go where we wanted."

"Wait. Who the hell is Wellington?"

"Nobody."

"Isabel Altagracia Benitez! You are blushing. I told you you aren't too dark to blush. Spill!"

"He's just the guy that sells fruit and produce every morning."

"The older guy whose shirts are so tight, the buttons look like they're going to pop off?"

"No, his son."

"Ooooooh, he has a son? Is he cute?"

"Yes. I mean, I guess."

"I need more deets. Oh my God, you're going to get your first kiss in a whole other country!"

"Stop. You're mad loud and embarrassing right now. There's other people here." I laughed.

"Girl, ain't nobody worried about you. What does he look like?"

"He's a tall moreno."

"Yessss! You're finally embracing your Blackness. It's about damn time."

"I've never not embraced my Blackness!"

"Okay, flat iron city. You'd rather let your hair pouf than wear it natural. I need more info!"

"I'm wearing it in braids now."

"I see that. Stop changing the subject! Do you have a crush on him?"

"I mean, he's cute or whatever, but I can't stand him."

"Why?"

"I just can't. He thinks I'm uppity."

"Well, you have been a bit snobby since your family left the projects and moved to Mount Pleasant. I'm just saying," she said, sipping on a straw.

"I gotta go."

"I'm just playing, Isa, damn. You are always so sensitive."

"I know. I'm just tired. I'll call you later this week when I have more info."

***

Talking to Yesenia was just what I needed after an afternoon of rejections. For a brief moment, the sadness I felt was lifted. I walked to a small park with colorful tires painted and used as benches. As I sat down, the heaviness of what was happening to my mom returned to my mind again. Abuela had said she was so sad she wasn't eating or working. I've never known my mom to do that. I had a lump in my throat when I remembered that my sibling had just died. I started to cry uncontrollably. After a few minutes, I exhaled, wiping my tears. A stray dog walked by and I wondered if anyone had fed it.

"Are you okay?" I turned around to see Wellington walking towards me.

"I'm okay. Wait, where did you come from? Aren't you done selling in this neighborhood?"

"My family lives on the next street over. I'm staying with my tía 'til my dad returns tomorrow."

"Oh, you're leaving tomorrow? Where?"

"Back to the birthplace of Larimar, popi."

"What's Larimar?"

"Wait, you're Dominican and you don't know what Larimar is?"

"I have to go before it gets too late and my abuela worries."

"Let me walk you home then."

"Okay," I said.

"Larimar is a precious stone. You know amber, right?"

"Yeah, from Puerto Plata."

"Exactly, Larimar is like that, but blue and more magical."

"Magical?"

"Yeah, it's used for healing."

"What kind of healing?"

"All kinds. Stress. Sadness. It's very powerful."

My eyes widened as I thought of my mom.

"Where can I get some Larimar?"

"They sell it all over, but the most powerful is right from the mine in Barahona. That's where my dad works to make extra money."

"Can you help me get some Larimar?" I asked, swallowing my pride. "I need some urgently."

"Yes. Larimar is so powerful it can even change you from a popis that hates this beautiful country to someone that loves it."

"It's not for me. I need it for my mom."

"Is she okay?"

"I don't really want to talk about it. But how do we get the Larimar?"

"You can come with me tomorrow. The trip is about six hours. You can ride up with me very early in the morning."

"My abuela is never going to let me," I said as we arrived at her front porch. "Thanks for walking me home."

"If you figure something out, I'll be waiting tomorrow at 6:00 a.m. at the park with the colorful tires. I wouldn't mind the company."

"I don't have money."

"My dad can get us into the mine for free. Find a piece for your mom and hop on a guagua back to Santiago in time for dinner."

"Even if I can pull it off, how am I going to get the Larimar to my mom in Providence?"

"We'll think of something. It's a very long ride."

That evening, I sat at dinner stabbing my spaghetti noodles with a fork. Wellington's plan was wild. I can't travel six hours across the country with him, go inside a mine, and then get back.

"Mi amor, you seem so distracted today. Are you okay?" Abuela asked.

"Yes, just thinking about enrolling in school tomorrow. I probably need to leave early."

"That makes me so happy! High school isn't so bad here. You can finally make some friends."

"Um, yeah, exactly." I felt terrible lying, but the need to help my mom was overpowering.

"Let me get you the tuition. Are you sure you're okay to do all of this? My blood sugar's high with the dulce de coco I had and my knees are hurting. But take my cell phone and call me if you need."

"Gracias, Abuela."

***

At 5:00 a.m. the rooster's crow awoke me. By the time my abuela was rubbing Bengay on her joints and praying the rosary at 6:00 a.m., I was ready to leave the house.

"So early, mi amor? Let's pray first."

6:05 a.m.

"Cion, Abuela," I said, asking for her blessing.

"But not without something in your stomach first, corazón." She walked toward the kitchen to make a hot avena for me to drink. I loved the oatmeal breakfast drink, but I kept looking at the time.

6:15 a.m.

"Aren't you going to sit? You're going to burn your tongue if you don't let it cool down."

"Can I take it to go?"

"Of course, mi vida." Abuela poured the hot avena into a thermos.

6:25 a.m.

I walked to the park and looked around. No signs of Wellington.

"Dang!" I must have missed him. My heart sank. Until I felt a tug at my backpack.

"Isabel, you made it."

"So, you do know my name," I said to Wellington, pursing my lips.

"Claro." He smiled and led me toward the public transport car. Once we arrived at the bus station, we walked toward a large bus. "I got your ticket. I know you're low on funds."

"Awww, thanks. My abuela did give me some money before I left so I'm not completely broke."

I sat by the window, and he sat next to me. Our arms brushed and it made my heart race.

"What's in that thermos?" he asked, peeking over as I opened my backpack.

"My abuela's avena. It's best with bread, but I left before she toasted any."

Wellington smiled and opened his backpack. "I brought sandwiches for us."

"For me too?"

"Of course."

"How did you know I would come?"

"I didn't, but I really hoped you would."

We ate our tostadas with avena and looked out the window. The mountains were green and so beautiful. I used Abuela's cell phone to take pictures.

"Selfie?" Wellington said. "Para que no me olvides when you go back to Rhode Island."

I gave him the phone to take the picture. He leaned his head against mine and we both smiled.

"You look so pretty. I really like your hair."

"Thank you," I said and looked away toward the window. Cows grazing at pasture, motorcycles zooming past us, and the smell of coffee and cacao in the air.

We arrived in Santo Domingo in less than two hours. I had never seen the capital. It was big and intimidating. I was relieved to be there with him. We walked outside and he signaled to a man.

"Have you ever been on a motoconcho?"

"Nope," I said, a bit scared.

"A la guagua de Barahona," he told the man as we followed him toward his motorcycle. Wellington got on it first and told me to sit behind him and hold on tight to him. I was scared, but there was no turning back now. I did the sign of the cross and off we went.

We weaved in and out of heavy traffic until we reached a smaller guagua to take us to Barahona. It was packed, but I could still see the most beautiful blue ocean views I've ever seen in my life.

"Why don't you live with your dad?" I asked him about halfway through the ride.

"He asked me to come with him to Santiago, but I stayed in Barahona with my mom. Honestly, once you spend time in Barahona, you'll see why I love it so much. There really isn't any other place like it."

We arrived in Barahona a few hours later. When we walked off of the guagua, Wellington disappeared for a minute. When he re-appeared, he had two coconuts in his hands.

"Bienvenida a Barahona!" he said. "Selfie? So you don't forget the coconuts?" The coconut water was cold and delicious. Now onto the hardest part of the day– the mine.

"Are you ready to go to the mine?"

"I can't be going with you," he said.

"What do you mean you can't go in there with me? I've never been in a mine."

"It's basically just a cave. I really wanted to go in with you, but I have to take care of something urgent for my mom. My dad's waiting for you at the entrance and he'll let you in. When you find a piece of Larimar, bring it out. Show it to my dad so he can account for it and call me."

"If I make it out alive."

"Nothing is going to happen to you. I'll be back soon. I promise."

***

The cave was filled with creepy sounds. Droplets of water fell from above, causing me to jump. Could I find bravery I never lost because I didn't have it to begin with? Could a cave rescue me from fourteen-year-old pendejismo? Could it compel me to find courage? I hear wings wildly flapping. Bats?

Do bats even exist in caves in the countryside of the Dominican Republic?

Mosquitos, yes, but bats? Dulce de coco con piña, yes, but bats? Waterfalls with brave boys jumping and women washing clothes, yes, but bats? Fincas full of coffee and cacao, yes, but bats? Doñas doing chores daily, yes, but bats? Bats!

Bats bite. Thoughts of bat bites made my heart race and my forehead sweat.

"Run, Isabel, run," my brain implored.

"Not today," responded my feet glued to the sticky floors of the cave.

I put my hands in my pockets and touched a small cardboard box. The matches my abuela gave me this morning to light the gas stove. Trembling hands held one single match and struck it.

Nothing new happened. I couldn't get the match to light. My hands were too shaky. I tried again. The box was damp, and the match was wet. I breathed on it and blew, hoping that that would help. I struck again. Light consumed the cave.

I noticed a butterfly dancing near me. The cave wasn't so creepy after all. It was then that I realized that caves create courage and beautiful sounds.

Filled with new-found courage, I walked through the dark until I saw a glimmer of a blue rock before me. I turned the lit match toward it and gasped at the beautiful stone. But how do I get it out?

"Looking for this?" It was Wellington. He returned with a metal pick and his dimpled smile. He used the metal pick to carve out the piece of Larimar for me.

"It's more beautiful than I imagined." I stared at the piece of blue rock the size of my thumb.

"There's something else I want to show you just as beautiful." He took my hand and we walked out of the cave. I breathed a sigh of relief. I did it. The bats were butterflies, and my fears did not get in the way of getting Larimar for my mom.

"Your mom will heal in no time!" Wellington said as we walked down the mountain where the entrance of the cave was. My heart fluttered. I held the Larimar in one hand; he held my other hand.

"It was scary at first, but I'm proud of myself. I feel braver here in Barahona. I see why you love it." We made it to flat land and walked toward the ocean. Turquoise waters as far as my eyes could see, the sea salt breeze blowing in my hair, cars driving by with bachata beats blaring. It was the happiest I'd felt all summer.

"I knew you weren't a pendeja," he said, and smiled. He leaned in and moved a strand of hair that was blocking my eyes. My heart was beating fast as he leaned in and gave me a soft kiss on the lips.

I thought about that kiss the whole way back to Santiago.

Wellington was right.

The Dominican Republic is a special place and I could find happiness here while I wait to be reunited with my family.

{ **12** }

They Outdid the Gray Sky

NATHALIE D. MEDINA

Janelle looked down at her purple, scaled, muscular arm and beefy fist with an expression of savage satisfaction.

"Janelle!" I shouted. I latched my arms around her chest and pulled her back, though she was no longer straining to fight. Instead, my former best friend shook free of me.

"Bet you won't run that mouth again," Janelle said to Karina, the sobbing blonde girl on the floor, who was clutching her swollen face and wailing in pain. Karina's friends buzzed around her in the narrow school hallway as blood ran down her mouth, dripping on the linoleum floor.

"What are you doing?" I hissed at Janelle. "Fighting is bad enough, but did you have to *shift*, too?"

"I think you broke her jaw!" shouted one of the girls around Karina. "Lizard freak!"

"Who wants another one?" Janelle snarled, stepping forward, and this time I wrapped my arms around her shifted limb and yanked. Her scales felt hard and rough against my skin, her muscles unforgiving beneath them.

"Janelle, *stop!*" I pleaded.

Janelle turned her head slowly to look at me, her dark brown eyes steely. "The teachers are here anyway," she said as the girls around Karina clamored towards a squad of them thundering down the hallway. The lights cast a miserable greenish tint over her purple scales, making them look like an oil spill in motion.

"You're proving right every awful thing people say about shifters," I said in a rush. "Sometimes I think you *want* to be every awful thing people say you are." Janelle looked half-feral—her scaled arm huge, black hair in her eyes, and a snarl on her lips.

"I'm sick of rolling over for Karina like some kind of dog, Amaya," Janelle snapped, flexing her shifted hand as though she ached to slug Karina one more time. "After all this time, you come over here to talk to me like you're the principal? I thought you understood me. I thought *that* was why you even came over here—"

"No, I just couldn't stand watching you destroy your life!" I raked my hands through my long micro braids. I wished I had seen this coming, so that I could have done more than hold Janelle back in vain. Or that I'd let myself see sooner how cruel Karina's bullying had become. "This is why we aren't friends anymore!"

"Is that it? Or is it because I won't let myself get pushed around by a pathetic, fake little bully like Karina?" Janelle tossed back her ponytail, a tangled sheet of black slipping over her shoulder. "She thinks I should be ashamed of being a shifter. Well, I'm not!"

"Shift back!" shouted one of the teachers, keeping his distance. "Shift your arm back, or you'll be in even more trouble, Miss Hernandez!"

A beat of silence passed, intercut only by Karina's hiccuping sobs. I stared at Janelle hard, willing her to obey the teacher. Janelle's black eyes were rageful and defiant, but she closed her eyes to my gaze pointedly.

She shifted her limb back to its human form. Smooth brown skin remolded around muscle and bone, the sleeve of her t-shirt shredded. Bits of cotton drifted around her arm like confetti. "It's safe now," she said to the teachers, and I didn't miss the heavy sarcasm in her voice.

The teachers surrounded Janelle, marching her to the principal's office between them. But the heart-piercing look Janelle shot me over her shoulder lingered.

* * *

I shifted for the first time that night.

I'd thought it would be my back that shifted first, where twin knots had been burning for weeks. But the wings that were lurking beneath the surface refused to emerge.

Instead, the change snuck up on me. One moment I was agonizing over a math problem I couldn't get right, wishing I could shake myself till the correct answer fell out, and the next there was a flash of muscle and bone in my aching hands. Suddenly my dark skin turned a rippled sandy color, like desert earth with crevices through it. My nails became diamond-hard talons. My pencil dropped to the carpet, rolling in a pointless semi-circle.

I stared at my hands in disbelief. Panic flooded me as I heard my parents coming up the stairs. They couldn't see me like this. I focused hard and fiercely, and a second later, my skin and muscle reformed. My hands were my own again, down to my pink and black nail polish. And it had to stay that way. I took a shuddering breath. Nobody could know. I was a grade-A student, my parents' only, golden child— not a shifter, cursed by God and my own distorted genes, skulking on the edges of society.

This was the last thing I needed, I thought, but my tears didn't fall. And I felt lucky for my self-control, because not thirty seconds later, my parents stood framed in the doorway of my room. They hadn't knocked—they never did.

"We need to talk to you," my father said. I blinked, forcing my tears to dissolve by sheer willpower, looking down at my normal, human hands. My mother hovered by my father's side, looking serious and concerned.

"It's about that friend of yours...Janelle," my mother said. They sat on my bed, and I turned in my chair to look at them before they could claim I was being disrespectful.

"We're not friends anymore," I repeated, as I had for the past year when they mentioned her. Janelle's face flashed through my mind with the same ache in my chest that usually accompanied it, her dark eyes and copper skin and black hair that was always up in a messy ponytail. I had avoided her at school, as my parents had demanded; I had stopped picking up her calls or answering her texts. I had let our connection erode by neglect.

Now, I called and texted the girls on my volleyball team, more "appropriate friendships" according to my parents. Now, I hung out with the kids from the school newspaper or the literary magazine. Now, I took honors classes and volunteered my time as a peer tutor. What else could my parents possibly have to say about Janelle to me?

"Well, we know the school is making you tutor her," said my mother.

My fingers clenched around the back of the chair and my hands ached again. I had stupidly confided in my mother that I had been assigned Janelle for peer tutoring. Of course, she had taken that information directly to my father.

"We're uncomfortable with that as well, so if you need us to, we're ready to call the school about your peer tutoring assignment, " my mother continued.

"No," I said, and swallowed under the weight of my parents' stares.

I couldn't keep anything a secret from my parents. They were as interested and invested in my education as though they walked the hallways instead of me. I knew I was supposed to be thankful for it, but I felt their care and concern like a circle of barbed wire slowly crushing in around me. Seeing Janelle again, even only as tutor and student...

It was worth trying to lie.

"No, um...peer tutoring looks really good. For college," I said. It sounded weak at first, but I made an effort to strengthen my voice.

"All the best colleges love community service like that. And since it's right at school, you don't have to drive me around anywhere."

"But I know it will be hard for you to tutor that girl," said my mother, scowling. She hated shifters even more than my father did and was always calling them loathsome words when she saw them on the news. I'd stopped challenging her, as it only ever resulted in explosive days-long fights.

"I can do it, though," I said hurriedly. I straightened, hoping they would get the horrifying thought of calling the school out of their heads. "Don't worry about me."

Their anti-shifter attitude was one reason among several that my parents hadn't approved of Janelle as my best friend. Janelle shifted easily and often, ignoring the rules of the school that policed her form and bearing her punishments without, it seemed, any intent to change. Teachers picked on her, sending her to the principal's office so often for infractions they let slide on other students that it was no wonder she was failing. She wasn't popular in school, either, and hadn't been even before I stopped hanging out with her a year ago.

"We just want you to be careful," my father said. "She's a bad influence, her and the rest of those demonic shifters. Avoid them, and you'll live a long and decent life, Amaya. That's what we want for you."

"To produce something useful for society," said my mother firmly. "To be a proud citizen, not like these crazy monsters stirring up trouble."

"I know. I'll be careful," I said. My tone had dropped back down to dull and obedient, as they expected. Both of them smiled at me, and my father pressed a heavy hand to my shoulder on his way out.

"We're very proud of you, Amaya," he said before closing the door.

I saw Janelle's face, heard her low alto again, thrumming with indignation. *"She thinks I should be ashamed of being a shifter. Well, I'm not!"*

The knots in my back burned.

***

"Your parents are gonna hear us," Janelle snickered. We were thirteen years old and it was my birthday, so I demanded that my best friend come over. Janelle's shifting hadn't emerged yet, and though my parents weren't her biggest fans even back then, they relented.

"They will not," I declared.

The plastic stars I'd stuck up on my ceiling glowed with the low lighting as we sat on the shag rug in my bedroom. We were telling each other's futures.

"You'll marry...*Nathan*," I said, bursting into giggles. Janelle muffled her laughter with both hands over her mouth. The idea of either of us marrying Nathan, who had braces and a tendency to spray when he talked, was hilarious.

"And you'll have *six kids* and live in *Beverly Hills*," I concluded, wiping tears of laughter from my eyes. "Wow, I'll miss you when you're Mrs. Nathan Perez."

"Never," Janelle swore. She rolled over onto her back, her black hair like a river of ink through my rug. "The Magic 8-ball says that's *never* gonna happen," she said.

Somehow, it made me warm and happy to hear her say so. "Do mine next," I urged.

"Sure." Janelle rolled onto her tummy, bits of orange shag in her messy ponytail, and took over the notebook we were using for our fortune-telling game. "Says you're gonna marry Cooper. Gross!" she said with a bark of laughter. "Imagine!"

"Yeah, I need the person I end up with to have at least a brain cell. At least one," I said.

"He's not good enough for you." Janelle grinned at me over the notebook, her eyes shining. "I don't care if it does say you're gonna live in..." She checked the page. "The Taj Mahal."

"How many kids?"

"Zero."

"Phew," I said, miming that I'd wiped my forehead. "At least there's that."

"I'll give you some of mine. You want some kids? I got some kids," said Janelle, sitting up and pretending to open a trench coat from which, presumably, babies dangled like fake watches. Tears of laughter streamed down my face as I made little snorting sounds, trying to keep my volume down.

"Stop!" I wheezed faintly.

"Fine," Janelle said with a grin. After a moment, her grin faded. "Hey, Amaya?"

"Yeah?"

"Can I tell you a secret?"

"Of course," I said, widening my eyes. Janelle already knew all of my secrets: where I hid the joint I'd found under the gym bleachers but was too scared to smoke, the fact that I wore eyeliner at school and scrubbed it off before going home, the crush on Mr. Bonilla that had lasted until he gave me a B+ on a paper instead of an A-. Janelle, by contrast, seemed to live with an openness and honesty that escaped me.

"It's serious."

I tilted my head. "What's up?"

Without preamble, Janelle said, "I'm a shifter." She picked bits of fluff off her pajamas as I gaped at her. "Yeah, since last night," she added. "I felt a horrible pain in my shoulders, and before I knew it, my arms shifted."

"Really?" I pitched my voice low, so that my parents wouldn't hear. "What's it like?"

Janelle shrugged. "It stopped hurting as soon as I shifted, so... that was good."

I sat back, my palms on the rug, considering her. Janelle looked no different to me than she normally did. Even at thirteen, we saw the way shifters were perceived. But she just looked like my best friend to me.

"Are you freaked out?" Janelle asked, looking terribly vulnerable for a moment. My heart twisted at the fear on her face.

"Not at all," I promised.

The next day, after Janelle left, my mother told me she had overheard what Janelle said to me and I was no longer permitted to be friends with her.

***

The day Janelle came back from her suspension, everyone gave her a lot of space. Whispering trailed her wherever she went.

"I heard she broke Karina's jaw," said one person.

"And part of her nose!"

"She used her shifted arm to do it," said another. "Knocked Karina back so hard you can still see a dent in the lockers."

"I hear she said she'd do it again, too."

"Monster."

"*Freak.*"

I didn't know how Janelle could stand it. The cruel whispers would have destroyed me, but she kept her head up high, gliding through the halls like she didn't hear the other students tittering behind her. I couldn't help but admire her.

She bore the weight of the whispers alone the whole day long, and that was because of me. Karina had bullied Janelle for months, but the other students had shunned her long before that. Because I'd publicly stopped being friends with Janelle, and I was well-liked, others avoided her too.

I wanted to tell Janelle I was sorry, but the clock ran to the end of the school day without me summoning the courage to do it. I knew just what she would say, anyway, with the same certainty that had us finishing each other's sentences back before I'd deliberately forced us apart.

"I don't need your sorry," she would say. And then she'd smile, the rakish smile that had captured my interest since third grade, when we'd first become inseparable. And then, I hoped, she'd say "Let's go," and drag us both away from this awful place.

***

As I headed out of class, my phone buzzed with a message from Janelle. I couldn't ignore it since she was my peer student, an excuse I hoped would work on my parents if they went through my phone again.

"Victory Vittles," the message balloon said, naming a favorite band of ours. Last year, when we were still friends, we'd spent hours sharing earbuds and listening to their debut album. "Free. The park. After school. Come with me."

I debated deleting the message, but some suffocated spark inside of me howled with protest at the thought. So I messaged, "I can't."

The message came back instantly. "You can."

Then after a moment, my phone buzzed in my hand. "Don't be scared."

I ducked between locker banks so as not to impede the flow of students. "Not scared," I shot back with a frowny face.

"Then come."

I thought of her open and honest smile, imagining it curving her lips as she looked down at a message from me. I hadn't given Janelle anything to smile about lately. I kept our tutoring dry and boring, resisting her attempts to push me into the intimacy we'd shared even though I missed it, longed for it with all my being. It was hard, especially when she tossed that crooked smile at me.

But she was a shifter and a delinquent, and I was *not-a-shifter* and a good girl, and it had to stay that way. I had to be firm and tell her that.

"OK," I texted.

Wait a minute.

I stared at the screen. The message had been sent and received. A second later, Janelle sent a thumbs-up.

***

A misty rain fell. Sweaty, damp people pressed in around me as we waited for Victory Vittles to come on, but Janelle stayed by my side. She wore a plain red t-shirt under a crinkly black bomber jacket, looking cool as hell with her hair up in a careless bun. Chin-length tendrils framed her heart-shaped face. Her shoulders were slightly hunched, her hands jammed into her jacket pockets, but the look she bestowed on me was filled with joyous anticipation.

"This is gonna be so good," she enthused.

For a moment I let myself bathe in the radiance of her black eyes, but only for a moment. "Maybe if it stops raining," I said.

She sighed. "You and the rain. It's just misting." She bounced in her boots, the heels digging into the muddy ground slightly. "It's been forever since we did something together like this," she observed with a sidelong glance at me.

"I know," I said shortly. I was ashamed and sick thinking of how long I'd spent toeing my parents' line, but I felt trapped, as though my hands were chained at my sides and I didn't have the slack I needed to reach out to her. "I shouldn't even be here."

"So why'd you come, then?" asked Janelle.

"Why'd you ask?" I retorted.

Janelle's smile twisted slightly. "I thought—after you tried to stop me from fighting, I thought maybe I wasn't so invisible to you anymore."

The fiery knots at the bases of my shoulder blades burned again, a bright flare of pain that made me stagger for a moment. Janelle reached out and steadied me by the elbow, a look of concern gracing her features. "Amaya?" she said, looking at me closely. "You okay?"

"I'm fine," I managed, and offered a patently false smile, but Janelle let it slide, releasing my arm. I felt the impression of her hands like ghostly little fingertips impressed on my flesh.

When the band finally appeared, the crowd screamed to life and roared around us, defying the gray weather. I felt like I could almost see the notes dancing around us. The music poured through my spirit, nourishing something in me that I didn't understand. I turned my face up to the foggy drizzle and sang until my throat hurt.

Then I saw them.

It was the girls from my volleyball team, their perfect ponytails somehow still bouncy in the humid weather. Their gazes crossed mine in the crowd, and the girls looked startled before the next song started.

"Oh no!" I gasped.

"What?" said Janelle, following my gaze. "Oh." She rolled her eyes at the girls. "Just ignore them."

My back burned harder than ever, and I reached out to grasp my shoulder, feeling my flesh begin to move beneath my skin. I tried to focus on pushing the feeling down, but one of the girls, a tall blonde named Lisa, was making her way through the crowd toward me. Any second, she'd see Janelle. Any second, all my hard work to stay away from her would be undone.

"Never mind her," said Janelle, placing a concerned arm over my shoulders. "Are you okay?" I pressed my lips shut against the pain and threw her an imploring look. "Do you need to get out of here?" I nodded, tears sliding down my face and mixing with the rain.

"All right. Don't worry," Janelle said. She glanced around and said, "There's a bunch of trees at the end of the lawn. The band's still going, no one will follow us. Come on!"

She tugged me, and we pushed through the crowd, losing Lisa in the press of bodies.

At the edge of the crowd, the going was easier, and we were able to run toward the forest. I was grateful for my volleyball conditioning, though I wheezed with pain as I leaned against a cold, damp tree. My back burned, and it felt like a pair of fists was rumpling my flesh from the inside out.

"You're shifting, aren't you?" said Janelle.

I groaned, but said, "No. I'm not," as the pain in my shoulders kept my back doubled. I pulled my long braids through my shaking fingers, clinging to the sensory feel of the hard beads at the ends. "I'm not!"

"Amaya, it's okay!" Janelle said urgently. "It's okay if you shift. I'm here for you."

Guilt surged in my throat like nausea. I felt freer to speak in this quiet space, away from the jumping and screaming of the crowd. "I haven't been here for you," I said. "Janelle, I'm—I'm sorry."

I swallowed hard. After a few moments of silence, she said, "I don't need your sorry," and smiled, the smile that used to get me to do anything. The crooked smile that I still found incredibly hard to resist. "Like I said, I'm here for you."

She raised a hand, and in a brief burst of muscle and skin, she shifted her arm. Purple scales over hard muscle glistened in the misty drizzle as shreds of her jacket sleeve drifted into the mud. Her shifted limb was so much larger than her human arm that it had burst her jacket's seams.

"It's not scary," Janelle said. "It takes no time at all, and if you focus, you'll shift right back." In the span of a second, she had shifted her arm back into a human limb. She grimaced sheepishly, her arm bare in the misty damp.

"I can't," I groaned. "My parents..."

"Fuck your parents." She held my eyes steadily. "They're bigots and you know it."

"I know," I said, gasping against the pain as I tried to keep the pressure in my back from exploding. "I'm just so scared they'll find out."

"It's just me here," said Janelle, her tone gentle and encouraging, like she was teaching a little kid how to walk. "And there are tons of shifters out there in the world, and we make out alright. You're gonna be just fine."

Finally, my shoulders unfurled.

The relief from pain was immediate, and I straightened, my heart still pounding. I craned my head over my shoulder and saw that I had great scarlet wings with feathers of royal blue, canary yellow and leaf-like green that shone so brightly, they outdid the gray sky. Awe was written across Janelle's face as she looked up at them.

"Amaya, they're stunning," she said. "They're beautiful."

I wiped my face, moist with sweat and fog and tears. I could feel my wings trembling as they flared to their fullest extent, and slowly I folded them behind myself. My back no longer burned, though I feared my shirt was shredded past saving. "They're okay," I said thickly, holding my shirt up over my chest.

Janelle immediately untied her zippered sweatshirt from around her waist and offered it to me. I threw it on backwards with a smile of relief. It would do.

"They're super pretty," Janelle said, looking up at my wings with wonder on her face. "Way prettier than me."

"Don't say that," I insisted. "You have your own kind of prettiness. You're powerful and confident. I admire that about you."

She tilted her head to the side with a playful grin. "So you think about me being pretty, huh?"

I was thrown, feeling too naked and vulnerable to know what to say with my huge wings folded behind me. The right answer, *All the time*, bubbled too easily to my lips. I bit them, and Janelle's gaze dropped to my mouth.

"Amaya!" came a loud voice. It was Lisa, the tall blonde from the volleyball team and one of the last people I wanted to see aside from maybe my mother and father. "Amaya!"

Something in the moment shattered, and Janelle looked at me expectantly. I realized she was waiting for me to shift my wings away. Raindrops trailed down her bare elbow and inner forearm in long, curving paths.

Of course, she was waiting for me to shift again. Waiting for me to lie, so she could support my lie, so the girl from the volleyball team wouldn't know the truth, so the truth wouldn't get back to my parents, so that I'd be comfortable. I could see in Janelle's eyes that she was ready and prepared for me to throw her away again despite the help she had offered me. I could see that I was already forgiven.

"I'm right here," I called back.

"Your wings," Janelle hissed.

I shook my head. "I know."

Lisa stumbled into the little clearing we were in, and her eyes widened to see me and Janelle standing there. I reached out and grasped Janelle's hand. Janelle grinned openly.

"It's okay," I said to Lisa. "We're fine."

"I was gonna say—" Lisa stammered, even her sprightly bangs slightly depressed by the weather, "um, Amaya, if you wanted to—" Her gaze was pulled towards my back, where my great wings must have been visible even though they were folded. "We're in the crowd."

"I know," I said again. There was a dizzying freedom in the words, like I'd dropped over a cliffside only to find that my wings were indeed strong enough to hold me. "I'll find you guys later."

Lisa's brow twitched, as though she had expected to walk in on some kind of drama and was confused to find us just standing by a tree, holding hands. She darted an uncertain glance at my wings and backed away hurriedly. "Okay, see you then," she said and took off.

As Lisa left, it seemed like the clearing itself released a breath. I shifted my wings away from one breath to the next and stepped forward, closing the distance between me and Janelle.

"Amaya, what are you doing?" Janelle said, and I took a deep breath, my fingers tightening around hers. I leaned forward to press a kiss to her cheek just as she turned her face toward me. Our lips brushed, and she made a soft sound of surprise and interest, gripping my hand more tightly as she pressed forward. My eyes fell shut as we kissed, my heart thrumming like a butterfly.

When we parted, I said all in one rush, "I'm sorry. I'm sorry for letting my parents control me. You're not any of the things they say you are."

Janelle rested her forehead against mine, her eyes warm. "I don't need your sorry, Amaya. Stop beating yourself up for it." I could have cried, but instead, I smiled, and Janelle's answering smile seemed to light the gloom.

The rain had let up, and the crowd was still rocking. Somewhere in there, Lisa and the girls were probably wondering where I was. Janelle glanced out at the sea of people consideringly, then back at me. "Do you want to head back?" she asked.

I gripped her hand tightly. "Let's go," I said.

{Sci-fi & Fantasy}

{ 13 }

Beyond the Mist

TAYLOR RAMAGE

While Alena tossed feed to the chickens strutting on the steep incline behind her house, she gave thanks to Yilra and, for the thousandth time, prayed for the goddess's revival. The chickens clucked contentedly as they pecked at their morning meal and hobbled behind the plantain trees that jutted out from the mountainside. Alena felt the day's humidity gathering. Not even the highest peaks were spared from Oyarén's heat, though the mountains cooled at night.

Leaning on the wooden railing that lined the deck around her house, Alena peered toward the ocean. Beyond the thick palm trees and groves of green tropical plants covering the mountains, she could see the mist wall. It hung over the water no matter how warm or windy, giving the Lunesos the perfect cover for the inevitable invasion. Dejected whispers among the villagers said once their ships broke through the mist, they'd already be on Oyarén's shores. But if conquest was only a matter of time, why wasn't there even more urgency to secure Yilra's protection? Oyarén needed it now more than ever, and Alena's visions, which had grown stronger since Papi disappeared, only added to her unease. Yet most days, Alena felt like she was the only one who still cared about the goddess, still believed in her protection.

As a child, Papi had told her that before the great storm trapped Yilra, the goddess would dance among her creation, the coquí's call her guiding melody. Alena thought these were just sweet bedtime stories, until her visions began. Dreams of her people from long ago. Disjointed flashes—churning waves and crystals, nonexistent walking snakes and giant birds, and then darkness. Mami never wanted to hear about it, but Papi understood. These dreams and visions made the singular blue plantain tree in their yard nothing for them to balk at while Mami muttered and blocked it from her sight with her hand every time she passed by it. Every inexplicable thing proved that Yilra was still somehow at work, despite being imprisoned and separated from her people for so long.

The door behind Alena creaked open and Mami appeared, hair tied in a tight bun. "Nena, we have to harvest the plantains before it gets too hot. Hey," she tapped the floor of the deck with her foot. "Stop staring at the sea like that. Your father did that before he left."

Alena started and gripped the railing of the deck, but otherwise didn't move. Left, disappeared—whatever the word, Papi was gone from them and he'd taken his stories with him. The visions called him, the same as Abuela, and he walked down to the sea on an important mission. The fisherman whose canoe he'd borrowed said Papi was muttering about "ending the legacy of the storm" and "chasing away the invader." Then, he rowed into the ocean toward the mist wall and never came back.

Papi talked about the visions all the time with Alena, especially after she started having them herself. His eyes shone with pride as he told her they were part of their family legacy. "They're pieces from a story we don't fully know, so we pass it down and try to find the truth."

Papi taught her that everything from the chickens to the coquíes told of Yilra's return, begging him to spread the news. Stay devoted, just as their ancestors had been. Yet visions without context made it hard to keep faith in the details.

The night before Papi disappeared, Alena dreamt about the storm that had trapped Yilra. It was so vivid she swore she felt the swirling clouds yanking her limbs in opposite directions, threatening to tear her apart. Beneath the ocean's chaos, she heard a low, commanding voice. She couldn't make out words, but the tone was firm.

Alena shook herself from her memories and looked at her mother, now standing still in the early dawn light and looking toward the sea despite her reaction earlier. Had she stood like this to watch Papi go to the ocean?

"Do you think...if Yilra was free—"

"¡Ay, nena!" Mami snapped. "There's no freeing her. She's gone from us like your father and all we can do is hope we're too far up the mountain for when the Lunesos come and stay for good. Come help with these plantains."

Alena didn't argue. At fifteen years old, she knew when Mami was finished hearing about Yilra. In the three years since Papi's disappearance, Mami had even less patience for the goddesses' name. Like most others in Oyarén, the only thing Mami believed in for certain was the inevitable Luneso invasion. Generations of tense peace and tentative trade at the mist wall had crumbled into threats of conquest as Luneso's crops ran low. But that was their punishment for Luneso's goddess, Gualíne, trapping Yilra in the first place.

Without a word, Alena followed her mother back inside to grab the machete. This used to be Papi's job, pulling down the dried leaves of a ripe tree and hacking the stem until the tree split and he could harvest the bunch. Alena had helped him enough times to know what to do, but she still missed him more and more with each strike.

As the morning passed, the rooster crowed and the occasional horse clopped along the road. Soon, only the blue plantain tree remained. The weird one. The one Papi had loved the most and whose early night-colored ripe fruit he'd prepared into a mash before he disappeared. The tree before her now had grown from the roots harvested from its predecessor—grown from the last suckers she and Papi had planted together. Most of the fruits had turned from green to a ripe blue. They were ready, but Alena looked hesitantly at Mami.

"Should we do that one? If the Lunesos attack, we can eat the plantains and hide. Use their own trick against them."

Mami bristled. Alena knew she was thinking of Papi.

"Take it down and we'll burn it all. I won't eat cursed Luneso fruit," Mami said, releasing a long sigh. "Only our forsaken goddess knows why one of *those* trees is in *our* yard."

Burn them? These plantains were the closest thing she had left of Papi. Alena tried to hold back her anger. "We don't have to *burn* them. Maybe they won't invade if we give them those plantains to take home."

Mami laughed without humor and gave Alena a sidelong look. "Nena, the world isn't that simple. If we give them a little, they'll just take more." Mami carried the bunches they'd harvested inside, but Alena still held the machete. She hacked down the blue plantain tree, channeling her frustration into chopping it to its root. She'd sneak the harvested fruit inside later when Mami went out to buy fish.

Something small hopped from the fallen tree onto Alena's head. She flinched, but before she could swat it from her hair, she heard a distinct, two-tone call from a close proximity.

Coquíes? In the middle of the day? But they never come this close to people.

Alena waited, thinking the tiny frog would hop away in a few seconds. Instead, it crawled to the edge of her scalp near her forehead.

"Alena Velez?" the voice that spoke was deep and large, too big for such a small creature.

"Y-yes?"

"Good. You can understand me. I hope my servant didn't startle you, but I needed to reach you immediately. I'm afraid there isn't much time."

"Servant?" Was this a new vision? Usually, Alena felt a jolt before a vision started, letting her know she wasn't quite seeing reality any longer. But if that line was blurring now, maybe her time to walk into the ocean was coming.

"Alena!" Mami called from inside. "You okay?"

Alena gripped the machete handle. Never in a thousand years could she tell her mother that she was talking to a coquí. It was too much like what happened to Papi. "I'm fine! Just taking a break."

But Alena's stomach twisted as the coquí continued to speak with its master's voice. "I am Korú, king of the coquíes, servant of the goddess Yilra. You can hear me, so please listen. Yilra must shift the skies again or Oyarén will be destroyed. At sunset, you will meet me at the beach."

"But Yilra's trapped."

"You will free her."

"Me? How am I supposed to free her?"

"Trust in the stories you know, even the fragments."

"But—"

"We must act quickly. Sunset. Tonight. This is the work your father started."

Before Alena could protest further, the coquí hopped off her head and disappeared into the luscious green. King Korú? Alena had never heard of him before. Yilra had been trapped, unreachable for centuries, but Papi had done *something* and now, somehow, Alena was supposed to free her?

The Lunesos—that had to be it. The fragments, visions, and dreams had only gotten stronger after Papi disappeared. Now, she was talking to animals, just like Papi and Abuela. And if the coquí was right, Alena would feel the ocean's call soon enough.

***

What were you supposed to wear to meet a king anyway? Alena hoped that King Korú wouldn't be offended by her plain dress and work pants. After finishing her chores for the day, she'd told Mami that she'd go to the beach to request tomorrow's catch from the fishermen—the perfect ruse to leave without making Mami suspicious. It took a couple of hours to descend the mountain on the dirt road from her house, and as day faded into night, the rocks around Alena became fine grains of sand. With the evening came the stars, the warm ocean breeze, and the steady chattering of thousands and thousands of coquíes. Despite how loud they sounded, you never saw them up close.

Unless their king wanted to meet with you, apparently.

Alena stood where the tide lapped the sand. The pattern of the beach looked like jagged teeth. She didn't often come this close to the ocean, but here, the mist wall appeared even more foreboding. No matter how clear the day was, it hung heavy, blanketing the ocean in a swirling, gray quilt. Neither sun nor summer storm chased it away. It obscured most of Luneso on the other side save for an imposing silhouette.

The Lunesos used to stay on their side of the mist wall except during trades when they would meet Oyarén ships. But lately, Oyarén fishermen had reported more Luneso ships lingering on the waters, creeping closer and closer to Oyarén's side of the sea and practicing battle formations. Between that, the visions, and Papi's disappearance, Alena feared that they wanted to finish their generations-long task of destroying Yilra for good, as the stories said. The mist wall was a remnant of the battle Yilra had fought against the Gualíne. Since she guarded Luneso, they were simply waiting for her command to invade.

"You need to stop taking your father's stories so seriously," Mami would say as she struck the side of the guisado pot with her spoon. "Look where that got him. He left us because of them."

But gazing out into the mist wall now, Alena felt wary. Fighting Gualíne had created the mist wall and sealed Yilra away, making her unreachable. Yet the way the mists swirled in the growing night was so out of place compared to the life and color of Oyarén. How could something so dreary have come from such vibrant goddesses? Alena didn't know nearly as much about Gualíne as Yilra, but Papi had seen her in some of his visions. She was the soft light of an ocean at sunset while Yilra was the bursting pink of a sunrise. Not even Gualíne was a goddess of such depressing colors.

Sometimes, the vast oceans brought lost travelers from distant lands to the shores of Oyarén. Alena had seen one once with skin lighter than dry sand and hair the color of ripe plantains. He left after his navigators had found their way again. Maybe the mist wall was the spirit of one of those lost travelers that got caught up in battle.

Suddenly, the coquíes went silent. It was so easy to tune out their songs as a steady backdrop to the night, but the world felt wrong once they stopped. Alena turned back toward the path she'd taken down the mountain. A big shadow rustled behind the palm trees. Alena tensed and glanced down each side of the beach for a place to run as the shadow stepped into the open.

A massive coquí—the largest animal that she'd ever seen—towered above her, its head reaching half the height of the palm trees from which it had come. It had algae-green skin, a pale belly, and long toes that kicked up piles of sand as it crawled toward her. In the clear moonlight, Alena saw a sparkling pink spiral marking between the creature's eyes.

"I am King Korú," he said, his voice inflating his throat. "I helped your father and now I'll help you."

Alena gasped. "You said I'm supposed to finish his work. What happened to him?"

King Korú nodded. "He left for Luneso after the last of his memories awakened and he failed to free Yilra."

A million thoughts spun through Alena's mind as she stared up at the giant frog, digging her feet deep in the sand. "Why? What did you do to him?"

"Nothing. I only used Yilra's essence within me to unlock his mind. I could not see inside it. The rest was the work he was called to do."

"If you serve Yilra, then why didn't you stop him from going beyond the mist?"

"My role is to awaken the key within each generation and trust Yilra with the rest for as long as she is imprisoned. I cannot interfere with the key beyond that."

Alena crossed her arms. "What's the key?"

King Korú lowered his snout to the sand, presenting the spiral marking to Alena. It glowed faintly with a pinkish light like the one that streaks the skies at sunrise: Yilra's color without a doubt. "Yilra knew a great danger would come to Oyarén after the world's creation, so she made a key—splitting her essence between me and your first ancestor, her most devoted follower. I am the keeper. However, my own memories have been lost for many generations—since the storm that trapped her. But Yilra's essence has returned some of them to me and for the past three generations, I have used her power to restore your family's memories. I reveal myself only when each generation must fulfill its role."

What sort of role would compel Papi—and Abuela for that matter—to go beyond the mist? How did leaving Oyarén help Yilra at all? Alena would never go to Luneso, no matter what she remembered.

King Korú lowered his head again. "Part of your father's role was opening the place where Yilra was imprisoned. It had been masked from human discovery before his magic awakened in him. He told me of the place before he left. When I awaken the key in you, your path will be clear."

The pink spiral on his head glowed brighter and before Alena could react, the light enveloped her. She closed her eyes as warmth spread on her forehead, chest, and palms. And then, she was open—thousands of memories raced through her mind at once, too fast to process. The light passed as the regular night returned. Alena looked at her hands to see spirals had marked her brown skin.

"The key is strongest in the youngest. You have more of Yilra's power than your father."

A loud bang sounded from the sea as a bright flash of red light filled the sky. Alena saw at least ten ships passing through the mist wall, heading straight for the shore. The Lunesos were coming for Oyarén.

"Quickly! Get on my back. I will take us to Yilra."

Alena scurried up King Korú's front leg and laid herself flat on his neck while cannons blasted from the invading ships. She smelled the smoke in the air as they bounded along the beach and onto a path leading back to the mountains. In the brief flashes of brilliant light, Alena caught glimpses of the ships' decks, but couldn't see anyone on board. The ships were completely empty.

No. The Lunesos were of the evening like their goddess. They must've eaten the blue plantains Gualíne granted to them, making her soldiers invisible at night. The same ones from the tree that Papi loved.

And since the sun had set not too long ago, Oyarén was in for a long, long night.

***

King Korú climbed a steep, barren cliff far from the battle on the beach below, but the sounds of fighting carried in the breeze. At last, they came to the mouth of a pitch-dark cave.

"Yilra's prison is inside," King Korú said. "You can free her."

"I don't know how."

"You do," King Korú said with confidence. "Each story and memory is your inheritance and your guide. I will guard the cave entrance and command my servants to help with the battle."

Alena slid from King Korú's back and faced the cave entrance. This cliff reached higher than any other part of Oyarén and the only path to the cave was a jagged, narrow rock edge. Even if anyone over the centuries had thought to look for Yilra up here, they wouldn't have been able to reach it without King Korú's expert climbing.

As Alena considered the cave, guidance like suddenly remembering a vivid dream told her that here Yilra was safest from the voice in the storm. The goddess designed the key to pass through Alena's ancestors, the first of whom had stayed by the goddess' side as the storm grew. Images in her memory showed her that Papi didn't have enough strength to free Yilra, so his last directive was to leave. Only Alena had the power.

Alena stepped into the pitch-dark cave with no clue of how to actually break the prison. The cave smelled like wet rocks and she couldn't see a thing.

Then, the marks on her palms started glowing and warmth covered her: the key. Outside, she heard King Korú guiding all the coquíes in Oyarén with a singular call. The sound was so powerful that it stirred the rocks in the cave. At the beach, the sound must be deafening.

Alena felt pulled deeper into the cave and the spirals shone brighter on her body. She followed the twisted path until she stood before a glowing pink crystal that stretched from the floor to the ceiling. It cast just enough light to see Yilra curled up inside, black hair floating around her like a cloud. A white dress was tied at her waist and a necklace of shells hung down to her chest.

"Yilra!" Alena said, taking a few steps toward the resting goddess. But as she did, she heard a shuffling that wasn't the echo of her steps, or King Korú, whose calls she could still hear in the cave.

Someone was right behind her.

Fear and instinct overtook Alena. She whirled around and shot her arms out toward the sound. Pent-up key magic burst from the spirals on her hands, illuminating the outline of an otherwise invisible figure. The pink contrasted the dark blue of a Luneso soldier enhanced by Gualíne's plantains.

"Who are you?" Alena demanded, keeping her arms raised.

The soldier cursed and in a flash, she became fully visible. She was about Alena's age, a little taller and more muscular, her black hair braided over her shoulder. She had eyes the color of palm tree bark, and the way she stared made Alena's cheeks warm.

But the feeling quickly faded when the girl drew a knife. As she did, Alena noticed ocean blue spiral marks on the back of the girl's hands.

Did Gualíne give her own key magic to this girl's ancestors?

"I won't let you awaken Yilra," the girl said, her knife hand shaking. She gritted her teeth and lowered her voice. "Get it together, Carmen. Gualíne needs you."

"Why is Luneso invading?" Alena demanded, standing as tall as she could and projecting her voice. "We've done nothing to you."

Carmen laughed bitterly, her voice wavering. "Your goddess is the reason Gualíne's imprisoned–why the mist wall keeps growing and killing the plantain trees that keep us safe in the night."

"What? How can Yilra be responsible for any of that when she's been imprisoned here?"

"You're her key! You tell me. She clearly has a plan and I'm supposed to stop you."

"Her only plan is to restore memories. Maybe *your* goddess is the one with an evil plan."

Carmen raised her knife. "Gualíne told me to come here to help her, but she couldn't say more than that. I follow orders."

Although she sounded less confident, she charged at Alena, who jumped to the side and shot more of Yilra's light at Carmen. The power felt more tangible the more she used it and soon her shots chipped rock from the cave walls. Alena ducked behind the crystal just as Carmen's knife jabbed toward her. The blade bent and snapped against the gem.

Alena draped her arms around the crystal, exhausted. She needed *something* that would break this crystal and free Yilra, but she felt nothing besides the goddess's essence flowing through her.

A flash of blue from the other side of the crystal caught her attention. The Luneso girl's spirals glowed, emitting a swirling haze. Memories told her the energy had been present at the imprisoning. *Yilra's power is of the growing dawn while Gualíne's is of the coming night,* Alena—or fragments of her ancestors—reminded. Whatever Carmen threw at her, Alena had to throw it back.

Alena focused her key energy into her hands. She prayed that Yilra would be free, that Papi would come back and the people of Oyarén would be safe.

Ancient power burst from both of them, colliding in a blinding flash. When Alena could see again, dozens of cracks snaked through Yilra's crystal prison.

Then, it shattered.

The cave rumbled as Yilra awoke, freed from her prison. Once it passed, she floated between Alena and Carmen, who now grabbed her bent knife and backed herself against the cave wall.

"If you're going to kill me, do it quick!" she said, trying to steady heavy breaths and sound braver than she looked.

"Killing you is the last thing I want to do, Carmen of Luneso," Yilra said, her voice gentle. "You carry my sister's essence."

"Sister? But didn't Gualíne trap you?" Alena protested. "She's sent her people to destroy Oyarén!"

"Gualíne did not do this," Yilra said with a sigh. "I am sorry for all of the generations that have suffered because of what we had to do. Please understand that we had no other choice."

Alena exchanged a confused glance with Carmen as Yilra placed a warm palm on each girl's forehead. Alena felt her spiral marks spinning. "You both have been given pieces from your ancestors. Now, here is the thread you need to understand them."

A vision overtook Alena. There were the two goddesses in the days of creation, hovering above the blank ocean. Together, they formed a single, beautiful island and filled it with plants and beaches and jungles and so many animals and fruits. Then, they filled it with humans who made colorful music and art from the vibrancy all around them. But the goddesses were not the only creators in the world. Jealous eyes fell upon their space—Helthar, who ruled stormy lands far, far from here. He sought to destroy the island so he could rule over every part of the world. Gualíne and Yilra saw his treachery coming from the east and prepared. Yilra granted her essence to a tiny coquí who then grew as large as a tree. Then, both goddesses touched the forehead's of two girls: Carmen and Alena's ancestors, who enjoyed the goddesses' closest confidence.

Helthar came, a storm so destructive that Gualíne and Yilra could hardly fight it off. His was the deep voice in the chaos. He yearned to decimate all creation and memories of the time before his rule. This was why the goddesses had hidden their essences between King Korú and two humans. Their memories were sealed for their protection. Helthar had already erased so much.

But now, Alena clearly saw that Gualíne and Yilra fought him *together*. They fought him with everything they had, but he was too powerful, splitting the beautiful island in two during his attack. He forced the goddesses into a compromise: if Gualíne and Yilra sealed themselves away, he would leave their island alone. His mist wall had already descended in the space between the islands, a haze that caused the people to believe the goddesses were at war with each other, fueling division. The weary goddesses sealed themselves away with a spell and left their creation. Their only hope was their keys.

When the vision ended and the cave returned, Alena had no words. This was the deep truth, passed from Yilra to her first ancestor, then from Abuela to Papi and now her. The truth had been revealed.

"We have to stop the invasion," Alena said, looking at Carmen. "It's the right thing to do."

Carmen nodded solemnly, the spirals on her hands glowing a soft blue. "Yilra, can you free Gualíne? I can't see any other way for my people to trust you. They'll exile me for not stopping you."

"Both of you have served your roles," Yilra said. "Now let me serve mine."

Yilra drifted out of the cave, heading toward the beach now alight with the flames of battle. Alena and Carmen hopped onto King Korú's back; the frog king carried them back down the cliff.

"If you're Gualíne's key, why would your people exile you?" Alena asked.

Carmen sighed. "I'm not supposed to be the key. Well, I *am*. I just wasn't trained for it. There was another girl in my village who'd had all these prophecies given about her, but when the awakening came, I got the markings instead of her. I guess somewhere along the way we lost track of the real lineage. Anyway, my people said they'd acknowledge me as the key if I helped our troops invade, even though Gualíne told me to come here anyway and follow you. They didn't believe me, but also didn't force me to stay with the ships. I'm no good in a big fight anyway."

"Are you joking? You almost killed me in that cave a few times," Alena said.

Carmen laughed. "If I was a better soldier, I wouldn't have stalled so much. I think that's why they sent me here—to die so the key could pass to someone more worthy."

"You wouldn't be here if Gualíne didn't want you to be," Alena said. She was puzzled at how someone who looked so strong could be so negative about herself while carrying a goddess's essence.

Carmen flashed a soft smile in the moonlight. "Well, if you say so, I guess I have to accept it."

King Korú slid onto the beach as Yilra glided above the fighters, making many stop mid-strike. The Luneso soldiers must've made themselves visible when they landed because bands of them lined the beach where the tide stopped. Everyone stared at the goddess as she spread her arms. The night itself split open and a section of the sky turned the soft pink of sunrise. The sky gathered before Yilra as she brought her arms in front of her, then pushed across the sea. Alena felt her key magic pulse.

Yilra's power burst into the mist wall and the cloudy mass sparked wildly as it dissolved. Alena heard a deep, terrifying groan roll through the air, the sound so sudden and loud that she jumped and grabbed Carmen's hand without thinking. The last dregs of Helthar's work were disintegrating. When the last of it dissipated, the shores of Luneso appeared just a short distance across the sea. Some of the mist wall still hung around Oyarén, though. Again, Yilra split the sky and gathered it before her. When she sent another blast of her power at the exposed Luneso, a mixture of despair and cheers arose from the fighters. Luneso was bathed in sunrise light for a moment and then a figure rose into the sky from the center of the island. She was dressed similarly to Yilra with a glowing blue light surrounding her.

Gualíne.

Now, the Lunesos cheered and next to Alena, Carmen's spirals glowed brighter. With both of their goddesses free, their magic coursed through them completely, a sealed and perfected covenant. Gualíne and Yilra mirrored each other's movements in the air. The land and the sea rumbled as the sky flashed pink and blue. The goddesses pulled toward each other and Luneso grew closer and closer and closer to Oyarén until only a shallow strip of ocean lay between the shores.

As morning bloomed, all the fighters laid down their blades and clubs, one people returning to each other and protected by their living goddesses. Yes, the world had once been this way—one island, not two. No warring strangers who didn't remember each other. With the mist cleared, people began streaming from the Luneso side to Oyarén, cousins and friends suddenly and tearfully remembering their ancient connections. Alena scanned their faces, hoping for the impossible.

"Alena!" shouted Mami. Alena turned and found her mother staring back at her, eyes wide. "You're...glowing. Both of you."

Alena and Carmen glanced at each other and Alena couldn't tell if the surge of warmth was from Yilra's magic or Carmen's smile. Alena quickly looked back at her mother. "Yilra has always cared for us, even when she couldn't be with us."

Now, Mami didn't scrunch up her face or grumble at the mention of Yilra. She considered Alena and Carmen and clearly saw the way the goddesses' powers flowed freely through them. No more denying or dismissing it as a pointless, fractured tale.

But Mami's eyes locked on something behind her. Alena turned toward Luneso and the people walking through the shallow water.

There with his long hair braided in the Luneso fashion and his wide, welcoming arms, was Papi. A grin of pure joy split across his face when he spotted Alena.

"Papi!" Alena cried, releasing Carmen's hand and running to him.

"My brave girl," Papi said, kneeling and holding her tight. "Yilra's key. You did what had to be done."

Alena could only cry into his shoulder. She never wanted to leave his arms.

Water sloshed right behind her.

"Carmen," Papi said, "I told you being the key would fit you well."

Alena pulled away from Papi, wiped her eyes, and looked between him and the still-glowing-with-key-magic Carmen.

Carmen scratched the back of her head. "I guess it does."

"It's your inheritance, no matter what anyone says," Papi said in a more serious tone.

"You two know each other?" Alena asked.

Carmen nodded. "He came to Luneso on the awakening day, just after Gualíne revealed her essence in me. He told the village elders that the real key would lead them right to Yilra."

"And they believed that? Even though you weren't a Luneso?" Alena asked.

"I told them I'd come to help them, which was true. They took me as a traitor to Oyarén and decided to trust me. But I think Yilra's influence helped with some of that."

Alena still had a thousand questions and a thousand missing pieces, but her world was now stitched together again. And on this beautiful day where the magic of sunrise and sunset danced together, King Korú extended the coquíes' song.

This is your inheritance, Papi had said.

All at once, the island was made anew.

{ 14 }

When They Come

LINDA RAQUEL NIEVES PÉREZ

The worst part of dying is coming back from the dead.

Salt water burns my lungs, igniting fire throughout my body. I'm suspended in space, my body feeling light as a feather but as expansive as the universe. Then comes the cold, a sharp needle that shapes the angles and curves of my bones again, and the fire that makes everything come together.

I am whole again.

The water around me guides me through the shores in Estrellada, lulling me until I'm in the Fountain of Souls. When everything is still, I open my eyes.

The first breath is always painful. No matter how many times I've done it, a gasp escapes my lips as air runs through my chest. Everything becomes clear: the salt in the air, the murmur of the fountain, the orange hue of the light that makes its way to this room.

The stone ceiling is decorated with an image of Principio y Luz, the creators of the worlds. Principio, sitting by his brother, is shaping the worlds with his hands while Luz breathes life into them. The mural allows us to reminisce in the powers that made us be every time we reincarnate from water.

"Su Alteza."

A voice calls from behind me, and I slowly sit up. A tall girl stares at me, her face betraying no emotion. She's wearing the Templo del Agua pale blue and deep purple. Her skin, glowing like polished onyx, looks as cold as her eyes. After giving me a quick look, she stares at the thin board in her hands. "You've finally come back."

"Márahe," I reply, giving her a sharp nod. Her hands are busy scribbling something on the board so she doesn't see me.

"Cemí Guari has been waiting for you."

"Sounds... ominous."

I try standing up but my legs aren't strong enough to hold my weight yet; Márahe takes a few steps to help me balance. After I've regained enough strength, she lets me go and returns to her board.

"Follow me."

Cemí Guari is my Mother, la Diosa del Agua. Cemí are the most powerful dioses, the ones that keep the three worlds in harmony and balance. Most cemí, like my mother, live in Ceki, the world of humans, managing the different Templos and keeping semidioses like me controlled. A few others live in Almia, the home of the creators of the worlds, and Turey, the paradise for souls and dioses.

As I follow Márahe, my mind goes back to that morning. I was sure I had caught Saymar unguarded. I'd studied patterns, checked schedules, and gave myself a five-minute window to kill her. But when I entered the room where the fuego semidioses gathered, it was empty. My first mistake was stepping in. As soon as I did, the door closed and Saymar was behind me, her body as warm as always.

My second mistake was turning around.

***

By the time Márahe prepares a temporal teleporting portal, Cemí Guari has changed into her goddess gown. Even with teleportation,

Márahe had carried me half of the way here, making sure I didn't fall again.

Mother turns around, a small bag of intertwined yellow palm leaves in her hands. Her eyes smile at me as she takes a few steps in our direction.

"Andreia! You're back. Just in time. I need you to come with me."

"Where are we going?"

"Palacio de la Luz."

My eyebrows shoot up. Palacio de Luz is the place where espíritus gather in the human world. If we're going there, something important must have happened.

"I can feel your brain thinking, Lluvia."

My childhood nickname almost brings a smile to my face.

"What happened?"

She sighs, another sign that something unusual must be the cause of this reunion.

"Fantasmas have been attacking the Puerta del Turey."

"They've attacked the Puerta since I can remember. Why would the espíritus call us now?"

Mother chuckles. "Always running off without letting the other finish. As I was saying, the fantasmas are attacking and espíritus managed to keep them away, but they keep rising in power. And... they've come to us because they suspect a semidios is helping them."

Dioses and espíritus hold the balance of the worlds; one creates while the other gives life. If there's a semidios helping fantasmas attack espíritus, they are attacking themselves.

"Can I ask why you're taking me with you, Mother?" Márahe would be the obvious choice for this. Especially after reincarnation. I can barely stand straight; I won't be good in a negotiation.

"If you want to become a cemí, you need to learn. This competition with Saymar is fun, but being a cemí isn't a prize for winning a game. It's a responsibility. We hold the balance of the worlds in our hands..." She stops, reaching out to pull me into a hug. "Come here. I don't want this to be a lecture. Would you come if I said I just want you to be there with me?"

"Of course, Mother."

Shaking the bag, she creates a small circle of water and I stand inside.

Teleporting is one of my attributes, but I'm too weak. I could barely teleport from here to my bedroom upstairs, let alone halfway across the world. As Mother drops a few water drops over me, I think about what she said. It's true that in the beginning the competition had been about becoming cemí. Saymar and I were children, eager to be just like our mothers. But after a while, the only thing fueling our competitions was winning. Not a place as cemí along with the other dioses, but over the other. I can see why Mother doesn't want me to continue competing with her, but this is about more than winning; it's about proving to myself that I can do this. Many semidioses want to be cemí.

If I can't win over Saymar, how can I expect to be chosen?

***

Palacio de la Luz is in the middle of Karaya, the main island in Ceki. It's a crystal temple that's closest to a work of art. The exterior is so intricate it reflects the sunlight at noon and the pale moonlight at midnight, creating columns of light for an hour each day. Surrounded by forest, desert, and shores, it's a magical place to see the beauty of nature. The sun's risen enough to shine over the mist hanging in the plants and trees. Nature's chorus of birds and insects has dwindled, but there's peace in the air. Mother's appreciating it as much as I am. Her eyes are closed as she takes a deep breath.

"It's been a while since we've been here. It's still as magical as always."

Standing behind me, she braids my hair. I realize I came here straight from the Fuente de las Almas. I'm sure I look hideous in the white clothes we wear during reincarnation. As Mother tries to untangle my hair, the rhythmic gallop of horses approaching interrupts the coquíes around us. Cemí Atana, la Diosa del Fuego, jumps from her black horse, two guards in dark green uniforms dismount after her. Her gown matches the green of their uniform, and her red hair is back in a long ponytail.

"I hear my girl got you again, Andreia," she says, her smile almost as smug as her daughter's had been as she slit my throat that morning. "Of course, that's to be expected. She has the best teacher."

Mother rolls her eyes and laughs. "Don't enable them, Atana."

"Oh, come on. They're just having a little fun. Koroce and I used to do that all the time."

"And look how you two turned out."

"If I was anyone else, that would offend me," Atana says, smile growing wider.

Mother ignores her, finishing my hair before tugging one of my braids affectionately.

"Speaking of him, did he ever reply to any of our messages?" Mother's voice betrays her concern, which isn't a feeling she normally has. Koroce is the third of the cemí that lived on Karaya's island—the Dios de la Tierra. He's quick to banter with Atana, not as serious as Mother, and he's extremely reliable. Normally, he would be the first one here.

Cemí Atana's mood turns somber. "His semidioses say they haven't seen him in over a week. I've been trying to find him, but there's no information. I was hoping to ask los espíritus for help."

As if on queue, the bells of the Palacio ring.

Los espíritus are here.

＊

The first thing I feel is the cold. Espíritus travel on the freezing wind from their mountains.

The second thing I notice is the smell of decay. Something is wrong.

Mother and Atana notice and gesture for the guards to get into formation. The doors blast open and Maru, the queen of los espíritus, runs inside.

"They are everywhere!" She screams, before collapsing on the floor. She is nothing but a pile of grey dust.

That's when the fantasmas come.

I can hear the guards screaming outside. There's no escape; we must fight. When the first fantasma enters the room, one guard strikes at it, killing it immediately. Then, a horde of fantasmas is on us, entering through the doors and windows. Animal, human, monster fantasmas surround us, making the big temple feel as small as a carriage.

They outnumber the guards. They outnumber the dioses. I try calling my water, trying to access my powers. But there's only a soft hum. There's too many of them.

Time slows down.

Mother turns around, fear in her eyes. She mutters something, but the screams of los espíritus drown her. She grabs the water bag hanging on her hip and empties it around me in a circle, slaying a fantasma in the process. My hand shots out to punch a fantasma that gets too close as I desperately try to take hold of my dim connection to water. I can't reach anything around me.

The fantasma turns around. Translucent eyes fixate on me as it morphs into something resembling a bird. With a flap of one of its wings, the fantasma sends something hot my way. I don't have time to focus on the sharp pain that envelops my knuckles when whatever it is cuts skin because Mother is suddenly in front of me, sending needle-like shards of water that turn the slimy monster to dust. She grabs the water bag hanging on her hip and drops a few drops in a quick circle around me as I kick another fantasma. They seem to grow in number. My sore body can't fight for much longer. Mother forcibly takes my hands in hers.

"Stay safe," she whispers in my ear. She kisses my forehead and steps back.

A bubble of water surrounds me, blurring my vision. All I can see are the figures of Mother and Atana. The guards fighting the fantasmas are nothing but small moving lights. She's concealed me. Mother is close enough that I can read her features. Her eyes have lost their focus since she can't see me, but she whispers again.

"Stay safe, Lluvia," she whispers once more.

A commotion steals her attention and her eyes grow wide before the sound of things being fired fills the room. I turn around and try to focus on what's happening around me, but the bubble makes that impossible. A gasp brings my attention back to my mother.

Red fills my vision. There's red in my mother's pale gown. There's red in her mouth.

A stone arrow is buried deep in her chest. Trapped in the bubble, I slap my hands over my mouth. If I make a sound, I know it will burst and all of this will be for nothing.

But inside, I'm screaming.

Mother falls to the ground, the arrow shaft protruding through her spine. I crouch beside her, reaching out even though I know I can't touch her. Her hands turn the soft gray of polished marble.

Someone approaches, close enough that I can see it is a man wearing a cape. He kneels beside Mother and, for a second, I hope he's trying to see if her essence is fine. But then he produces something shiny, and I freeze. A knife.

I close my eyes as he cuts her and bile rises in my throat. I can hear her words in my head. *Stay safe.* When I open my eyes again, his shadow is still close. I don't need to look to know that he's cut her just enough to take her essence.

He goes through the other bodies too, taking essences from every dios he sees. Even with the movement invisibility allows me, I can't make out his face. His cape obscures his features except for a bruised jaw. Once he's finished, he holds the essences in his hands—deceptively simple rocks that reflect the fire around the room. He scans the bodies, and a chill travels up my spine.

He's counting the bodies. What if he realizes someone's missing?

But he turns around and calls the fantasmas, instructing them in words I can't understand. He walks away slowly, until he is nothing but a point of light. Soon, only the bodies and me remain in the Palacio. A sob makes its way out of my chest, and the protective bubble vanishes. I approach Mother.

Stay safe. My mother's voice reverberates in my chest. Her face is cold marble except a small smile on her lips. She is only a tragically, beautiful statue. Beside her, Atana is stone too, her guards carved into fighting stances for eternity. The espíritus' ashes cover the floor—a gray nightmare.

They are dead and there will be no reincarnation for them. Their essences have been ripped from them.

And I just stood here, silent, and let it happen.

I scream.

***

Simple instinct pulls me to find Saymar. It's the same thing that made me hide in her room when Márahe fell for one of our pranks and stormed around the templo looking for us. Back when we were children. Before our fights started. I take Atana's horse, who is faster than any other animal I've ridden. It's been only a few minutes when the Montañas de la Luna, the mountain chain where Barrio Alto's located, appear on the horizon.

Two hours later, I'm walking through the food district. Barrio Alto is famous for its restaurants and taverns. But if Saymar is in town, I know she'll be at Fuego's Memories, her uncle's tavern.

The building was constructed in the shape of a cloud. It stands out among the others, but it's the batatas fritas that makes it famous. My stomach growls, a reminder that I've had nothing to eat since I reincarnated.

In front of the tavern, a few groups chat. A man plays guitar a few feet away and two men are singing and clapping as their friends dance to the rhythm of Barrio Alto's melodic tunes. A dog wags its tail, mimicking the happiness of the groups.

The heaviness in my heart is a vivid contrast to everything I see.

As I get closer, more people join in dancing. I'm startled when a hand drops on my shoulder.

"Andreia! That's you, right?"

Ceba, one of the fuego semidioses, smiles at me, recognition in his brown eyes. He's wearing his guard uniform, so he must have come here right after finishing his shift at the Templo de Fuego.

"It is you! Man, Saymar is not gonna believe this," he continued, making way for us through the crowd. "You really came back fast. Didn't she, uh…"

"Kill me this morning? Yes. Nice gift, by the way. She told me the blade was yours."

His ears turn bright red, but his smile never falters.

"What brings you around here? I don't think I've seen you here since… well, never."

That isn't true. Saymar and I spent most days hiding from Koroce's lectures under her tío's bar, betting on who could find more fire lizards around the tavern. But none of that is actually important right now.

"Is Saymar here?" I hear my voice and flinch at the severity of my tone. Ceba notices, too, and loses his smile.

"Why? Are you looking for revenge?"

"No. I just need to talk." It's not revenge I need from her.

He doesn't look convinced, but he greets the guard at the door nevertheless and leads me in.

"Here, here! The reason for our celebration has arrived!"

When Ceba opens the door to the tavern, chaos welcomes us. There are groups everywhere, some louder than others. Their yells compete to be heard above each other.

I find Saymar quickly, her bright red hair braided in a cascade down her back. She's surrounded by people I barely recognize, but they seem to be having a lot of fun. Once we're close enough, I register that she's telling a dramatically embellished version of this morning's fight. Any semblance of goodwill I have evaporates.

"Saymar, can I speak with you?"

"The diosa herself!" she says, clapping slowly. "Everybody, thank Andreia for dying again!"

The chorus of giggling 'thank yous' that followed only add to my anger.

"Saymar. We need to talk," I repeat, emphasizing each word and trying not to scream in frustration.

"Don't let it eat you. I know it sucks to die, but it's not your fault. We just have different experiences," she says, winking at the semidios beside her. "Oh, and talent, too. Can't forget that part."

Ceba laughs, along with a few other fuego semidioses I've seen in other celebrations like this. Saymar finally turns to look at me, a lazy smile on her face. One look at my face and it all fades away.

"What's wrong, Andreia?"

And, even though I'm angry, even though I've rehearsed what I wanted to say, the words get stuck in my throat. I just stare.

"Come with me," she says, taking my hand and pulling me away from the screams and racket. We pass a series of doorways and make our way upstairs toward the attic room. She opens the door with a set of keys and ushers me in. I trip over one of her bags and she grimaces, but leads me to the farthest corner, where my favorite coat, the one I was wearing earlier today, has been laid out on a sofa.

Behind it, a window opens up to the forest, displaying the green giants of Barahona and the purple hue of the darkening sky. I register its beauty while my brain tries to force my mouth to speak, to make any sound, to work. Saymar hands me a glass of water and sits beside me on the sofa.

Her eyes are soft as I drink. "What happened, Andreia?"

The mouth that had been grinning a few moments ago turns into a thin line as I tell her.

"Are you sure about this?"

I bite down a harsh reply and I remind myself that Saymar just learned that her mother had died. *Our mothers*, a voice in my head reminds me as I fight tears. I can only nod.

"What's the plan?"

I blink. "Plan?"

"You came all the way here instead of going to your temple. There must be a plan."

"I didn't think that far ahead," I answer honestly, and her eyes look at me incredulously.

"Then think. Is there anything else you remember? Did they mention anything at all?"

"Why do you want to know?"

"If I'm going after them, I need to know where to start."

I go through the events scene by scene in my head. "He spoke to the fantasmas in the Laiko dialect. I could only understand a few words."

Saymar stands and grabs the bag I stumbled on, filling it with random things around the room.

"Then I'm going to Laiká."

"And I'm going with you."

She rolls her eyes. "Of course you are. Are you strong enough to get us there?"

I hadn't teleported here before, so I hadn't used the energy I'd regained after reincarnation. Still, it had been less than a day. I couldn't be sure that I'd be strong enough to make the trip from Barrio Alto to Laiká, and even less if I could do it twice and bring us back.

"I can try."

She sends a small grin in my direction. It's not the big smile she was wearing earlier, but it's real.

"That's all I'm asking for."

***

"Remind me what part of 'try' means 'I'll throw us in the middle of Bosque Barahona, right where the aquias hunt for their next meal', please."

My powers hadn't been strong enough. While we passed over the trees of Barahona, Saymar fell through the trees, and I went right after. With a splash, we landed in one of the forest's lakes. As soon as we hit the water, five small aquia dragons attacked. Saymar had to fight all of them off, which, considering she was soaking wet, was harder than it should have been. Or maybe it was because she had to drag me out of the lake when my body became sluggish with exhaustion.

"I already said I'm sorry. Besides, they attacked me too!"

"Aren't you supposed to be a goddess of water? I thought you could control water monsters."

"*Saltwater*. And I'm still a semidios, I can't do that."

We've been walking for some time now, with Saymar complaining consistently. As the forest thins, I wonder how we'll find anything in Laiká. With hundreds of thousands of inhabitants in the capital, it'll be near impossible.

The towers of Laiká welcome us to the city.

***

Laiká is nothing like my memories. When Mother was a minor god instead of cemí, she would often take me on trips to the Breathing City, where espíritus, dioses and humans lived in harmony. It was a city full of color and music, strange food and the latest fashions. You couldn't visit Laiká without experiencing something new. Now, the streets are empty, dry leaves gathering in the edges. As we make our way to the city center, empty carts and destroyed shops litter the ground, making it hard to walk.

"It feels like a ciudad fantasma," Saymar says, and I silently agree.

Once we're in the plaza, the rich smell of wet grass replaces the rotten odor. Plants and trees have taken over the heart of Laiká, growing over cobblestone and fences. It feels like something wiped out all the humans and left a picturesque paradise for nature.

Or it would be if we weren't being watched. The hairs on my neck stand up as we get closer to the buildings around the plaza. If it was any quieter, I could hear my heart echoing through the city.

"We're not alone," I say. Saymar nods.

"There's fire inside a few of the houses we've passed. I can't tell much more than that."

It's dark enough now that we can't see the things that litter the street. Saymar makes a small ball of fire in her hand.

"Maybe if we go back to the plaza, we might—"

I register a movement behind Saymar. A small girl runs towards us, face hidden under a dark cape. She's around 12 with brown skin, the pale hue of someone who doesn't spend time in the sun.

"What are you doing?" she hisses. "You'll get all of us killed."

She approaches Saymar, but stops when she sees the fire dancing on her palm.

"W-what?" She studies us quickly, disbelief and hope fighting in her face. "You're dioses?" We nod. "Hurry, come with me." When we hesitate, she looks back and whisper-screams. "Now!"

Saymar looks to me for direction. "I think we should go. We're out of options."

"Whatever you say, jefa. After all, I'm just here to save you if you need it...again."

I smile and run after the girl. She waits for us to dart inside the door before bolting it.

She takes off her cape and I realize I was wrong—she's short, but about our age. A small child crawls to the girl and Syamar reignites her fireball. The girl glares at us.

"Turn that off! They'll see you from the outside."

"They?" Saymar and I ask at the same time.

The girl hoists the child on her hip. "Follow me and don't trip. You've made enough noise."

She guides us down a few stairs that are carved into the rock under the building. The more we descend, the less I can see. I touch the wall to guide me but it hardly matters with the stairs being so irregular. I miss one but before I can trip, Saymar has grabbed my arm, holding me up. The girl scoffs and keeps walking. Once we've reached the bottom, she unlocks another door and the light is blinding.

Behind the door, there's furniture and belongings piled precariously on every available surface. Spoons inside pots inside cubes over one small table. They've stacked boxes in zig-zagging towers, and there's a small patch of earth in the only corner in the room with windows. Clothes of every color hang from the ceiling around the room, creating small halls between the different piles.

"Ama, they're dioses," the girl murmurs to a pile of clothes in the back corner. Then it moves, revealing a woman sewing shirts. She limps in our direction, throwing a worried look at the girl.

"You seem to know who we are, but we know nothing about you," I say.

"You can tell them," a third unknown voice calls. A taller woman moves to stand behind the girl and the other woman. She clutches a soup mug in her hands and the deep marks under her eyes don't hide the distrust she directs at us. "My name is Etma. I'm the owner of this house."

"I'm Lia," the old woman says. "And this is little Sam and Claudia." She holds up the baby's hand so he is waving at us. "We found them after the first attack."

"You keep mentioning attacks and a 'them.' What are you talking about?"

Etma motions us to sit while Lia walks Sam and Claudia behind a patchwork curtain.

"He came one morning, full of bruises, and Etma took him in," Lia said, her eyes trained on Etma's face. "He was a lost man, looking for something or someone. But he never said what." Lia falls silent, twirling the thin fabric of her dress between her fingers.

"Then one day, the fantasmas arrived." Etma's voice cuts through the silence. "They started attacking everyone–human, dios, espíritu. If you moved, the fantasmas were after you. At first, we tried fighting them off. But by two weeks later, fantasmas had us cornered in our houses with no way to escape. They closed the city and people hid wherever they could."

"Why did we never hear of this?"

"But you did," Etma says, exchanging a look with Lia. "Los dioses sent someone here."

"And they killed him," Lia adds. "That's when Darel showed his true nature."

"He ate the dead dios' heart!" Claudia says from behind the curtain, her voice muffled. Lia moved it back to find her standing with a sheepish smile. Lia looked at Etma, but she just shrugged.

"He didn't eat his heart, Claudia. He mixed his heart with the dios so he could have his powers. No eating involved."

"But Ada said—"

"She was only trying to scare you. Go back with Sam. This isn't a conversation for you."

"You know that I'm just as old as they are, right?" Claudia pointed to us and closed the curtain, separating all of us from Sam. "Besides, we still don't know if we can trust these two. They were walking through the streets like they were looking for trouble."

Something clicks in my mind as Saymar explains that we didn't know there was trouble here.

"When did this happen?" I ask, and four pairs of eyes focus on me. Etma answers.

"The attacks? It's already been two months."

"No, I meant when did they kill the dios."

Claudia jumps at that. "It was a week ago, probably. Maybe nine days."

I turn to Saymar, but she seems to read my mind. "Cemí Koroce."

"If you didn't know anything about the attacks, why are you here?"

Saymar is about to answer when a rumble shakes the building, dust raining from the ceiling.

Lia and Etma pale.

"They're here."

***

Outside, the night has thrown its blanket over the sky. The moon shines bright enough to give the streets and the buildings shape. The crunch of gravel sounds, as if someone is standing on it. Etma sends Lia and the others downstairs. She grabs a gun, which I hadn't seen earlier, and leads us to an alley. From there, we can see the streets around the plaza—an enormous shadow lingers.

Etma lets out a sigh of relief.

"It's not them. It's only a wolf fantasma. If we ignore it, it will go away soon."

I tense. If we ignore it now, it might go away. But what happens if it brings others with it? What if it told the fantasmas working with Darel? What if they came to Laiká, destroying more than just buildings?

Saymar seems to hear my internal battle because she turns to me.

"No one needs to play the hero," Saymar says, clasping my shoulder. Shrugging her hand off, I stand and make my way closer to it, making sure it can't see me.

I couldn't save my mother. But at least I can get rid of this fantasma and help the people of Laiká. I run out of my hiding place and call the water to me, ready to turn this fantasma to ashes.

The wolf focuses his attention on me and I realize my mistake—my powers refuse to respond. It attacks and I'm helpless as its claws rip the clothes and skin on my right leg. I wonder why the water won't listen to me as I fall to the ground. Its other paw cuts through my arm.

I feel Saymar's scream in my chest as she fires fireball after fireball at the fantasma. It turns to ashes a few feet away from me. And then Saymar is beside me, faster than I could have ever expected, cradling my head in her arms.

"You stupid girl. What are you doing?!" she mutters under her breath. My body is nothing but pain. It feels like it belongs to someone else.

Lia and Etma look conflicted when Saymar places me on their sofa. Claudia sings a lullaby to Sam behind the curtains. They linger about, standing in front of the kids as if that could protect them from all of the bad in the world.

"We're sorry, but you can't stay here."

***

Lia and Etma take us to a building a few streets away.

Before long, Saymar has dusted the room and laid me down. She's been oddly silent.

"Drink this. It'll make you sleepy, but Etma says it's the best she has for open wounds."

I drink the medicine, aware of Saymar's stare. She's finished cleaning the cuts on my leg and wrapping it with salve and strips torn from her cape. She inches closer to me.

"Are we okay?" I ask, unable to keep the question inside.

Saymar turns her face to the chalice, soaking up the piece she tore from the cape. I hiss as she softly applies it with pressure on my arm. "Why wouldn't we be?"

"That's what I don't understand. Other than throwing us into a lake full of vicious water dragons, I've done nothing wrong." I try to smile at that, but she doesn't react.

"There's nothing to understand. Just...give me your arm and let me clean your wound."

I give her my hand again. As Saymar bandages my arm, I try to read her expression, but she's closed up. But I can tell she's angry by her scrunched eyebrows.

"I feel you're holding something back and I don't like it. If there's been any constant in my life, it's your need to say absolutely everything you think. Where's that honesty now?"

"Honesty? Goddamn, Andreia. You're cruel," Saymar exclaims, placing a hand on my cheek and staring into my eyes. "You almost died in my arms. You ran out there without your powers. And for what? There was no real threat, no need to fight. It was one fantasma and you almost died. So, how dare you ask if I'm holding something back."

I'm speechless. The last thing I expected was a scolding.

"What?" I ask, trying to get a smile from her. "Are you scared someone other than you could actually kill me?"

"No." She's still holding my face in her hands, her eyes conflicted. "I'm scared you'll never notice me if you really die." And then her lips meet mine. Fleetingly, like a red butterfly in my mother's gardens, dancing across my skin. And then I kiss her back, longer, deeper; her body relaxes. Eyes closed, our foreheads touch and I can feel the fire inside Saymar.

Burning.

For me.

I wonder if she can feel the storm inside my chest, the waves of feelings crashing in my bones.

The fire flickers and we both open our eyes, staring at each other like it's the first time we've seen in full color.

Then her face clouds and Saymar takes a few steps back, walking to the door.

"I'll let you rest."

***

"Su Alteza, I expected you to call me sooner."

When those words make their way to my ears, I sit up immediately. "Márahe?!"

She's standing close to the door, blue uniform perfectly in place. I can feel her eyes scanning the room before focusing on me.

"Saymar called for me last night. It's a pleasure to see me, of course. Can't say the same about..." Márahe gives my hair, torn and bloody clothes, and obvious bandages a once over. "You."

"You're as insulting as ever," I whisper, my voice catching in my throat.

"Apologies. Analysis is an occupational disease of mine."

Although her words are cruel, she helps me stand like she did in la Fuente, and makes sure I'm sitting before moving away. Whatever Etma gave me yesterday worked fast. I stretch my arm and the cut barely stings. My leg is sore, but it's nothing that would stop me from moving.

Saymar enters, carrying what looks like breakfast on a tray; she refuses to meet my eyes. There are four sets. I'm about to ask who the last is for when I see someone following her.

"Gooooood morning!!"

Ceba's voice roars from the doorway, way more chipper than I expect anyone to be before the sun has risen. If we were still staying at Etma's house, she'd kick us out again for the ruckus.

Márahe closes her eyes, visibly shuddering. "Ceba."

"Márahe." His voice grows softer as he tries to catch her eye, but Márahe is already turning back to me.

"As you can see, Ceba here suffers an astonishing lack of social skills. No one would blame you if you felt the urge to bash him over the head with a blunt object." She grabs the lamp from the nightstand and puts it in front of me. "Oh, look. Here's one. May I do the honors, Su Alteza?"

Ceba is smiling even more broadly than before, obviously entertained. Whatever affected him before is gone, as the vibrancy returns to his voice. "Oh, Márahe, no need to be shy. I know you've missed me."

Márahe mimes swinging the lamp and I laugh, interrupting them before chairs start flying.

"I guess you two know each other?"

"Unfortunately," Márahe confirms. Ceba playfully shoves her shoulder. Márahe glares at him. And if looks could kill, he would not be safe.

Ceba ignores her look and pats her hand. "Don't worry, we're usually like this."

"Don't lump me in with you. Disgusting."

Once Ceba is seated, we tell both of them what we've learned from Lia and Etma. Saymar talks without looking at me. Márahe nods throughout while Ceba listens quietly.

"Like you asked, I found a little information about Darel," Márahe says. "There's not a lot about him. He came from the wilderness of Maguayo after monsters exterminated his family. The few things the historiadores could find was that he seems to believe dioses ordered the attack, and he's been studying the archaic magic in the temples, trying to bring his family back from Turey."

"So that's why he's been attacking the Puerta," Ceba says. "He needs to open the portal to Turey."

"And that's probably where he's hiding now," Saymar adds. "We have to go there."

"Agreed," Márahe says, and they turn to look at me.

I refuse to look at my bandages. I know what they're thinking.

"It's okay if you stay here, Andreia." Ceba is the first that breaks the silence.

"We need as many hands as we can, but you're hurt. Don't feel forced to come with," Márahe says. Saymar stares out the window, ignoring me. It hurts, especially after last night, but I push it aside.

"I want to go. No, scratch that: I need to go. If there's any way to stop this monster, we'll figure it out. Plus, I'm feeling better. My wounds don't hurt as much as I expected."

Saymar looked like she wants to say something, but she holds back. After we all agree on going, Márahe looks for the things she needs to teleport all of us to the Puerta del Turey temple. Ceba follows her. Saymar stands up to leave, but I stand up, too.

"Can we talk for a second?"

Saymar looks around the room, evaluating every escape route. Instinctively, I block her way to the window, even when I know she's not about to jump to postpone this. Or at least I hope she isn't.

"Are we okay?"

She stares at me, a mix of fear and hope in her eyes. "I should be the one asking that. I shouldn't have assumed. Or kissed you like that."

"Did you forget I kissed you back?"

Her whole face is as red as her hair now, and she's silent. She nods.

"I know this isn't the time or place to talk about this, but I… I hope you won't run away as soon as this is over. Don't you think we owe it to each other to see what this is?"

Saymar nods again.

"Now that's out of the way, can I kiss you again?"

She smiles. And I move toward her, promising myself that I'll do everything I can to make sure this isn't the last time.

***

Márahe took us as close to the Puerta as she could. With only a few rooms between us and Darel, my heart pounds in my ears again. Since I'm the only one who's been to the Puerta, the rest stand behind me. Saymar's closest to me, making sure she's ready to attack in case someone finds us.

We silently walk through the usually chaotic halls of the Puerta. The quiet is deafening. Unease strengthens its grip over my heart as we make our way to the portal. Something tells me this isn't going how it's supposed to.

So when we get to the room of the Puerta and I see Darel standing there, like he has no cares in the world, a sinking feeling hits my stomach.

He's rubbing a golden locket between his fingers, but drops it the moment we step into the room. It catches the light as it hangs on his neck.

"I was growing a little bored, starting to think you wouldn't be able to find me." His voice isn't what I expected. I wanted him to sound evil, pure evil. As if the tone would be another confirmation of all he's done. But his voice is normal. A little deep, but otherwise unremarkable. He laughs, as if our silence is amusing. "Well, it seems like we won't be able to have a conversation before we kill you."

Ceba opened his mouth this time. "You and what army?"

Darel smiles and the fantasmas make their presence known. We're surrounded, at least two dozen fantasmas inching closer with each passing beat. Darel's smile transforms into a grimace, distorting his face into an unnatural visage of madness.

"It's almost poetic how delusional you all are. You really think four semidioses can stop me at this point? I've become a new dios, one that won't forget about the people who trust him. One who will create new worlds. Now I just need to open the door to a new future."

At that, he turns around and makes his way to the door. He flicks his hand and the fantasmas attack.

Specks of saliva hit my face as the fantasma screeches. It shoves me to the floor, gripping my wrists. I wriggle on the floor, trying to hit it. Until the pressure lifts off my body, Ceba kicking it into dust. Helping me stand, he slices through another fantasma.

"Are you alright?"

"Yeah," I answer. He nods and spins around to cut through another fantasma. A snake-like one approaches me and I try to reach the water within me. The answer is weak. I summon two streams, enough to turn the snake to dust. They grow stronger as more fantasmas approach, but my connection still feels weak. *It's too soon,* my mind keeps repeating. *I can't use this many powers so soon after reincarnating.*

But we don't have the days, not even hours, to wait for my strength to come back normally. I have to make do with what I have. I jump as a fantasma with horns and sharp needle-like fangs runs to me, throwing two water daggers that evaporate as soon as they reach their target and turn the monster into a gray cloud of dust.

"You're not half bad in a fight," Saymar screams somewhere behind me. I can't turn around, but I feel the smile in her voice. "I'm surprised."

"Does she ever shut up?" Márahe asks, her eyes tracking Darel as he reaches the other side of the room. A warning scream leaves my lips when a stone arrow flies past me in her direction. She spins, spotting it and hearing me. She jumps and explodes into raindrops reappearing crouched in front of Darel. She kicks him in the chest and then dissipates and returns to my side.

"Since when can you do that?" I asked, astonished.

"I've been your guard for all your life. Did you really expect me to be bad at fighting?"

"No, but you did nothing when Saymar attacked me." I hit the snarling fantasma of a beast with a spear of boiling water. The energy is flowing through my body, each move I make strengthening my connection, though it's still weaker than normal. "She's never tried to kill you."

"The hundred times I've had to reincarnate beg to differ."

"You know what I mean."

I do, but I can't contemplate that now. More fantasmas fill the room and Márahe hands me a dagger before we separate.

Two fantasmas are slithering their way towards me. I send a small rain of hot water over them before something crashes into me, pushing me to the floor and sending the dagger spinning away just a breath too far for my fingers. I try to stand up, but a snarling fantasma keeps me down, unable to move more than my hands.

I can feel Saymar's scream before the fantasma flies away from me, its body swiftly turning into dust when she lights her palms and pushes him again. My hands grab the dagger in front of me just in time to throw it to a burly fantasma running towards us. Saymar helps me up, but there's no time for snarky remarks this time. Four fantasmas surround us again and we fall into a rhythm: her fire daggers attack the flying fantasmas as I throw spear after spear of boiling water to the fantasmas crawling around the floor.

Darel makes his way over to the door but he can't open it. He spins around, eyes angry as he looks around the room. A scream erupts from his mouth and fire burns.

"Why are you fighting now? *Now* you do something? When your people, your dioses, are dying, you use your strength to protect them." Darel throws everything at us that he can. Stone arrows, fireballs, boiling geysers—all the things he stole from the dioses, anything that came to mind. "But when it was my family dying, my people perishing, you did *nothing*. Los dioses haven't served us for a long time. Now this is your judgment."

"Judgment?" Saymar spits the word out as she turns the fantasmas in front of her to ash. Her voice had lost all the lightness from earlier, replaced with an anger so powerful it could burn all of us. "How is this justice? You're killing dioses, threatening cities and destroying dioses, espíritus or humans who refuse to think like you. That's not justice. That's just slaughter!"

Six fantasmas remained, but Ceba and Márahe kept them occupied. Saymar and I inch closer to Darel, her fire creating a barrier between us. He throws his hands out at us, sending more projectiles flying our direction. Shielding me, she leans down toward me. "He's growing desperate," she whispers.

"Do you have a plan?"

But I shake my head. "We won't need one." Darel drops to his knees, clawing at his chest. The veins in his arms have turned black, creating dark spiderwebs on his skin. The fantasmas are still roaring behind us, but the balls of fire, stone, and water stop. He's struggling to breathe.

"We should immobilize him now," Saymar says, fire licking at her hands.

She's about to hit him with a blast when Márahe puts out a hand to stop her. To our left, Ceba blasts the last fantasma into ash and limps our way. Márahe is by his side in an instant, holding him carefully. His whole body seems to relax as he leans against her, exhausted.

"There's no need. He's already dying," Ceba says, out of breath.

"W-why?" Darel chokes out, falling to the floor.

"Your soul is being consumed by the essences of the dioses," Márahe answers. "Did you really think becoming a dios was this easy? We train constantly to keep our bodies and souls strong enough to hold our essences at bay. Power with no control only destroys."

"Lack of justice and strong ideals are what push the world toward rebirth," Darel whispers. "I might die, but you can't stop this."

"There are many things that need to be fixed," I say. "But not like this. There are other ways. You don't know what the lack of balance between the worlds could cause."

"It can't be worse than what your indifference has already cost us."

"The world is a blend of unconcealed and hidden aspects," I say. "When some people rejoice, others weep. One man's justice could be another man's evil. It's part of existing. What makes you so certain that you're on the right side?"

Letting his head drop, he glares at me and then answers with a smile. "What makes *you?*"

And with that, he's still. His body slowly turns to ash, leaving behind the essences of the dioses he defeated in his attempt of justice. They pulse and glow, full of life and ready for their journey over the Fuente de las Almas. Ready for a new beginning.

He's gone, but there's no joy in our victory. Instead, the four of us gather around and mourn for the man that was so lost he thought he needed to make others suffer to regain happiness.

For our friends.

For our family.

And for those of us left behind.

{ 15 }

Dark Space

STEPHANIE SLAGLE

Gabriela's Trip Diary
Day 1

I can't believe I'm here and I'm typing this right now. I'm sitting in my cabin aboard *The Grim Ranger*. It's my first day as part of the crew. We're leaving soon for Japera, some mining moon at the edge of the galaxy. After that, well, I'm not sure where we're going yet. I met the captain earlier—Captain Rosa Juárez herself, one of the most famous treasure-hunting space marauders in the five closest star systems! But she only said hello for a brief moment. She and her crewmembers have been busy getting the ship ready for flight and I guess they think a newbie's gonna get in the way. They're probably right.

But let me start at the beginning.

I sent in my application six months ago. I had to write a five-page essay sharing why I wanted to join Captain Rosa's space crew, what sort of skills I could bring to the table, blah blah blah. Writing the essay wasn't the hard part. The hard part was waiting six months to learn if I was accepted or denied.

Mama tried to hide the comm slip when it came. She gave it to our little white dog, Fiero, hoping he'd bury it in the backyard. Luckily, Papa caught him in the act and brought it to me.

"This came for you, mija," he said.

I was stumbling around, sleepy-eyed, as I got ready for another day of work on my family's spice farm. When I saw the symbol on the back of the comm slip, I snatched it out of Papa's hand to read it: *Ms. Gabriela Lopez, we are pleased to extend an invitation to you to join* The Grim Ranger. *Please report to flight deck 7 in the Landa II spaceport promptly at 1600 on the 14th of Juniper 2687, if you wish to accept your position.*

I'm pretty sure my scream of excitement echoed through the whole neighborhood.

Mama was furious at Papa. She had tears in her eyes as I packed my suitcase. The comm slip had taken so long to reach me, I only had twelve hours to get to Landa II—practically on the other side of the planet.

"I don't understand why you would want to join a space crew at your age," said Mama, her hands on her hips. "You're only seventeen, Gabriela—"

"*Eighteen,*" I corrected her. My birthday was just last week. She'd already conveniently forgotten.

She brushed my words away with a hand. "It's too dangerous! You have no idea what you're getting into."

"Abuelita said it's exciting and I'll have the time of my life!" I shot back. My abuela was the one who had spent hours helping me write the essay and fill out the application. *She* supported me.

"We can't stop her, Elena," Papa said to Mama. "She's old enough to decide for herself."

Mama's eyes cast flames in his direction. I don't envy Papa. He'll probably have to sleep on the couch for a full week just because he was sticking up for me.

I feel bad for Mama too, of course. I'm her and Papa's only child, and they've always hoped I would stay on the farm and take it over someday, to keep it in the family. But Papa assured me they have enough hired hands to harvest the spices without me, and there are plenty of buyers who would take over the operation if I turn it down. I have bigger dreams—namely, space adventures. Traversing the galaxy, finding long-lost planets and treasures. Who would pick a boring life on a farm over that?

"I'll get the transport ready," said Papa, heading out the front door.

I leaned down to scratch the scruffy fur on Fiero's belly. He responded by doing his favorite thing—licking my hands. "I'll miss you, little guy."

When I stood up, Mama had closed herself off. Like she didn't want to acknowledge the fact I was really leaving.

"Goodbye, Mama," I said softly.

As I turned to go, she rushed over and pulled me into her arms. "Be safe, mija. You're my little girl, don't forget that. And don't forget your family. Promise me that, okay?"

I squeezed her back, burying my face in her shoulder for a moment. "I promise."

After that, I got in the transport with Papa and we took off for Landa II. I'd only been to the spaceport one other time. My family makes a good living with their farm, but Mama hates taking excursions off-planet—the space sickness hits her hard—so the only time I've been allowed to go anywhere was a couple years ago on a school trip to Rognon, a floating colony on a nearby gas planet. That was the trip that convinced me I had to get off this planet. There are so many interesting places in the galaxy I want to see, and joining a space crew is the only way I'll be able to do it.

"You sure you'll be all right on your own?" Papa said as he pulled our small skimmer transport to a stop in the short-term parking dock.

"I'll be fine. Thank you—for everything, Papa." I leaned over to give him a quick hug. His scruffy beard always itched my cheek when I got too close.

He planted a kiss on my forehead. "Go have some adventures so you have stories for me when you come back home."

I grinned. "I will!"

So, I'm gonna document every single adventure I have with the crew. I still can't believe I'm actually here on a spaceship, and we're about to fly off into the far reaches of the solar system. I'm the youngest crew member aboard by far. I'm not exactly sure what my job is yet—I think I'll be doing various odd mechanical jobs, helping with cooking and cleaning, that sort of thing. Hopefully, I'll learn a lot. Hopefully, I won't let my fellow crewmates down.

Gabriela's Trip Diary
Day 3

I was right about the job thing. As the newbie, I'm the grunt of the crew—any menial task anyone else doesn't want to do gets thrown my way. Some things aren't too bad...but other things stink (literally). Oh well. I don't care what they make me do, as long as I get to tag along on whatever treasure-hunting missions Captain Rosa takes us on next.

Speaking of, I know where we're headed after Japera! I found out earlier when I was talking to Sebastian. He's one of the engineers and the second-youngest member of the crew. He's super tall, tan skin, with black hair dyed blue at the tips. Yes, he's totally swoon-worthy. He's the first person I met on the crew. In fact, I made a fool of myself the first time he saw me, racing across the Landa II spaceport and colliding with one of the cleaning bots, my belongings flying everywhere. My face was as red as the sun. But he was cool about it, thank God, and now I've *almost* stopped being embarrassed around him.

Anyway, this morning after breakfast he asked me to help him with an engineering project. I held a rag and handed him tools as he asked for them. But I also paid careful attention to what he was doing—I want to learn everything.

"You're quiet, huh?" he said as he tinkered.

"Me?" I snort-laughed. "Oh, no, not usually. I'm just a bit over-whelmed by everything."

"You can ask me anything you want to know."

"Well, I was wondering…how many other applications did the captain receive for the open crew spot?" Yesterday I learned that there are only four other people aboard ship, besides Captain Rosa and myself, which really freaked me out. There was only one spot open, and she picked me. Surely, there were many, many people like me wanting a chance at a life in space.

Sebastian paused in his tinkering, frowning. "Hmm, you know, I think we only got ten applications."

"What? Really?"

"Yeah." He shrugged. "People get scared. Not everyone's up for this kind of life."

"Oh." I twisted my mouth. "What are people so scared of?"

"Hasn't anyone told you where we're flying to?"

"Japera, right?"

"Yes, but Japera's just a pit-stop. We'll refuel there, catch up with the chatter in the local bars, and then we'll blast beyond the outer rim and head to dark space."

Dark space. My breath caught in my throat at those words. Dark space means uncharted space—places past the edge of the discovered galaxy, where few humans have ever gone before. Most space maraud-ers and privateers don't have high-tech ships capable of making it that far. Others are simply too afraid to make the trek and face the unknown.

"We're going to dark space?" I asked.

"That's the plan." Sebastian didn't sound too excited.

"Have you ever been there before?"

"Just to the edge of it. I've heard the captain went there a few years ago, before I joined, and—"

"And what?" I pressed.

"And she was out there for an entire year. Everyone thought she was lost forever, but then she finally made it back. Her ship was brimming with artifacts from some long-lost alien civilization, worth a ridiculous amount of gold. But the weirder thing was, she only thought she'd been gone for a day. Probably went through some kind of wormhole."

A shiver ran down my spine like spider legs. I'm still not sure if it was from fear or anticipation.

"So, why go back now?"

"Because there's always more to discover," said a voice behind us.

I jumped and almost dropped the tools I was holding. Captain Rosa herself stood looming above me in the corridor with her long, velvet-lined black coat whipping behind her. She has long, thick, shiny black curls, the kind I envy. At the moment, she was chewing on a piece of rat jerky.

"There's something out there. A planet rumored to hold a host of mysteries. So, I hope you're up for some danger, Gabriela."

"Oh, you bet I am, Captain," I replied.

"Good," she said, winking at me. "Because we'll land on Japera in a few hours' time, and then tomorrow, we're heading into dark space. Make sure you take care of any last comms before then. Once we cross the border of the galaxy, we'll have trouble getting in contact with anyone for a while."

I glanced back at Sebastian after the captain left. "How long will we be out there?"

He shrugged. "No idea."

He went back to tinkering. In the silence, I tried to ignore the nerves buzzing in my stomach.

Mama wouldn't be happy if she knew where we were going. Papa and Abuelita wouldn't be either, for that matter. I'll have to keep it secret until we're back safe and sound.

Gabriela's Trip Diary
Day 6

It's official. We're beyond the solar system, in dark space. Two days ago, we left Japera. It was a short stop, and the place was a literal junkyard. Yesterday, we flew through an asteroid belt and a wormhole. *That* was anxiety-inducing. And then we entered dark space.

It's weird. It's the same view out the window—distant specks of suns blanketing the black black black of space. I wouldn't be able to tell we were off the map of the known galaxy if I hadn't seen the dot of our ship disappear from the navigation charts with my own two eyes.

We do actually still have a map, though. Our pilot, Freddy, showed it to the whole crew at dinner earlier. He and Captain Rosa started putting it together on their previous trip into dark space. We'll be using it to chart our course to the planet we're trying to find.

"A rogue planet," Captain Rosa said. "Meaning it's not caught in the orbit of any star. It's wandering through the vastness of space, just like us."

I don't get most of the science talk, so I don't know how we're going to find a planet no one else has ever found before. But Captain Rosa seems certain we'll find something extraordinary there.

Gabriela's Trip Diary
Day 17
Sorry it's been a few weeks since I last wrote anything. I honestly thought space travel would be a lot more exciting than it is. Or maybe it's just dark space that isn't that exciting since we're just wandering through unexplored territory. It turns out the reason why most of it hasn't been explored before is because there isn't much out here. Random floating bits of space dust. That's about it.

I spend my days mopping floors, cleaning latrines, helping Sebastian with more of his projects (I'm becoming quite the novice engineer, in fact!), and helping Mary, the cook, develop her recipes.

Mary has some great stories, let me tell you. Before she was a cook, she was a soldier in the Great Solar War. A badass fighter pilot, too—but she says now she prefers making delicious concoctions. That's why she's only Freddy's co-pilot on occasion when it's necessary for the mission. Seriously, if not for her and Sebastian, I think I'd be out of my mind out here.

I've gotten to know the last crewmember—Dante, the medic—a bit, too. He doesn't talk much and Sebastian says he never has. But Mary says he used to a long time ago until something happened during a mission and he started keeping to himself a lot more. So, I haven't exactly talked *with* him all that much, but I took Mary's advice and started chatting with him even though he didn't say much back. I told him about my abuelita and how she taught me to make the tamale recipe passed down for generations in our family. Or how she would always insist on playing games with me in Spanish, even though my mama and papa never taught me much Spanish growing up. I told Dante Abuelita insists we still carry the blood of Mexico in our veins from all those centuries ago on Earth. She says we must keep our heritage alive, even if no one else thinks it's important anymore. Dante seems to like it when I talk about Abuelita. I swear I saw him smiling.

Captain Rosa gives us a pep talk every morning, tells us soon we'll have a real adventure. I cheer along with everyone else, to keep up the mood, but I really hope she's right. Even Sebastian doesn't seem all that hopeful. And if I'm being completely honest, a tiny part of me is maybe starting to regret signing up for this.

Gabriela's Trip Diary

Day 34

We found it.

The rogue planet.

It's the strangest thing because, since it doesn't orbit any sun, it's impossible to see until you're close to it. But Freddy could tell something was there because the ship sensed the planet's gravity.

And then, it appeared, right outside the viewport. I don't have a window in my cabin, but if I wanted, I could walk down the corridor and see it again right this second. We're still a few days away from landing on the planet, since Freddy and the captain will have to do some assessments of the terrain and whatnot first, to make sure it's safe for us to land in the first place. But I can't wait!

Gabriela's Trip Diary
Day 37
Well, I'm officially annoyed.

Today, we landed on the rogue planet. Or, I should say, everyone *else* in the crew landed on the planet, in the small spacecraft they took to the surface. *I* was given the "highly important" task of staying behind on the main ship to keep an eye on things. Because Captain Rosa was what? Afraid someone was going to steal our ship out in the middle of dark space? Or some tech would break down and I, the newbie-with-minor-mechanical-skills, would be able to fix it? It made zero sense.

But that's exactly what happened. Sebastian was grinning ear to ear even as he squeezed my shoulder in apology. "Sorry, newbie, we've all been there. I'm sure next time you'll be able to come." I glared at him and everyone else as they entered the spacecraft and left me all alone.

I've been up here going on seven hours now. Hopefully, they'll be back soon. Sebastian better not still be grinning, or I'm gonna smack it right off his face.

Gabriela's Trip Diary
Day 38
The crew is safely back aboard *The Grim Ranger* and I still can't believe I didn't get to stand on the rogue planet.

I made Sebastian tell me all about it as soon as he got back.

"What was it like? What did you find?"

"It was fucking cold," he said, pulling off his spacesuit helmet. They all had to wear spacesuits when they went down there, since Dante was concerned about the oxygen levels. "And dusty. Not much to see besides rocks. Oh, and it was windy."

"So, you didn't find anything?" I asked. "No alien artifacts? No priceless records of a long-lost civilization?"

He shook his head, his face grim now that I could see it. "We didn't find anything but rocks."

Behind him, Captain Rosa came stomping out of the spacecraft. She wasn't happy, and she didn't say a word to me as she passed by. Not even a "Thank you for looking after the ship, Gabriela."

So, yeah, apparently the trek down to the planet was a bust. It wasn't what the captain thought it would be. Maybe it was just the wrong rogue planet, or maybe whoever told her she would find something extraordinary on its surface was a liar.

Gabriela's Trip Diary

Day 39

I didn't sleep well last night. Something felt strange inside the ship. Different.

Sebastian went to bed way earlier than usual. Like, usually he'll stay up into the wee hours of the morning, finding something to fix. This time, he went to bed before anyone else—except for the captain. I never saw her after she stormed past me when they got off the spacecraft.

"Everything okay?" I asked him. I figured he was tired after how much time they spent on the planet, but wanted to make sure.

"Yeah. I just have a headache." He wouldn't quite meet my eyes.

I guess I didn't sleep well because I was worried about him. And because I couldn't warm up. I had goosebumps all night. I'll have to ask Mary if she felt weirdly cold, too. Maybe something's wrong with the temperature controls.

***

I don't usually write more than one post in a day, but Sebastian seems to be avoiding me, so I don't have anyone else to talk to.

Things have been weird all day. Captain Rosa came out of her cabin this morning, grabbed a can of food from the kitchen, and grunted something about how we're gonna take a day to rest before we chart our next course, and then left again. Mary and Dante didn't seem that concerned by it.

"She gets like this sometimes." Mary shrugged. "She'll be back to her old self in a day or two, once the sting of the mission failure wears off."

Dante, not surprisingly, didn't say anything at all. He was very busy fixing a sort of turban around his head, made of what looked like sheet metal. He'd been wearing it since they left for the planet's surface. He had an odd, nervous look in his eyes, which were constantly shifting around the room.

"Why don't we go down to the surface again?" I asked. "If the captain was so certain we'd find something, shouldn't we give it another try?"

"Oh, no, I don't think she wants that. We'll be off somewhere else soon." Mary gave me a perky smile and started humming under her breath as she put her plate away. Weird—she's usually so serious.

I don't get it. I mean, what was Captain Rosa expecting to find on a planet without a sun? From what I understand, it's not like any life forms could survive there, and if it's been floating through dark space for God knows how long, it seems like she should have kept her expectations low.

I really wish I knew what exactly happened on the surface and saw it for myself. All day, I kept trying to talk to Sebastian, to press him for more information, but he just complained about his head hurting and went back to his room.

I still have goosebumps all over my body, by the way. The temperature hasn't gotten any warmer, even though Freddy said he checked and the controls are set the same way they have been this whole flight. When I asked him if the controls themselves could be broken, he shrugged it off.

Why is *everyone* acting weird? Except for Dante, I suppose—he's no weirder than usual. It's like something happened to them on the rogue planet, and no one wants to admit what it was.

I'm going to bed now. Hopefully, I'll sleep better than last night.

Gabriela's Trip Diary

Day 40

Oh, Gabriela, you sweet, naïve child.

Yeah, so the sleep thing didn't happen at all. I didn't get one wink.

I lay down not long after I wrote that last diary entry, and I closed my eyes and tried to think of peaceful things to get myself to relax. Right before I was about to drift off, my cot started shaking.

The entire *ship* started shaking.

It was like an earthquake back home—went on for a full three minutes. I tried to get on my feet at one point, but that didn't go well. I fumbled to turn on my comm and shouted Sebastian's name, since his cabin is closest to me, but apparently, he didn't hear me.

Then the quaking stopped. But something worse happened. The ship went *silent*. The air stopped blowing out of the ceiling vent. The two lights in my tiny cabin shut off, drenching me in darkness. And I started floating.

I was scared out of my mind. Because of course, my mind went from—the air system is shut off, the lights are shut off, the artificial gravity system is shut off—to—what if the *oxygen* is shut off?

I clutched my throat, gasping for air. It took me a full minute to realize I was still breathing; I wasn't dead. Yet.

I haven't had much experience in low gravity, except for the couple times I went in one of those low grav machines at school. It's kind of fun, but it's also annoying. You can't move the same as you do at normal gravity levels. It's even worse when you're floating in low gravity in a dark spaceship, and the whole time you're terrified the oxygen is lessening and you're dying from hypoxiation.

I managed to get out of my cabin and into Sebastian's, only he wasn't there. I started yelling again—his name, Mary's, the Captain. No one answered.

I figured my best bet was to get to the cockpit, because hopefully, Freddy would know what to do. I hoped that's where Sebastian had gone too, since he was the engineer who'd be able to figure out what the hell had happened to the ship systems and turn on the backup power generator.

I don't remember much of what happened next. My head was getting woozy because of the failing oxygen system. As I went up the ladder to the next level of the ship, shouting for my fellow crewmates the whole time, I floated into someone. Literally.

I couldn't see who it was in the dark. I just started grabbing at them. "We have to fix the ship!"

"Shh," said Dante. He finally spoke! "They'll hear us," he hissed.

"What are you talking about?" I gasped.

"The ones who came aboard."

"What—who came aboard?"

"*Them*," was all he said. "I told the captain they wouldn't like us landing on their planet without an invitation. We shouldn't have come here."

My eyelids were getting heavy by this point. Dante had a spacesuit on, hence why he was talking and breathing just fine. And thank God he was. I could barely keep up with what he was saying. Some kind of life form that lived on the rogue planet? And they had come aboard our ship when Captain Rosa and the others returned?

Dante did the responsible thing and dragged me after him through the corridors of the ship until we got to the room with the spacesuits. He helped me into one and turned on my oxygen tank, the relief was instantaneous. But it still took me a bit to get my bearings.

"Okay, so hang on," I said. "How did something get on board? I haven't seen any aliens."

"These ones are so tiny you wouldn't be able to see them," said Dante. "They have to be, to survive on a rogue planet. But they can burrow into the brain. Like parasites. Make us do things we wouldn't normally do. Like—"

"Shut off all the ship systems," I finished, catching on. My heart was going haywire. If the oxygen was failing, Sebastian and the others were all in danger. "We have to turn on the backup generator, and get the systems up and running again. Or at least get the others into these spacesuits too, before they all die!"

"It's too late for them," Dante said, flicking on the light inside his helmet so I could finally see his face.

I stared at him. "What?"

"The parasites are already inside them. The captain and the others. It happened back on the planet. I knew it as soon as the boy said his head was aching." He meant Sebastian. "I told them to take precautions, but they didn't believe me."

"How come the parasite things didn't get inside you? Or me? Or...*are* they inside me?" I started panicking again—really panicking, reaching for my own head like I might wrench it off. Could there be an alien inside my brain without me knowing?

"I took precautions." Dante tapped on his helmet, pointing at the sheet metal turban underneath it, still wrapped around his temple. "And the captain did you a solid by leaving you here on the ship. They've already found hosts. They won't bother you."

Their hosts—Sebastian and Captain Rosa and the others.

"But...but can't we do something to...to get them out of their hosts? We can't just let our friends die!"

Dante shook his head solemnly. "Even if we had the technology, it's much too late for that. All we can do now is wait. The parasites will leave once their job is finished. Once they've killed their hosts. Then, we can take back control of the ship."

I didn't believe him. I didn't want to.

I pulled away from him and left, making my way toward the cockpit again. I knew where the backup generator was. I would figure out how to turn it on myself.

Soon Dante's voice was just an echo, and I was alone.

I heard their voices as I neared the cockpit. Sebastian. Mary. Captain Rosa. Freddy.

"...The others will be dead by now," said Captain Rosa. "It is time for us to go."

"What fools they were," said Mary. Her laughter sounded different —cold.

"Humans are always fools," spat Freddy.

"You'd think one day they would listen," said Sebastian with a low chuckle.

My heart cracked when I heard his voice. So warm and friendly before, but now it was hollow, a shell of his former self.

I realized at that point the four of them were moving out of the cockpit, so I backed up from the door as quickly—and quietly—as I could, praying they wouldn't be able to see me or sense me in the darkness. I felt a shift in the air as they moved past me in the corridor. My fellow crewmates and captain, their minds invaded by some alien host.

I wanted to reach out to Sebastian, to see if maybe, just maybe Dante was wrong and the real him was still in there somewhere, still alive. But I didn't. I was too afraid.

When they were gone, I broke down in tears.

Dante found me like that, sometime later. He took my hand and pulled me gently after him into the cockpit, and we sat together and watched as the spacecraft carried our friends back to the surface of the rogue planet. A frozen place where their bodies will turn rigid and lie in wait. Maybe someday another foolish space marauder will discover them and believe they've found the remnants of a great, long-lost civilization.

My heart breaks for Sebastian. He was just following Captain Rosa's orders, just going along with her mission, here for the excitement and the adventure. I don't think he had any idea there was a civilization on that planet, or he would've told me.

But then again, he knew there would be danger. He told me so. That was part of what excited him.

"We need to warn people," I told Dante. "Make sure no one ever comes back here."

"We can try," he said grimly. "But the planet will keep drifting. Someday, it'll find its way back onto a map. And then humans will learn again the hard way that not every unexplored planet has a treasure worth discovering."

We found the backup generator, and I figured out how to turn all the systems back on. Our plan is to sit like this for the rest of the day, and keep wearing our spacesuits just in case, and then we'll get the hell away from this planet and back to civilization.

All I want to do right now is hug Mama and Papa and Abuela as tight as I can. Dante warned me that my family might be a little older than they were when I left. We might've been gone a lot longer than a few days in their time, since we traveled through a wormhole and will go through it again to return home. I'm trying not to think too hard about the implications of that.

What I'll do after I go home...I don't know. I could go back to working on the farm, but that still sounds awfully boring.

Dante did tell me he plans on starting another space crew, one that will stay within the confines of the known galaxy, and there's a spot for me if I want it. He said he's got a hookup so we can transport goods between the planetary nations. There will be steady pay and a lot less danger, but plenty of sights to see. I have to admit, it's tempting.

Breaking News

LAUREN T. DAVILA

How the prom committee thinks they've turned this gods-awful gym into a passable Greek temple is beyond me. I stand in the foyer, heels digging into the linoleum floor as if the flimsy material could keep me safe. I'm early and dateless and the sound of faint drums meets my ears. Did they really decide to go with war drums as the students enter?

American idiots.

Pushing down the anger, I try to calm my stomach, focusing on images of marble statues as I walk past the gaudy, white-and-blue streamers hung from the ceiling. The poor chaperones are lined up along the wall, squeezed into tight suits and dresses they haven't worn since this time last year. Different students, same outfits.

My ankle wobbles as my heel catches a divot on the floor of the basketball court. At least that's what I tell myself. It's easier to chalk it up to human error rather than the panic clutching my chest when I spot the papier-mâché horse in the corner of the gym. The editor-in-chief of the newspaper, Elaine, and her boyfriend, Brad are posed beneath it, tight against each other. And as the photographer's flash goes off,

I see her smile waver. See the way the beach volleyball captain's hand squeezes the flesh at her hip. Hard. Too hard.

And even though the flash disappears, and her smile is painted back in place, the little nagging in the back of my head that I've come to know so well tells me I must help her. It would've been nice if the nag had appeared in the last journalism staff meeting. But no, it's gotta be tonight, of all nights.

As I make my way across the gym toward that horse, I realize I've stopped counting the new lives I've led, the prophecies I've given. The first couple of times, I tried to make it back to Troy. I prayed and prayed and prayed until the prayers turned to screams.

I'd warned that young French girl not to lead them into battle. That they wouldn't trust the voices she heard in her head. They martyred her anyway.

I'd tried to hide the young princess from the paparazzi. But she was everywhere, the car crash on the front page of the tabloids.

Too many others to count or think about. Too many lives and countries and years. Too many deaths. Names and lives distilled into a textbook chapter or Wikipedia page or headline. So in this life, I decided to try to be a part of the narrative, shaping it all by writing headlines and interviewing people. Maybe someone will listen to me if my name is in the byline. Maybe someone will hear me if the headline is snappy enough. Maybe someone will finally see me. Maybe—

"Cas, what are you doing?"

I stop abruptly at the sound of my twin's voice. I try to peer around him to calm the buzzing in my chest, the need to keep moving. But his uncalloused fingers lift my chin toward him. I miss his battle-worn hands; I wonder if he misses holding a sword.

We look nothing alike in this lifetime. Not that we ever do anymore. I think the gods like playing games, making it impossible for us to find each other. It gets harder every time we are brought back.

This time around, my parents are immigrants from Mexico City. I'm short and brown and speak with an accent. At least my name is mostly the same this time. My parents sing my name, lilting over the dropped S, caressing the vowels throughout. I wish I could love them the way they love me. I wish I could be their Casandra.

My brother moved here from South Carolina with his uncle. He's tall, almost too tall. He's white and lanky and his hair is a shock of platinum white, like a blanched seashell. He sat next to me in homeroom last year, introduced himself to the class as Harry. I didn't look twice at him until he slid a bookmark my way with a cartoon drawing of the Parthenon. That's when I knew he'd found me.

I'd skipped journalism to meet him in the hallway. I thought we'd hatch a plan, figure out who we were supposed to help, figure out how to make them listen this time around. No matter how often I was overlooked or called insane, I always knew at least I had him. But it didn't happen like that. Instead, he told me he wanted to live this time around. He'd grown tired of trying to figure out how we could find peace. He'd said he wanted to be normal for once, and as I looked into his eyes, which were the only constant to his many forms, I couldn't refuse him this. I couldn't make him die again.

And looking at his eyes now, bright from what I'm sure is cheap alcohol, it hurts knowing what he's going to give up if I don't get this right.

"They're giving us another chance, Helenus."

"No, Cas, they're not," he says, voice low and deep. It reverberates down my spine, matching the pace of the weird drum beat the DJ is playing. "The gods are playing you again."

"But what if this is the time I break the curse? What if Athena's on our side finally? What if it's not a trick?"

He glances toward the horse, wincing just like I did. I'm sure he's reliving the part he played in giving up Troy to our enemies. But then again, that was a long time ago. Maybe he's just cringing at the lopsided papier-mâché eyes.

"Maybe. But I wasn't kidding, Cas," he says, taking a step back. "You're on your own this time."

My knees lock. I've never done this on my own. He's always been there, a heavy protector. I was comfortable being his shadow. I was comfortable standing behind him, peeking out only to offer words they wouldn't listen to. It was easier with him protecting me. But for the first time, in this smelly gym, surrounded by hundreds of my classmates, I'm suddenly exposed. And it's terrifying. Because even though my blood is pulsing, it feels for the first time like I can do this.

On my own.

"Okay, H. I hope you find what you need here."

And I do. I really do. Maybe he'll get to live. He'll go to college and buy a motorcycle. He'll win bets and the lottery and every game of luck he's up against, because well, that's what we do. He'll smile a bit too wide, and he'll grow into his bright hair. He'll move back to Greece and open up a bar, where the bachelorette parties are loud, and the wine is strong. And he'll fall in love by the sea as he did so many years ago. Gods, I wish I could be there for all of it. I want to say more, break down, or beg him to reconsider.

All of this must show because the strong face he plastered on wavers, and I can see he's on the brink of following me. Like he always does. So, for the first time in our history, I grab his hand, squeeze it tight, and unlock my knees. And I set out on my own. I don't turn around, knowing that if I do, I'll break. I start walking toward where I last saw Brad and Elaine.

My brother fades into the mosh of teenagers as I make my way over to the refreshment table. They say refreshments but really, it's just stale cupcakes our chemistry teacher, Mrs. Liang, pretends she baked, and radioactive punch the teachers pretend isn't spiked with every kind of alcohol stolen from unlocked liquor cabinets. I fill a cup and knock it back, wincing as the liquid burns on the way down. This is nothing like the wine we used to have at every meal. Back when everything was simple. Back before that night in the temple. Back before they refused to listen, before our city burned to the ground.

The buzz flares to life and I know she's close. I check my phone and it shows 9:01 p.m. Still pretty early in the night, and Principal Martinez hasn't announced prom king or queen yet. In other words, there's still enough time for me to royally screw this up. I hear the unsteady clacking of stiletto heels before I see her.

The first thing I notice is that Elaine is wasted. Which seems impossible compared to Brad, who's slumped over with his teammates on the pull-out bleachers. Her red hair's pulled back in intricate braids, complimenting her impeccable make-up and fashion-forward, metallic midi dress. She knows she doesn't belong in this tiny town. She belongs in New York, walking a Doberman through Central Park. Eating fancy Italian food in the West Village with her model friends. Managing one of the upscale imprints for Condé Nast—maybe Vanity Fair or Vogue. She doesn't belong in this gym, where her fresh gardenia perfume is smothered by the smell of teenage hormones and Axe body spray.

I fake a cough, so Elaine knows I'm here, and when her hazy eyes meet mine, she gives a half-hearted wave. She fills another cup of punch before putting it down on the table.

"I'm gotta find a bathroom, babe," she whines, running her nails through his curly hair. "Don't let my camera out of your sight; I've gotta use it to take pictures of the prom court."

Brad grunts, not looking at her as she careens into the foyer toward the family bathroom; I follow her quietly. She tries the door, but as most drunk girls do, she doesn't bother trying to read if it's a push or pull. She pushes; it's a pull. After three tries, Elaine staggers over to the wall opposite me and crouches down, ignoring a pile of wetness near the water fountain.

"Cas, do you know if someone's in there?" she says, voice faking steadiness and cheerfulness.

"Yeah, I think I saw someone go in."

No matter what year or what country or what their problem is, they always start off unassuming. Like they don't want to upset others around them. Whether the person I'm supposed to be helping is a future queen or a CEO's assistant, they're always so, well, *nice*. They've been trained to be agreeable and cordial and at ease. Even if that's the last thing they want. And that's the problem.

But maybe Elaine will be different.

I shove my hands into the pockets of my sparkly blue pantsuit, trying not to feel the pressure of the buzzing in my chest. I'll need to use my lifetimes of experience to ask the right questions.

"So, who's your pick for prom king?" I say brightly, craning my head at the bathroom door. "You're here with Brad, so I'm assuming him?"

She lets out a tiny laugh then stops, as if she's surprised that a sound escaped her. But she recovers quickly.

"Um, yeah, it'll be Brad. Some computer genius on the volleyball team hacked the admin's Google poll and rigged it."

Now it's my turn to laugh. These teenagers are resourceful, I'll give them that.

"Oh, shit!" she says, neck turning red and blotchy with embarrassment. "I totally shouldn't have said that! I'm not even supposed to know that. Brad got pissed when I found out and said I'd better not run an exposé. Don't spill or you'll be writing the Horoscopes for the last three issues, too."

No one reads my news articles or op-eds. No matter how extensive my research is or how creative an interviewee. But they all laugh at my horoscopes. They're funny and trendy and no one takes them seriously. Little do they know that they're all right. But no one believes.

Stupid curse.

"No, I won't tell," I answer. "And I'll write the horoscopes, it's fine."

"They're always really good, Cas. Thanks."

We both go quiet, taking turns looking at the bathroom door. She crouches over all of a sudden, before pushing herself back up to stand. She wobbles on her stilettos and hits the wall hard. She won't remember it except for maybe a bruise tomorrow morning.

"Maybe the bathroom next to Principal Martinez's office is open. Wanna come with?"

I nod and follow her along the edges of the gym. She rarely talks to me outside of staff meetings, but then again, bonds are strengthened when Svedka's all but replaced the blood in a girl's veins. We've almost reached the doors to the foyer when a tuxedoed arm comes flying out of nowhere and lands heavily on my shoulders.

I feel the immediate panic rise in my stomach: a push to run down the hallway. To escape from his grasp. To pray Athena won't ignore me like she always does. Instead, I grab his wrist and shove him off.

Brad just laughs and stumbles over toward Elaine. Her face is blank, revealing nothing.

"Hey, babe, where'd you escape to?"

"I told you already," she says, eyes darting to me as if to make sure I haven't left her. "I needed to find a bathroom."

"Well, Eduardo wants to leave soon, so hurry up. His cousin got the keg delivered already and needs to set it up."

"But I need to stay to see who gets crowned," she says, swaying more than she was earlier. "It's gonna be the cover story for this week's paper. Where's my camera?"

"How would I know?" he slurs.

"I asked you to keep it with you!" she says, looking him up and down as color rises in her cheeks. "I need it for the next issue's pictures."

"Babe, just relax. Let's just get out of here."

"Brad, it's important!"

He reaches out to grab her forearm, and the buzzing in my chest gets louder. Almost painful.

"I thought I was important."

Her smile slips, so quickly I almost miss it. But I don't.

I channel drunk, happy girl energy, and muscle myself between them.

"Elaine," I say, whining over the top. "I've really gotta peeee."

Brad smiles at me in a way that reminds me of rope on a ship about to snap. Tension, too tight. But he doesn't say anything, just presses a kiss to the side of her neck and slinks back to the gym.

Elaine all but runs into the bathroom, which is luckily empty. I pretend not to notice her hands shaking as she opens up her clutch and pulls out a roller tube of her gardenia perfume.

"So, remind me, how long have you and Brad been a thing?" I ask. The pressure in my chest pauses for a second and I know I'm on the right track.

"Um, since like October? So, I guess seven months or so? But I've known him since 5th grade, so it feels way longer than that."

I push, knowing that the more she talks the less she will remember of our conversation. Even if she did recall it, it'll be dulled and not just by the alcohol. She'd wonder why she was able to open up to a classmate that was practically a stranger. Why she felt comfortable pouring out her darkest secrets under the fluorescent lights the janitor never got around to fixing. Why, when she was so used to asking the questions, she felt comfortable answering mine.

"He's always been super sweet, you know?" she says, all in a rush. "My dad really likes him and he's going to Chapman for economics. Which is close enough to USC that it won't even be *actual* long distance. Way easier than Columbia like I'd originally wanted. Like, can I really ask for much more?"

Elaine twirls the bracelet on her wrist around and around with each excuse, as if hoping I don't hear the question at the end of all of her sentences. But even if she wasn't talking, I'd still be able to hear them. She continues, not waiting for me to say anything.

"I just keep thinking I'll feel more, but Brad is just so...Brad, you know? He's nice and, and, I don't know, I think I'm lucky to have found someone like him. He says he loves me and—"

She cuts herself off, looking at the spot above her bracelet where he grabbed her. We can both see the red imprint of his fingers.

"I'm fine," she says, glancing over her shoulder at me. Her eyes are completely dry. She thinks she's placating me, but I can hear the question, the quake in her voice.

Hoping I'm wrong, I reach out, letting my own hand cover the red spot. And I see it all in an instant.

I see the way Brad's hands always tighten too quickly on the controller in his hands when he plays video games. Sneaking beer from the extra fridge stocked in the garage. The pistols he admires because his whole family hunts. The shudder of doors slamming open against newly painted walls. The raw cut of his throat from screaming expletives at his dad at 2 a.m.

I see them later tonight, Elaine's shiny dress ripped. I see him telling her to get back in the car, to stop complaining, he hasn't had that much to drink, she was being ridiculous, he has to get her home before curfew. I see the semi truck that he doesn't see around the curve because he's too preoccupied with Elaine's crying. I see blinding lights, a long honk, and one scream. The smell of gardenias doesn't linger long, replaced with rust and beer in the air.

Her skin is stark white in the mirror and I know I've projected enough of it her way for her to feel. She'll chalk it up to drinking, but she felt it: she felt her future and the impact of the truck.

"*Does* he love you?" I ask her quietly.

And then, that little nag in the back of my head turns into a voice, as sharp as it was in my first life.

"*Tell her,*" Athena whispers.

Elaine refuses to look at me, but she hiccups as if her emotions are trying to break out of her diaphragm. As if she refuses to allow herself to feel it all. I break because I know what that pressure is like.

"I know how you feel, Elaine," I say, grabbing her hand. I clutch it so tight I can't tell if I draw blood. I know my voice will be so urgent it'll sound like I'm speaking in tongues. If anyone passes by, my Spanish would frazzle them, phonetics frantic and hurried. Later, Elaine will think it sounded ancient, all Greek to her. But the words aren't important. What's important is that she believes me.

"It started off perfect. He was so kind and sweet and he looked right at you like he understood. But then somewhere along the line, he stopped hearing you, stopped listening, and he took everything he wanted."

My grip tightens as I remember Apollo's smile, the sunlight in his eye that turned taunting. And even worse, how Ajax smelled of sea salt and sweat and rage. Night and day, but both ultimately the same.

"Elaine, don't leave with Brad to go to the afterparty. Call an Uber and head home. If you go with him, something terrible is going to happen."

"What do you mean something's going to happen?"

"Just, please, believe me. Please believe me."

"This isn't something to joke about, Cas," she says, tearing her hand from mine. "This isn't pretend like your horoscopes, so just stop."

"I'm not kidding, Elaine. Please believe me."

I remember when people didn't question me. When they didn't automatically assume I was kidding. When they didn't laugh at me. When I would sit in the temple and they'd line up. They'd come from far and wide and wait for hours for my predictions. I remember the absolute power. To have everyone listen. Back then, the buzzing wasn't gusts of winds looking for a way to escape. Back then it was just me and the future. But I'd give all of those memories up if this girl, this time, in this place would hear me.

Elaine puts her perfume away and glances toward the bathroom door. My heart rate ratchets up even more.

"Please," I whisper.

She doesn't look at me when she leaves the bathroom and walks back down the hallway. I follow her as she pauses in the foyer, the sounds of prom winding down are muffled out here. Principal Martinez's voice is garbled, but I'm sure she's announcing the prom court. Elaine staggers a couple of steps toward the gym doors but hesitates. One of her ankles wobbles and I see her heel roll a bit. But she's barely paying attention. She stares into the gym through the windowed panels in the door and I see Brad over her shoulder.

He's standing near his friends, a drunken smile on his face. And, I know she's thinking how simple it would be. How easy to go in and borrow his jacket, lying that she's cold. How easy it'd be to allow another alcohol-tinged kiss. And I'm so tired of trying and failing yet again. For thinking this time would be different.

But then Brad leaves the table and Elaine straightens up, head held high. He's left her camera on the table. And his cup of spiked punch falls over, leaking into the lens. It's ruined. Keeping her eye on him, she lurches back while pulling her phone out of the pocket of her dress. She starts toward the parking lot until she catches me out of her periphery.

And she just looks at me, blinking slowly. As she leaves the foyer, I feel the pressure lift off of my chest and the buzzing stops for the first time in this life. I recognize the sound of my brother shouting my name from inside the gym as he feels the curse lift too. Athena's laughter in my ear as I breathe in the disappearing scent of gardenias.

I push open the doors and Harry runs to meet me. Confetti is falling and Taylor Swift is being played by the local cover band and it's perfect. I finally did it and now, it's time to live. Enjoy prom. And then maybe I'll look up flights to Greece. Or maybe I'll give this life a chance.

Who knows.

I can't see what the future holds anymore.

{ **17** }

Written In Sand

ALEXANDRA CAMPOS

"You're going to stain the carpet," mutters Felix from the bed, head tucked under his two little fur paws, eyes barely squinting open.

I glare at my familiar and continue to mix the bright pink hair dye. "No, I won't." The smell of bleach fills the bedroom and I unlatch a window, allowing the ocean breeze to permeate.

Felix's mouth stretches open in a languid yawn. "Why don't you just wait for Julia to dye it for you?" He licks his paw a few times. "She's much better at this than you are."

At her name, I stir the hair mixture vigorously and pink sloshes from the bowl, landing on the beige carpet. I grit my teeth, sensing Felix's eyes on me. "Not a word out of you," I say, pointing at him.

I grab a ratty towel, soap, and water, and get to scrubbing. But the color only fades to a pale pink. A familiar burning sensation burns behind my eyes and I fight like hell to brush it off.

The entire dye job takes me longer than I thought it would. I wander over to the window, watching the sun set in front of my bay windows. Combing fingers through my wet hair, I wonder if Julia can see the same sunset as me.

The rays splash buckets of bright orange down my bedroom walls. If I listen closely, I can hear the faint sound of waves rushing the shore. I imagine Julia's footprints disappearing with each wave.

Lifting my hand, I whisper a quick spell, letting shadows play across the walls. Julia liked when I did that. Although, I mostly created shadows along the curves of her body, her laughter my guide.

The burning in my eyes returns and this time, I let it free. The shadows across my bedroom walls intensify, washing out the orange sunset outside and casting the room in darkness.

Felix's soft head bumps my arm, and through the tears and shadows, the corners of my mouth lift. He bumps me again. "What's wrong?" he asks.

A tear slides down my cheek—for Grandpa Nino, gone five weeks today. Then I shed another one for Julia, her absence only adding to the ache in my chest from when grandpa died. They continue to fall, these tears, faster and faster, my breathing working to match its intensity. I let the shadows grow until they threaten to swallow the room; the window frame begins to shake. With practiced restraint, I ball my hands into fists. "These shadows are *mine*. I'm in control." Slowly, the shadows dissipate.

"Celine?" My bedroom door creaks open. "Everything okay?"

It's my mom. Her eyes are rimmed red, cheeks puffy. Her emotion slaps me in the face and I simply nod, waiting for her, or maybe her grief, to leave. She closes the door without another word. I bring my knees to my chest and continue to watch the sun disappear beneath the ocean. Tomorrow I won't just have to face my mother's grief, I'll also have my grandma's. And maybe that's worse.

***

Grandma Chayo takes her coffee with a cinnamon stick the next morning. I normally wouldn't say anything, but when I set the mug down in front of her, she adds two teaspoons of sugar, no creamer.

Brows pinched, I say to her, "Grandma, is something on your mind?"

Her hand shakes above the sugar jar. "I dreamt of him again last night."

My hold on the creamer freezes briefly. "Did he say anything new to you?" I ask, grabbing a pencil from the jar beside the fridge, distracting myself with the list I started weeks ago. I cross off the third item on the list, 'sage cleanse', and wonder if I should try an herbal sleep tea on her again.

Grandma Chayo grabs the spoon beside the creamer and stirs her coffee. "You know he used to pick grapes and strawberries down by the border?" A smile touches the corners of her lips. "I made him a straw hat out of wheat and pumpkin seeds."

I slide freshly buttered bread across the table to her. "You've told me," I try to say it softly.

The first time she told me this story, I asked her so many questions, like where along the border Grandpa had worked, or what spell she'd used to create the hat, but she couldn't remember. I gave up trying to help her remember the details weeks ago.

"He told me he was sorry." Her hands struggle to hold the blue porcelain cup to her mouth.

I watch her carefully. "Sorry for what?"

"Leaving me alone so much," she says, a smile still stuck on her face, pulling her winkles taunt.

I take the seat across from her, wringing my hands beneath the table. "It wasn't all bad, right?"

Despite her shakiness, Grandma Chayo's grip on my hands is firm. "Not once you were born."

We drink our coffee and eat our toast in silence. Grandma Chayo's eyes are glazed over, her deepened gaze staring into the distance. I wonder if she'll start to see Grandpa's ghost while she's awake, too. I doubt there are any spells or remedies for waking nightmares.

I shove my chair back suddenly. "I'm going to head into work. Mom probably could use the help for the morning rush."

Grandma Chayo grips the tablecloth, readjusting her grip to hoist her body up. "I'll come too."

I rush forward. "I really wish you'd wait for me to help you," I scold, lightly. "I'm stronger than I look." I offer a smile as I tuck an arm around her shoulder and another under her arm. With my foot I push her chair back and help her stand. I'm close enough to hear how her breathing struggles.

She reaches up to pat the side of my face. "I still remember how to walk."

Grandma Chayo and I are halfway down our driveway when I feel him on my shoulder. Felix's soft black fur nearly pokes me in the eye. He yawns and readjusts himself inside my backpack.

"Your crystals are poking me in the butt," he complains.

Grandma Chayo chuckles, poking my backpack. "Celine, have you continued with his training?"

Felix's ears perk up. But training him means I have to continue my own training, too. "On and off," I lie.

A single brow arches, but Grandma Chayo doesn't push it. "And where is Julia these days? I haven't seen her around lately. And, oh! I found a nice sea salt scone recipe I think she'll enjoy."

I let her go on about the recipe and how she'll modify it to Julia's likings; my heart twists in my chest. It's been eight days since Julia left. It's not the longest we've gone without seeing each other, but between her leaving and losing my Grandpa Nino, I hadn't been in the mood to talk about it.

I decide to rip off the band-aid. "Julia's gone, Grandma. She won't be around anymore."

Grandma Chayo's steps falter and I stop, worried she lost her footing and hoping to prevent a fall. But she brings her hand up to cradle the side of my face. I blink in surprise. "Que paso?" she asks.

I shrug, unsure how much I want to say this early in the morning. "We're going in different directions." It wasn't exactly the truth but it was not a lie. Julia was always destined for the sea. I knew when I met her but I couldn't stop myself. She wove earrings for me out of seashells and spun flowers from salt and kelp. She made the ordinary feel extraordinary.

"It's for the best," I continue, breaking eye contact. The wind carries the ocean breeze along my face and I grip my grandma's hand. "I didn't want to hold her back from living the life she wants."

My grandma's face softens. "Asi es," she says, patting my hand, leading us closer to the pier, and Coronado Street.

***

There's a place along the boulevard where prickly pear cacti grow and the air smells of fresh bread and sea salt. Coronado Street Bakery was first established by my grandparents nearly fifty years ago when they first made their way up the coast from Mexico. The sign hanging above the door sways with the breeze, its white lettering faded from years of the ocean. The tinkling of bells alerts the store to our presence. The place is teeming with customers, several in line waiting at the register to order, and a few more sitting with the pastries I know Mom made this morning before the store opened.

"Buenos días," my grandma greets them, pulling herself free from my grasp, struggling toward each table to say good morning and offer more coffee.

Once she's done, I help her to her own table near the window overlooking the pier. I pull a chair closer for her to prop her leg up and set my backpack down beside her.

Felix saunters up gracefully and jumps onto the windowsill, giving us a big stretch. "Milk, please," he says. When I don't reply immediately, he meows loudly. Several customers turn to see him.

"Yes, yes," I say, tapping his head. I bring Grandma a glass of ice water. "Pan dulce, too?"

She waves me off, coughing into her napkin and squinting against the sunlight.

"Could have used your help earlier, Cel. Lunch rush starts soon," my mom says, throwing a brown apron at me. Her cheeks are flushed as she begins brewing a fresh pot of coffee. She spins around the kitchen, breaking cinnamon, refilling creamer, and checking on the glaze for our lavender scones.

I nod as I sprinkle flour onto the countertop. As I knead the dough, I finally start to feel some semblance of peace. I grab nutmeg and honey and add it in—just because it feels natural.

The door chimes and two customers walk in. The door chimes again and again. Soon, the bakery is flooded. The pastries mom made this morning slowly dwindle and I work to get the pastelitos and other pan dulces in the oven. Despite the sweat that forms at my brow, the magic stirs inside of me. In this bakery, there is no loss or grief, there's only fresh bread and tenderness. I work quickly but tenderly as I cut into the dough and spread it thin. I slip them into the oven with a spell to rise.

Grandma Chayo taught me how to make sweet bread when I was fourteen—back when the sweetened maise used to get stuck between my braces and the excess sugars lingered beneath my nails.

"A true Mexican woman knows how to make her bread at home," she'd said to me. I spent hours trying to perfect her recipe, but every time she showed me how to make them, she added in a few more secret ingredients. "Rosemary for earthiness, honey for sweetness, and lavender to balance it out."

When I finally had the recipe down per her instructions, I presented the corn-like bread to her. Her lips pursed and she shoved the plate back. "It's missing something." But she couldn't figure out what. Eventually, I had to tell her that there wasn't anything missing—this was just how my bread was.

She had smirked, slapping my butt with a dishtowel. "Fine but it won't be as good as the ones I make."

I've never told her that our customers haven't noticed a difference between my sweet bread and hers. Julia preferred mine. The thought enters my mind uninvited. I slap dough onto the counter hard.

By lunchtime, the bakery slows just enough for me to take a break and go find Grandma Chayo. I pause when I see the way she wipes at the tears streaming down her face. She rubs at her sore legs under the table and clutches her half-eaten bread. She must be missing Grandpa Nino. Every Sunday, they'd sit in that booth with their cafecito and sweet bread, sun hitting their faces, laughing.

I wonder if she remembers the things they used to talk about. I wonder if she remembers what it was like having two coffee mugs at the table, instead of one.

I leave her to her thoughts as the hours pass. Mom comes up to me, wiping down the counters.

"This came for you," she says, pulling a folded paper from her apron pocket.

I recognize the writing immediately and my stomach drops. "Who delivered this?"

"She was just here," mom says. "While you were washing dishes and she—"

I don't wait to hear what else she has to say. I run out of the bakery, apron still on, toward the pier where we always met. I'm greeted by familiar orange colors of the sunset and a cool breeze as the ocean shifts. It fades into a deep sapphire, calling me in like a beacon.

I run as sand breaches my shoes. The letter crumples in my hand at the sight of her silver hair.

My thighs are burning by the time I reach her. "I thought you'd be halfway to Hawaii by now." I mean for it to come out half-heartedly, but my tone is sour.

Julia shifts, her hair reflecting the sun. Warmth spreads across my chest when her blue eyes meet mine. "You didn't read my letter."

"Sorry," I say, heat rising to my cheeks. There's nothing else to say.

Standing this close, the urge is strong to breach the space between us—hold her hand or hear her laugh at my jokes. But the letter in my hand feels heavier as I remind myself that we aren't the same.

"Why didn't you talk to me yourself at the bakery?" I ask.

Julia's eyes dart between me and the sea, trying to decide whether or not to run away from me.

I've always wondered what the call must feel like for her. All I've ever known is this land, this shoreline, and Coronado Street. What was it like to yearn for more?

"I waited for you to see me off," she says quietly. "But you never came."

The sentence hangs in the air, chilling me more than the ocean breeze. The corners of her lips curve, trying to seem like she's just stating a fact and isn't hurt by me. But she fails. I can see the pain flash across her brows. It fills the space between her scales and her flesh, making her shoulders quiver.

My anger explodes outward, violent and unrestrained. A shadow flashes out of the corner of my eye. "I did show up that day," I say and take a deep breath. I don't hate Julia; I don't think I could ever. She made a choice and I could never fault her for it. "But how could I say goodbye to you when I had just finished saying goodbye to my grandpa? It was too much."

"I know," she whispers. "I'm sorry and I stayed for as long as I could but—" she looks out to sea.

"I know," I echo her. When the guilt hits me, I know it's for her. It's the guilt of knowing I was the one holding her back. I hand her back the semi-crumpled letter. "It doesn't matter what this says. I know you were made for the sea."

On a breeze, Julia surges forward. Salt and vanilla flood my senses. Her touch is cool and warm at the same time, hard and soft. Her blue eyes shine brighter. "Who says you couldn't find a home in the sea?" Julia's eyes widen, her voice turning frantic. "Come with me, Celine.

Let me show you it's possible." As the words form on her lips, so does her smile, like she's convinced herself it's a good idea.

I'd be lying if I said I never thought about what life would be like under the water, with Julia. Sometimes I even dream about it. But I would have to leave my family. I think of the story my Grandma Chayo has told me every morning since Grandpa Nino died, the one of making hats out of wheat and pumpkin seeds. I think of the story of him and my Grandma Chayo getting married in the worst storm Mexico had ever seen. Then I think of the stories Grandma Chayo still has for me, the ones she's losing to time—the ones I still don't fully understand.

I shake my head. "I can't leave my mom and grandma, Jules."

"Do you remember the first time you tried to teach me to make elotes?" she says, hands caressing my arms and sending little jolts of electricity through my body.

Julia is good at lots of things, but baking is not one of them. Yet she'd begged me to teach her how to make elotes because she wanted to learn to make my favorite. She listened intently, the tiny indent between her two brows making an appearance. She kneaded dough until her arms ached and sweat glistened across her forehead. Flour flaked along her cheeks and I laughed as I wiped it away. The day ended with flour-filled hands and sugared-coated lips, cinnamon kisses and honey-dipped tongues.

"I remember it too," Julia says, eyes darting to my lips briefly. The warmth in my cheeks must be making them red. "What I meant was, do you remember what we talked about that day? You said you wanted more than life at the bakery, more than a life on Coronado Street."

I do remember that conversation. I remember being scared to admit that out loud, and I'm scared now to even admit the conversation happened. I never want Mom or Grandma Chayo to think I'm ungrateful for the life they've given me, or what they've taught me. But when I see the way Julia searches the waves for adventure, or the way she soaks up the ocean air like it's breathing new life into her, I can't help but be envious. I want to yearn for something the way she yearns for the sea. Even growing up surrounded by love and magic, by spells and charms, there was still something missing.

Julia closes the space between us, her forehead coming to rest against mine, our breath mixing together intoxicatingly. "Let me show you how much more there is," she whispers against my lips.

My entire body lights up at her words, igniting a desire that goes beyond what we have. But even with her body against mine and the ocean lapping at my bare feet, something calls me back home.

Julia snaps her eyes shut tightly and her breath falters. "Celine, I don't want to leave things the way we did before." When she looks at me again, tears well up in her eyes. She presses the letter back into my hand. "Read the letter. I'll be back tomorrow night. Answer me then." She caresses my cheek and then kisses my cheek. Then she sprints for the sea, diving under the waves with a flick of her tail, scales of iridescent blues and purples the only clue she was really here.

When Julia's gone, I can't bring myself to go back to Coronado Street. Instead, I walk along the shoreline. I step into the water, then step out. I didn't even know it was possible for me to follow Julia to the ocean.

My mind takes me back to the moment we revealed ourselves to each other—the day I knew I loved Julia. Our relationship was like a whirlwind, coming in fast and violent. I knew if I wanted to continue seeing her, she had to know the truth.

We spent the majority of the day on the boardwalk playing arcade games and trying to win the stuffed animal we thought looked the ugliest. I managed to convince Julia to ride the Ferris wheel with me, despite her fear of heights. When we came back down, Julia's feet planted firmly, like she'd never leave land again. I remember laughing, wondering how this girl who made me feel like I was flying could be so happy to remain on land.

I waited until dinner time, when I rolled out the blanket and fresh bread I made for us on the sandy beach. The weather was perfect—not too hot, not too cold. I was sweating through my shirt.

"Julia, there's something I need to tell you," my sweaty palms nearly slipped out of hers, but I held tight. Julia finished eating the sweet bread I made for her and she nodded once.

"It may seem unbelievable at first, and I want you to know it doesn't change anything for me. It doesn't change the way I feel about you and how I think you feel about me."

Julia took my cheek in her palm. "Just tell me," she said, sweetly.

"I'm a witch." I watched the light pink in her cheeks move down to her neck. "I have powers and I can perform spells, but I've never used them on you. Well, I did once but that was because there was toilet paper stuck to your shoe and I didn't want you to feel embarrassed so I just," I paused to snap two fingers and a gust of wind tumbled in the space around us. "But that's it, I promise."

Several moments passed before Julia's smirk appeared on her face. The sun caught the tops of her cheeks, making her look shiny. Julia touched my lips once, the simple act set my skin alight. Then, she moved away from me.

This is it, I thought. She doesn't believe me. Or, worse, she believes me and thinks I'm a freak. I closed my eyes at the thought and tried to give her more space, but her hand stopped me.

"Can I show you something?" she asked, gently bringing me to my feet.

I began to protest when I noticed she was taking us to the water. Her silver hair rose around her, water rushing up to cover her legs, and in an instant, they weren't legs anymore. I fell to my knees as I looked at her. In place of her legs was a tail—a magnificent dark purple and blue tail, though as her tail dipped into the water, its colors became brighter.

"Don't you see," Julia said, breathlessly. "We are full of magic. We were meant to find each other." Her smile, all white teeth and promise, warmed the inside of my chest. My hands blossomed with energy and excitement. I'd placed them on her hips, and we'd sprung toward each other, our giddy laughter surrounding us as we melted into brand new kisses.

A wave hits me, shaking me out of the memory. I groan, conflicted about what to do. I raise a hand into the air, whisper a quick spell, and watch the water react, swirling around my feet, parting with each step I take. Not caring if anyone sees, I walk further into the ocean. I walk until the water is waist high, still swirling around me like a barrier, not a single drop actually touching me. But eventually, it will have to. And just like that, I release the spell. Water crashes in around me, taking me under for a few brief seconds. Then I emerge above the waves, mascara leaking down my cheeks.

As I make my way back to the shore, I see something shiny in the water and feel my pulse jump. But it's not the scale of a mermaid's tail. It's just a seashell that's caught the light of the setting sun.

***

When I arrive at Coronado Street Bakery, the lights inside are dim. Mom is busy wiping down tables and pulling up chairs. Her lips twist as she passes by Grandma Chayo and I can see her mouth move quickly, Spanish flying out. Mom suddenly throws her hands up, storming to the back kitchen.

I step in, my soggy apron in one hand and my wet shoes in another. Before I can say anything, Grandma Chayo groans and maneuvers her legs off the chair opposite her.

"I'd like to go home now," she says.

"Sure," I say. "Are you okay? Are your legs bothering you too much?"

She rears up, jostling the table and knocking over her half-full coffee mug. Brown liquid spills off the edge and onto her shoes. "I am ready to go home. Are you coming with me or not?"

Stunned by her outburst, I freeze. What just happened? I wonder if I've done something to upset her. Maybe she's upset that I left her alone all day? I have to remind myself not to take it personally when she lashes out like this but the older she gets, the more difficult it becomes.

"Mom, don't yell at Celine. She's not part of this," my mom says from behind the counter.

Grandma Chayo scoffs and places a hand on her hip. "Yes, she is. Why hasn't she continued her training, Sofia, eh? No es normal for a twenty-three-year-old bruja to not be recognized by the coven."

"You know why, Grandma," I start. "I wanted to go to college, to get a degree. Being a bruja isn't going to pay my bills."

Grandma Chayo points a finger at my mom. "You did this," she says. "You let her go to college and you let her think her magic was not important."

"I don't think that!" I say, my face flinching. "But that's not all I am!"

"No me grites!" she yells. "You can't keep letting fear stop you from doing *anything!*"

In truth, I was worried what continuing my training meant. I would be recognized as the familia bruja by our coven, and then what? Would I be stuck here forever?

I ask mom to take Grandma Chayo home, unsure of what I need. A break, I tell myself. I shake the thought away. No, I need to bake.

I press my hands into flour and water, coaxing them together. I whip sugar and butter and strawberries and try to paint a sunset on a cupcake. I take the leftover dough and twist the pieces, coating them in butter before baking them. I turn the lights off, casting the bakery in shadows. It's easier like this, to turn my brain off, and lose myself to the smells and feeling of soft dough.

In the distance, I hear the ocean waves crashing violently and I picture the moon hanging above them while they thrash. I fold my Grandma Chayo into the dough, mix my mom together in pink and orange frosting, sprinkling myself in sugar on top of fresh bread. I burn my fingers on the oven door. I should stop now, but I can't.

At the stroke of midnight, dough rises. Ocean currents rise. Bread softens. Waves crest.

I feel her the moment she steps onto moist sand. It jolts up my spine and I sigh as the oven timer goes off and the bread is done. I slide trays out and more trays in, waiting for her salt perfume to fill the room.

Julia appears in the doorway.

"I made your favorite," I say. I place the plate of sweet bread in front of me.

The tops of her bare shoulders glisten, still, with saltwater. Her shaky legs carry her to a stool.

I lean forward, inhaling the salt and vanilla clinging to her hair. "I didn't read the letter," I say, mirroring my earlier words. "And I have no idea if I want to stay at Coronado Street or if I even want to be a witch, but I do know that I love being with you, Julia." I step around the counter where I've left my freshly made pastries.

My family might hate me for this. But Grandma Chayo was right about one thing. I've been scared to advance in my magic. I've been scared to imagine what a life outside of Coronado Street would be. I've been scared to admit how I've felt.

I turn the lights off in the bakery. "If there's more to see out there, I want to see it with you."

When I'm back home, I don't feel scared to tell my mom and grandma that I'm leaving. I know it's not forever, and I know this is what I need to do. Mom's already sitting at the kitchenette with a cup of coffee when I arrive. Her eyes don't meet mine though; she peers behind me and I feel Julia's warmth at my back.

Mom gives a small smile. "You're leaving aren't you?"

"Is Grandma asleep?" I ask instead. Mom shakes her head and I turn, barely noticing the faint light coming from Grandma Chayo's room. Julia sits with my mom as I face my grandma.

I knock once. "Grandma? Can I come in?"

"Sí, mija." Her voice doesn't sound angry or rigid. It sounds soft, a little somber. When I enter, she's writing something down in a journal. I sit beside her. "I'm sorry about before, Grandma. And about my magic. I never wanted you to feel like I was shutting myself off from you or our family magic."

Grandma Chayo stops writing. She places her hand on mine, the wrinkles in her hands giving me an assuring comfort. "Do you know why your grandpa and I chose this place all those years ago?"

She continues before I can respond. "I had never seen an ocean so blue and so bright before, I said it must be because only the brightest people live here." Grandma Chayo sets aside the notebook she had been writing in. She taps me once on the nose. "And I was right. But maybe you shine too bright for just one place, no?"

Before I know it, I'm crying.

"It's okay, Celine. Your mama and I are okay. And look," she holds up the notebook. "Now I won't forget the things your grandpa used to tell me. I won't forget where he worked. I won't forget the hat I made him out of wheat and pumpkin seeds." Her lips turn slightly before she chuckles. "Well, I will try not to forget at least."

"I love you, you know that?" I say, as we both laugh.

Grandma Chayo nods once, then pulls out a new notebook. She hands it to me. "For your own memories. Sometimes forgetting can be the sweetest gift you give yourself, but remembering," she pauses, "that's its own kind of magic. Remember it all, Celine. The bad, but especially the good."

I don't know how Grandma Chayo knows I'm leaving before I've told her, but if there's anything I know about my grandma it's that she's full of magic and surprises. "I can't wait to tell you all about the things I'll see," I say to her.

I give Mom and Grandma Chayo a kiss goodnight, give Felix a pat on the head, and let the gentle night breeze carry me and Julia away into the ocean. The outside world fades slowly into blurred images of blue and black, and the light of the moon.

{ **18** }

Currucus

FLOR SALCEDO

Today is the nine hundred and eighty-third day without eating. Just so I can stay away from the killers.

I suck in the crisp morning air and mountain freedom, forcing away the dullness of never-ending days.

As the mountains ring with the cacophony of camel crickets, wrens swoop in and out of the nests they made in between the cactus needles, and quail softly call each other as they duck in and out of boulders, I crawl out of Dramático Cave, my preferred hiding spot along the top of my favorite mountain ridge. I didn't grow up in these mountains, but I made my way here over time. They're home now, the perfect cover for a hiding heart. I trundle down the slope.

I can barely remember what it was like to be the me from before, to anticipate any particular event. I half-wish for something to happen today. I close my eyes and focus on the fresh breeze again. The wind brings with it the smell of human cooking from the past. The memory tickles my whiskers.

There's a crack and a mild crash. I sharpen my senses, scurrying to the newest bird nest at the top of a flowering yucca. I stretch upward to check in. The little ones are still tucked in, brown and wiry.

And what about the massive ocotillo? Is it leaning? What could've disturbed it?

A blur of color. I lose my thoughts and freeze. "I see you," the scrunched shape says. I can tell it's a human; the proximity sends an electric shock swirling through my nerves. She crouches low, ogling eyes like black spheres, an oversized soft garment hiding her knees. She smells of anise—unnatural to these mountains. I should've noticed it earlier, but I'm not the sharp one I used to be.

I take a step backward, straight into the ocotillo. It pokes the back of my neck with its thick thorns. Out of the corner of my eye, the fire-colored flowers at the tips of its long limbs sway as I stare at the thin-skinned creature.

"Actually," the girl sticks her chin out triumphantly and grins, "all I see is the very bottom of your legs and your paws, and boy let me tell you, seeing only legs padding around like some Cheshire Cat trick is the biggest trip of my life."

Without a second thought, I disappear my legs.

"¡Ajá! So you do understand humans."

I cringe and leap to a high boulder.

She gasps and speaks slowly, sounding out every word like a cawing crow. "Cola de picos."

¡Maldición! I disappear my tail as well.

She yelps again, her foot sliding a few inches down the incline she's propped against. "¡Ajá! Español, too."

I grit my teeth. Fell for it twice.

"Those are the only two languages I know, so I can't test any others." She shrugs and lays her head on a boulder.

Twenty-seven, I think. I know twenty-seven. Or I used to. Some of them don't come to me so easily now. Some I haven't heard or practiced for hundreds of years.

I focus on the girl again while remaining still as a rock. Except my tail keeps nervously swishing over to a nearby shrub. She snaps her eyes to the shrub, and I double-check that my tail is still invisible.

I creep a few steps away, but loose pebbles crunch underneath me and I freeze.

She grimaces. "Please don't leave. I can't stand any more rejection this week. Five nos on college applications is enough for one week. And," she grins. "I'd love to see more of your adorable pawsies. You have big cat paws like my cat's. Well, about twice as big. Tiger died last year, though. Your face looks a little like his too. But that tail. Whew. I've never heard of any animal with a tail of spikes. I saw you grab onto that yucca with the end of your tail." Her grin grows wider, and she side-eyes toward my location. "But you're not really an animal, are you? Out here. All alone."

She looks around, eyes not focusing on anything in particular. She's lost me but doesn't seem panicked. She starts humming to herself. It's as if she's read me, seen everything, all these hundreds of years, and how I've been waiting for things to get better. But I know they never will.

My scales are vibrating as I scan the mountains and gulp in swaths of air. But the only scent is hers. Is it possible she really is alone and just happened upon me? Small groups of humans do climb this portion of the Franklin Mountains every so often. The mountains are right in the middle of their city after all. Bustling families, giggling friends, panting lovers. Doing things up here they think no one sees—urinating, spitting, humping, falling. I see it all.

I peer into the distance toward the human town, but El Paso's houses and buildings are just small specs from here. The people are unaware that I've been their neighbor for years, nothing but a climb away. But someone must know. This path is not a usual visitor trail. This girl knew I would be coming along. Someone sent her. Since she doesn't look like some scientist with a lifelong pursuit of finding creatures like me, she's here for something else. And I can't tell what. But that's the problem with humans: cheating hearts, power, and riches in their eyes.

I focus on her fingers. She's clearing rubble away from seedlings to make way for life. The old me might've fallen for it, but not today. I make a run for it.

My leaps toward the next mountain ridge are long and calculated. I scan the skies, sniff the air, eagle-eye every shadow and leaf flutter until I'm satisfied no one's following me. In the distance, the mountainside I just ran from is covered in a yellow-orange glow cast by the sun. I squeeze inside a small crevice and settle in for the long haul. I catalog the human's voice, skin, hair, teeth, limbs, fingers, clothes; all of it spins in my mind. It's been so long since I've been within a hundred feet of a person. I curse myself for having wished for something to happen. As if I willed it to happen. But I know that my magic is long gone. I have no desire to help any human anymore. I didn't call the girl. She just was. There. Suddenly. Inconveniently. The nervous twitching in my whiskers makes it hard to fall asleep.

My dreams are metallic and rainbow-colored. Golden pyramids and staccato dances. Feet thumping and bouncing cloaks made of straw. Vast rivers I used to love gliding in and powwows. Horse carriages rumbling in the distance and screeching railways. They mesh together in the same time. Dance, dance away. Mitote.

When dusk arrives, I'm visible again. Even though I'm buried in the earth, I'd prefer to have stayed invisible the entire time. How many years has it been since I was able to stay continuously cloaked? I've lost track. It's getting worse. Sometimes I wonder if I'm still that small imp I was when the space gods placed me and my siblings here on Earth. This could be some long dream of the future, granted by the gods, and I'm about to wake and find that it's still 1520, I still live among the Mēxihcah, and Motēuczōma Xōcoyōtzin didn't try to drown me to see if my life force would transfer to him. Or maybe I did die on that haunting night and don't know it yet.

I wish I could tell one of my siblings about everything that has happened since we were hunted down. What would they think of me?

The last of us, alone. Dying out here so far from our motherland. No importa. They're all gone. Thanks to the humans.

I traipse down the mountain to lick the dew off agave leaves. The dreams follow as if I've tethered them above me in engorged rain clouds, always pressing down, making my scales bristle.

My chest and tail are unusually cold and my heart beats slower. Is it because of yesterday's encounter? Or because it's been so long since I've eaten? Longer than I've ever gone.

A sharper flush of cold spreads in my chest. I thought I could hold out another year. But I don't think I can. Time to sniff out the prey that I've been avoiding. Even if it means I have to go further out to the edges of the mountains.

****

I take my kill to Small Mouth Cave. Not my favorite cave, but the encounter with the human girl has my scales raised. I'll leave the mess here and retreat comfortably back to Dramático Cave.

The mountain goat is still warm, and I delight in how my fangs sink in as if into butter. I've never had a need for the meat. I thrust my teeth deep and suction out the blood, slow and steady. The warmth fills me and my muscles relax. This is good. I wanted to wait longer, but this is good.

The last of the stars disappear behind the rapidly brightening sky. I try not to notice, but it's too late. I saw them leaving. A gloom comes scratching between my eyes. A longing for what was, or what I can't reach anymore.

Then, there's a voice. "Fiii-nally," she huffs and drops at the cave's entrance, sitting cross-legged, peering in. "I know you're in here. I heard you dragging something." She stretches her neck and her eyes zero in on my kill. "Oh God. Watching that dead goat wobbling on its own like a possessed blob is...gross."

I peer out into the skies to check for helicopters or any of those achichincle flying things the humans use to spy on everything, but it's an empty act on my part. Undoubtedly, she truly is able to hear me and is locating me herself. I didn't think those traits were possible in humans anymore.

She gasps loudly and almost falls backward into the escarpment behind her. "Wait, you're sucking it's blood out. ¡Chupacabras! It really is you. You're one of them. I mean, you're not. I mean, you're the one that makes everyone *think* there's such things as Chupacab—" she stops abruptly and watches me, or looks to where I am if she could actually see me. "I looked you up. You're Ahuítzotl and no one even knows you live."

My name flows out of her mouth so freely. It was the name my first master gave me because it was his name too. It's the only one I knew before I became "the creature" or "El Chupacabra."

She scoots under the scraggy shade of a dried-up bush, putting up a hand to shade her eyes. "Gosh, it's so bright out here already. Like my Má poured a thousand botellas of bleach over this mountainside." Her palms are scabbed, the skin thickened on the palms, a sure sign she's been out here often searching for me. How long has she been looking for me before yesterday? Days? Months? She puffs out air. "Why do I keep wearing this asinine, heavy sweater? Oh that's right, because it's stupid cold in the mornings up here." She fans herself with her hands.

I shift in place and swish my tail. Why don't I simply leave? I can find new places to live. I just wish she wouldn't pretend to be so fascinated by me when she knows she's going to be my death sentence.

All the lies that humans tell themselves, I made them mine. Ahuítzotl and me. We play, we swim. Las aguas negras glisten on his skin as I hold him up, make myself radiate, and his battle wounds close. I curl up at his feet at night, and he sings a song of eternity. He hugs me, and murmurs that I'm his life. He turns cold slowly when disease ravages him and he realizes I won't be able to heal him forever.

I know why you're here. It escapes me before I can stop myself, and she jumps back.

"You, you...you can *talk*? Well, you sent me your thoughts. Right? I mean, wow. I mean, wow!"

A sigh escapes me, and she goes quiet.

"My name is Josefina." She whispers the name like she doesn't believe it. "No, it's not. That's what I go by. So just call me Jay, I guess. You know, when you hopefully talk to me, more."

I say nothing until the sun is highest in the sky and sweat drips down her neck. She gives off a few grunts of discomfort and eventually gets up and leaves. The next day I don't spot or smell her, but then she's back the day after, trekking about, telling stories of these mountains and the animals she's seen as she's been hiking, giggling to herself, mouthing off curses when she occasionally slips. I lay still and put all my energy into staying invisible. When the cold feeling comes rushing up into my chest, I start wishing she'd just fall off a cliffside. But she continues showing up every other day. Seems like she's just practicing to see how fast she can locate me. She can move around the ridges so much quicker now.

Today she makes a strange noise from her throat. "Currr, currr. Come out now and be with me. Talk to me a little more," she pleads.

I hate how I can't make myself walk away. I'm more tired than usual today so it's going to have to be a waiting game—wait for her to get bored and leave. I lower myself on top of a clump of rocks as quietly as I can. She smiles and turns in my general direction. "Currr, currr." In truth, the sound is quite soothing and I put my head down to listen. Her smile fades. She clutches her hand to her chest and looks straight at me. "You're...flickering."

I move to get up but I flicker more and lie back down.

"Is it me," she asks. "Do I make you weak?"

I swish my tail and look away. How can I tell her it's not just her, but her kind? Those that I gave my everything to. They used me; the betrayal is a knife in my back that never comes out.

She moves one step closer, slowly bends her legs, and drops to cross-legged position in one move. "Curr, curr. Currucus. You are…" she sighs, "so beautiful."

It stings. Straight to my heart.

She'll betray me, too. She admires what she's here to kill without a hint of regret. I know she won't pull out a weapon and do it herself. No. She'll hand me over to them, and they'll lock me up and study me like a specimen for the rest of their lives. Then hand me to the next generation. And the next. I won't let them. I'll let go long before then.

I scoff at her remark and look away.

"They came looking for me," she breaks the silence and looks far away to the rocky cliffs. "Whoever they are, I still don't know. They said they're top-secret government so I called them The Feds. I heard it in a movie once." She shrugs. "There was a bazaar, the same one we have each year at Saint Anthony's Church. The kids were shrieking in laughter in the carnival games and the people chattering and stuffing their faces, but I could hear something through it all. Something no one else could." She shoots me a quick glance. "I heard your cries. The Feds were playing it. They were like human baby cries mixed with something else, something familiar that I couldn't place. I was inside the church. See, I wasn't supposed to be there, but I was scrubbing the floors because Má, Pá, and I hadn't had groceries for a while, and the church people said they'd give me a few plates of food to take home as payment."

She stops to rub her hands, and I think of the rough palms I thought she got from climbing.

"I went to the noise," she continues, "because I couldn't think past my gurgling stomach anymore. I went past the gordita and enchilada vendors and the stand where they were selling plants. They asked me my name, and I said Josefina. I've been pretending I'm her for so long so that CPS won't take me that it just came out. Josefina was two years older than me and she was illegal and so are my—I mean her parents. Well, my parents were illegal too, but I was born here and I'm legal.

Josefina and I would lie for hours in her room, playing quiet games of "imagine the future" while she hid the headaches she'd always get so her parents had one less thing to worry about. We'd talk about what we were going to become when we grew up. Josefina was going to be a doctor, of course, to help her parents and find out why her head hurt so much. But then she started losing her vision and when they found the tumor in her head, I hardly had a chance to say goodbye because she died a couple of weeks later. Her parents lay in bed, rotting."

She turns to me, eyes glassy as quartz, hurt reaching into the past. "I'm not exaggerating. They were becoming skeletons and like," she reaches for a word, "decomposing," she spits out, "and dying right there in front of our eyes. My parents did everything they could, even force-fed them a few times. We couldn't take them to the hospital because they asked to die right there next to their daughter's bed. They would've gotten deported anyway. My parents said there are some things you have to allow, even if you don't like them, because it's not your choice. So we left and my parents went to work, my mom and dad in the only car we had, my mom would usually drop my dad off first at his work. But they didn't make it that morning because some-one ran the red and killed them. A police officer came looking for me, but Rosario, who works at the hospital had already told me, and so I hid and neighbors told the cops that some relatives from Mexico had already picked me up and taken me to Mexico. I laid down with Josefina's parents and told them I would go with them and we would soon be with Josefina and my parents. Just like that Josefina's mom got up a few hours later, made dinner, and told her husband that it was not right to keep a girl hungry and to come have dinner. He got up, ate, showered and went out to look for work."

She stops and breathes deeply for many breaths. "They're my Má and Pá now."

I stop flickering and just let myself be fully visible. Her face has gone pale and she stares. "I didn't know that anyone could die of grief. But now I know. Because they almost did, and I'll never forget it."

She gets up. Her lips quiver and she smells of fear. I've seen the look: right before Motēuczōma Xōcoyōtzin took me down to the river. I knew it would come, I just didn't know when. "The Feds offered me a lot of money to find you. They said I would never have to scrub floors again. They said that I'd finally be free." She uncrosses her legs and gets up. She's leaving. "Adiós, Currucus," she says so quietly I barely hear it.

Where will she go now? To turn me in? To tell them where I am?

When she takes a step, I burst with raging, red thoughts. *You're what I wanted most of all.*

Her mouth opens like she wants to say something. But then I'm crashing through the barrel and prickly pear cacti, thorns piercing me, dust blasting into my lungs, claws digging into rock.

When I reach Dramático Cave, it's empty, and I puff out relief that no one was there waiting for me. The cold ground is an annoyance as I lay on it and lick the spot where I'm now missing a claw, my limbs getting colder and colder. My bloody tongue swells in my mouth. I'm useless. My life as protector is a thing of the past, I will never heal anyone, and I will never heal myself again. I have no will anymore. The weight of a thousand clouds lifts. Calm and clarity fills me. I killed for all my masters without question. All those souls I lured still spin in my mind after all these years.

I've been telling myself for ages that I'd do it all over again just to have those early moments of my life when all was glory. But the truth is I deserve this. Most of me died on the river that day anyway.

***

I catch her scent briefly as I limp down the mountainside. I'm leaving for good but wonder if it's pointless. My end is coming one way or the other. My cut-up tongue stings in my mouth and a gaping hole on my paw oozes out blood. As expected, I'm not healing.

I continue catching her scent as I trek further and further away from my favorite ridges. It's as if she's going up and down these mountains, but I never see her.

Until someone crosses my path. Small, covered from head to toe in cloths, only a sliver across the eyes and two dark pools reflecting the moonlight back at me.

"Currucus," she says. The faint chopping sound of a helicopter comes up over the mountain. It's right over Dramático Cave, beaming its lights down, dropping ladders and then tiny figures climb down. The helicopter moves, coming our way, shining its light over the mountains. She looks behind her then back at me.

A part of me thought maybe she was different.

All of me wanted it badly.

All of me was a huge imbécil.

"I'm sorry it came down to this," she cries. She lifts one leg and kicks me hard; I go over a cliff.

Then I'm falling and I think hard and steady and project to her. *It was time anyway.*

* * *

Unbelievable pain shoots from my foot to my skull. I'm still alive.

But it's over. If I don't die now, they *will* get me.

My leg is on fire; my chest turns as cold as a desert night. It's getting harder to breathe. I'm thankful it will happen fast. This is where I leave this earth.

There's a loud snap and then the girl is above me.

"Currucus."

I'm so sorry my brothers and sisters that I didn't fight harder to stop them from killing you, but now I'll see you again soon.

"It's just me." The darkness is heavy, her pupils dilated as her eyes rush all over me.

Let go, I demand from myself.

She sticks something into my mouth and a liquid oozes out, warm and thick.

"It's just an opioid," she says. "For the pain." She tries lifting me. "Crap, you're bleeding a lot." I feel myself being moved, turned. She bandages my leg tightly with quick hands then scurries up the mountain where she touches a bloodied rag to boulders and rubs it on the dirt. She moves like a weasel but holds the concentration of a pack of wolves. Then she's at me again, takes out a plastic bottle from her pack and squeezes a liquid out wildly onto the dirt. She turns to me with a feral expression. "My blood," she says. Then she's stuffing me in a bag almost the size of her body.

My eyelids are so heavy. I can't tell how long she's been moving, but her panting is heavy. The chopping noise zooms in and out. Even though I'm fading, I can still feel the violence of her heartbeat.

"My super-talented mom," she huffs out, "made these clothes and this bag for us. The patterns make us look like we're a part of the mountains, and it's all made from some space blanket stuff so that helicopter can try detecting our heat all day long but it ain't finding us."

Before I know it, the mountains are behind us.

Two white metal doors open and she's laying me inside a big van with blankets on the floor.

"I don't know if they were ever planning on giving me the second half," she grunts as she pulls me out of the bag, then squeezes into the driver's seat. "But I made sure to ask for a ridiculous amount upfront that they actually agreed to. Ha! Cash only, I said, because how could an immigrant girl with no papers and illegal parents ever get paid in anything other than cash, right? And now, how are they going to find said illegal girl and her family whose names they don't even know? That is *if* they decide the mighty Chupacabra didn't gobble her up." She smirks at me in the rearview mirror. "The money was enough to buy a raggedy small house with a huge plot of land up in Anthony, Texas. We're going to live there with my Má and Pá and there's enough money left over to take care of us for years, and I can even go to college. Well, a community college, but still. We're going to have a small farm with lots of goats and chickens and grow food and my parents never have to worry another day in their lives again. Though Pá is already set on fixing up the house and extending it." She chuckles.

"We're your protectors now and will be for the rest of our lives. My parents are waiting at the farm." She cranes her neck back and strokes my mane. "They're going to spoil you to death." Her jaw drops and she exclaims. "Currucus, you're glowing. Bet you The Feds didn't know about this one."

She throws her head back and laughs into the morning twilight as my wounds tingle with a healing warmth I haven't felt in ages. I think it's time to be someone else. Currucus sounds perfect to me. I lift my head and lick her hand. My protector.

The sun crawls up the sky, the breeze flooding through the windows. The engine rumbles steadily beneath us as we head toward Anthony. To our new lives.

I look at her and project one word.

Home.

Contributors

Alexandra Campos is a Latine writer from Los Angeles, California currently residing in Canada. She has multiple degrees in creative writing & recently acquired her Masters in Fine Arts from the University of British Columbia. Alexandra enjoys writing young & adult fiction about magical girls and their desire to belong. As a first-generation Mexican-American, Alexandra has struggled to find her place among family and culture, often reflecting that struggle in her work. *Where Monsters Lurk & Magic Hides* is her first publication.

Twitter: @Alex_Livier

Instagram: @alexlivier

Ashley Jean Granillo is a Mexican-American writer hailing from the San Fernando Valley. She currently teaches college-level writers, and in the past, has hosted creative writing workshops for middle schoolers. She has her BA and MA in Creative Writing from California State University Northridge, but she got her start as a writer at the age of five when she illustrated and published her first "book" through Telfair Elementary's Book Buddy program in Pacoima, California. Currently, she is an MFA candidate in Fiction for UCR's Low Residency program in Palm Desert. When she isn't writing, she's exploring LA's cat cafes, writing songs, wandering Disneyland, or cuddling with her dog, Emme.

Carolina Flórez-Cerchiaro is a Colombian journalist and international politics expert, living in Bogotá. She is represented by Janine Kamouh at William Morris Endeavor. As a lover of all things horror, she describes her work as a ghost-haunting tour around Colombia. She writes mostly speculative fiction with a horror twist, and romance.

Contributors

Flor Salcedo was born and raised in the border town of El Paso, TX, among the enchanted desert and mountains which make for the setting for this story. She is currently a computer programmer living in Austin, Texas and has been in this technological field for over a decade but dreams of transitioning to writing full time. She has a personal essay published in The Ocotillo Review Vol. 1, and a short story in the anthology, FORESHADOW: The Magic of Reading and Writing YA.

Twitter: @FlorSPower

Instagram: @florwithstories

Jaelin St. Clair is a multi-faceted individual who often tries to balance three things at the same time. They see themselves as an artist first, a human second, and they think lists are unimportant and silly. They studied at Cal State Long Beach, graduating with dual BAs in Creative Writing and English Literature. They hope to one day get their masters, a movie deal with Jordan Peele, and a driver's license.

Twitter: @DJxMatchax

Jarrard Raju (they/them) is an AfroLatine non-binary writer. They have a Bachelors in Sciences in Criminal Justice, and by day, are a barista in the coffee-fueled Portland, OR. They discovered their passion for putting words together in intricate ways when they were 12. And thanks to a couple of books, *Aristotle and Dante Discover the Secrets of the Universe* being one of them, they now piece together words in ways movies play in one's mind. If not consumed by the magic of the world that inspires their words, they can be seen on a longboard figuring out what to eat or watching astronomy docs on Youtube.

Judy Fernandez Diaz is a first-generation Black Dominican American living in Arizona. She was selected as a Spring 2020 Las Musas Books Hermana mentee. Her short story, FLOR DE CAÑA, is included in the upcoming anthology "Quislaona: A FANTASY ANTHOLOGY," published by Worldbuilding Magazine and DWA Press. Her poem "NOT YOUR TYPICAL DOMINICAN YORK" was included in the anthology "Ni de Aqui Ni de Alla" published by DWA Press (2021). In addition to writing, she juggles a career in human resources and being a mom to her beautiful nine-year-old daughter.

Twitter, Instagram, and TikTok: @JudyWritesMG

K. Victoria Hernandez is a speculative fiction writer and Environment & Sustainability Ph.D. student based in Los Angeles. She is a graduate of the Clarion Science Fiction & Fantasy Workshop, 2018, and since then her work has been featured in *khōréō*, *7x7.la*, *Cotton Xenomorph*, and *Daily Science Fiction*. Her latest piece was listed in the 2021 Locus Recommended Reading List. The granddaughter of Mexican and Guatemalan immigrants, Hernandez's writing is often inspired by her heritage and Southern California upbringing. She is a scientist, she believes in ghosts, and she hopes your hauntings are kind.

Twitter: @KVictoriahHerna1

K.C. Amira is a Ph.D. researcher and horror fiction writer studying at Northumbria University and living in Brighton, UK. Her research is focused on child autonomy and moral panics in Reagan-era American horror cinema. KC has a master's degree in forensic anthropology from UCL and studied signs of child maltreatment and child ill health in osteological material both modern and ancient. Her work has been published in *Bust Magazine*, *Death and the Maiden*, *The One That Got Away* by Kandisha Press and *Hear Us Scream*. She has presented her research at York St John University, University College London, Northumbria University, University of Liverpool and the University of Winchester. She is currently working on a project with MAI: Feminism and Visual Culture, Doing Women's Global Horror Film History.

Twitter: @horrorchromatic

Instagram: @horror_chromatic

Kiara Medina is a Puerto Rican exiled to Texas. She has a Master of Fine Arts degree in Writing for Children and Young Adults from The Vermont College of Fine Arts. When she's not writing, she's watching too many animated movies and cuddling with her three cats.

Linda Raquel Nieves Pérez (she/they) is an Afro-Boricua writer born on a rainy night in Arecibo, Puerto Rico, which they often blame for their obsession for writing water goddesses with stormy tempers. Their goal is to see more curls and fat bodies portrayed in the books they read. She has a degree in accounting and currently studies Law. You can find her short work in the *Reclaim the Stars* anthology (Wednesday Books, 2022).

Twitter: @MissLindaBennet

Instagram: @l.ndaraquel

TikTok: @linda.reads

Mariel Jungkunz: After a childhood move from Puerto Rico to the United States, Mariel Jungkunz learned to love and call the Florida Panhandle—and now snowy Ohio—home. She loves the mystery and allure of words, whether she's working as a research editor at Dictionary.com or writing picture books and a YA novel that's in the works. Mariel's first picture book about Los Tres Reyes will be published in fall 2023 by Astra Young Readers. She is represented by Caryn Wiseman of Andrea Brown Literary Agency.

Twitter: @marielbjungkunz

Nathalie D. Medina is a graduate of Haverford College, where she obtained her B.A. in East Asian Studies. She lives and works from home in the Bronx, New York, with her wife, comics and fiction writer Danny Lore, and her cat, a senior rescue named Lucy. Nathalie is inspired by anime like the Gundam series and Yu Yu Hakusho, video games like Mass Effect and Fire Emblem, and legends in sci-fi and fantasy like K.A. Applegate, Mercedes Lackey, and Lois McMaster Bujold. She writes weird, queer speculative fiction for all ages and enjoys bullet journaling and collecting plushes in her spare time. Her current project is a young adult fantasy. She is represented by Desiree Wilson at The Bent Agency.

Twitter and Instagram: @cosyfemme

Sabrina Prestes is a twenty-something author focusing on unconventional romance, magical realism, and character-driven horror. Raised in Brazil, the USA, and Mexico, she seeks to incorporate her varied experiences into her stories. At thirteen, she began posting original YA stories on Wattpad, where she's gained a cumulative 2,200,000 reads on her work. In 2019 and 2020, she participated in #WriteMentor to mentor other authors on their path to publication. Aside from writing, her interests range from history to math to esotericism and just about everything in between.

Twitter and instagram: @destaciax

Shayna Conde is a Jersey-born, NYC-based writer, actor, and model of Afro-Caribbean descent. Her words can be found in *Departures, McSweeney's, Allure, FOOD52, Well+Good, USA Today, Anti Racism Daily, Greatist,* and many more. She has been featured in ads and commercials for L'OREAL, Carol's Daughter, Bank of America, *Marie Claire* magazine, and more. Her theatrical credits span Moscow (Russia), Krakow (Poland), Cambridge (Massachusetts, USA) and NYC (USA). She also owns a substack called Heart to Arts where she talks about representation issues in the entertainment industry, food and wine recommendations in the NJ/NYC area, and mental health topics. In her spare time, she enjoys watching anything narrated by David Attenborough, venturing into boutique wine shops, and dreaming about a world in which Zutara is canon in the Avatar: The Last Airbender universe.

Instagram: @shaynarc

Twitter: @SRCondee

Stephanie Slagle is a professional freelance editor with over six years of publishing industry experience. She has read the slush pile for literary agents and edited books for small publishing presses. She majored in film production at San Diego State University. When she isn't editing books or working on her own novels, she enjoys playing with her dog, traveling with her husband, and singing in her local choir. She is represented by Chip Rice of Wordlink, Inc.

Twitter: @steph_slagle

Instagram: @stephanieeslagle

Taylor Ramage is a poetry and fantasy author of Puerto Rican descent. Her flash fiction has appeared in speculative and literary anthologies. Her published poetry includes the collections, *Forgive Us Our Trespasses* and *Lest I Know Your Weakness.* Taylor has an avid love of stories in all forms.

Twitter: @TaylorRamage

Instagram: @taylorrama

About the Editor

Lauren T. Davila is a Pushcart-nominated, Latina author, anthologist, and editor. She is represented by Susan Velazquez Colmant at JABberwocky Literary Agency.

She has edited multiple short story anthologies, including:

– WHEN OTHER PEOPLE SAW US, THEY SAW THE DEAD (Haunt Publishing, May 2022; Outland Entertainment, April 2023)
– WHERE MONSTERS LURK & MAGIC HIDES
(Bee Infinite Publishing; Nov. 2022)
– PLACES WE BUILD IN THE UNIVERSE
(Flower Song Press; Nov. 2022)
– RECLAMATION: AN ANTHOLOGY OF CLIMATE GENRE FICTION (Outland Entertainment; July 2023)
– LOCALE: AN ANTHOLOGY OF TIME AND PLACE
(Inked in Gray; Nov. 2023)

Beyond these titles, she is editing or co-editing multiple anthologies on submission.

Her poetry and short fiction has appeared online at *Granada Magazine*, *The Paragon Journal*, *Ghost Heart Literary Magazine*, *Peach Velvet Mag*, *Voyage Journal*, *Second Chance Magazine*, *Headcanon Magazine*, *In Parentheses*, and *Poets Reading the News*.

Lauren is currently pursuing her Ph.D. in English at Claremont Graduate University. She holds an MFA in Fiction Writing from George Mason University. After completing her studies, she plans to teach at the collegiate level while working in publishing.

She is editing her debut novel, AT THE STILL POINTE, an adult gothic mystery featuring ballerinas and the Greek Furies. She is also working on a YA superhero series, picture books, and poetry and short story collections.

Besides her personal and anthology work, Lauren has experience working as an Acquisitions Editor for an independent press. In her editing work, she prioritizes acquisitions of diverse and historically marginalized authors. She is also currently taking on freelance editing clients and information can be found on her EDITING SERVICES page. She is also a judge at NYC Midnight and Editor-in-Chief for Foothill Poetry Journal.

She lives in the Greater Los Angeles area where you can find her swimming, walking her golden retriever, and drinking one too many rose lattes.

For inquiries regarding invitations to anthologies, international rights, or IP work, please reach out to Susan at https://awfulagent.com/agents/susan-velazquez/

About the Artist

Mazziel Coello is an Illustrator and Character Designer from Miranda, Venezuela. Her illustrations revolve around interesting character dynamics and the intriguing worlds that surround them. All of this is often portrayed through delicate symbolism and atmosphere, with pure intention to connect with whoever views her artwork.

Mazziel is a self-taught artist, having seven years of intensive studying and experience in drawing. Currently, she works as a freelancer, making new ideas come to life every day through her semi-realistic illustrations. She has also volunteered as a drawing teacher at her local foundation, helping kids to delve into the fantastic world of creativity and drawing.

Bee Infinite Publishing

As a Black-women owned and operated space, we hold an Afrofuturist perspective at the core of our business. We're committed to amplifying the voices and stories of people of color, especially Black and Indigenous voices. Our books honor the infinite artistry of our collective community through the creative lens of compelling storytelling.

Our mission is to be an equitable, conscious publishing house. We want to put creative ownership back into the hands of those who dream of fantastical new worlds, who think in verse, and who draw when holding a pen.

Learn more about our books, projects, and products at www.beeinfinite.org.

Let's Connect!
Instagram: @beeinfinite_publishing
Twitter: @beeinfinite_